The Playboy, the Poet, and the Spy

A novel

by
Donna Drejza

This book is a work of fiction. The names, characters, places, and incidents either are the product of the author's imagination or are used fictitiously. Any resemblance to actual persons, living or dead, events or locales is entirely coincidental. If I have mentioned an actual person, place, or thing, then it is meant as a whole-hearted recommendation.

ISBN 978-0-9960615-1-3

Book design by Donna Drejza

Other books:

Palm Beach Busybodies

Renaissance Now

Swiss Mystery

Cats Don't Bark

To all of my lucky angels and my secret muses.

A list of characters and descriptions can be found on the last page.

Chapter 1

Lugano, Switzerland

The sapphire lake glistens in the rear-view mirror, making for a lovely drive. Too bad I'm a murder suspect in the back of a police car. I run a comb through my tangled auburn hair, and put some lipstick on, in anticipation of a brightly lit mug shot. We are in the Italian section of Switzerland, which looks just like Italy—only cleaner. A haunting Billie Holiday song plays on the radio, making me think we're about to go off a cliff —actual or proverbial. We pull up to an old stucco building, and I'm sent to a room that smells of pink cotton candy.

There is a flock of preschool ballerinas running amok in the hallway. The only clue to my dire fate is the chalkboard that says, "Police Station." A darkly handsome man enters and introduces himself as Detective Bernardo. With his liquid Italian accent, he explains, "The station burned down, so they're letting us use the kindergarten." He takes on a serious tone as he begins the interrogation. I'd be intimidated if he weren't sitting at a miniature plastic desk.

"Please state your age, Ms. Carano."

"Um. Thirty-eight."

"Are you aware that it's a crime to make false statements in a murder investigation?"

"Okay, I'm forty-one, but I was a preemie."

The detective looks at my bare legs. "Is there some reason you're not wearing pants?"

"Um. Yes."

Before I can explain, the detective falls off his chair. "Ah. Let's move on."

Despite the ridiculous setting, he implores me with his dark eyes and says, "Camille Carano, why are you here?"

"I'm here because the cops drove me here. Or were you looking for something more existential?"

"No, why are you in Switzerland?"

While I ponder his question, he opens a fancy box of Poire-William liqueur chocolates. In no time, I'm a chocolate-filled chatterbox, making me sure they put them in the budget to get people to blab.

Nervously, I start to babble. "Well, I was a food blogger in Boston, but my friend's mother fell down the stairs, so now I'm a private chef in London for her dog... after she had a little too much sherry. Mrs. Etherington, that is, not the dog, although he's been known to take a nip or two..."

The detective waves his hands in a wrap-up mode and says, "The short version, please."

"My boyfriend brought me here." I point to the lobby. "He's the one out there with the pale-blue shirt and the pale-blue eyes."

The detective gets an impish grin. "You mean the pale blue shirt with the bright red bloodstains?"

A few chocolates are left in the box, and he waves one over my head like a dog treat. "Please describe the victim as you found her."

"Well, her mouth was wide open, and her arm was raised like she was hailing a taxi."

"Hailing a taxi in her closet?" he says excitedly, "Or waving— like she knew her killer?"

"Let's see. I'd have to get on the ground…"

He motions to the floor. "Be my guest."

I carefully lay down on the carpeting to create a road-kill mime of the dead woman.

"I understand they found chocolaty smudges on the glass. Do you have any idea whose fingerprints these might be? Just off-hand."

I wipe my fingers on the shirt. *Boy, am I in trouble.*

Chapter 2

Four months earlier:
Boston, Massachusetts

Stella, my reluctant bridesmaid, stops in the middle of the aisle, letting me know she hates her chartreuse dress. She's not the best choice for a bridesmaid, but she's the only dog I have. She's an elderly pug with dead-ringer Betty Davis eyes. When I catch my reflection in the hall mirror, I am grateful this is just a dress rehearsal. I can't get my wedding dress to zip, so I get a brilliant McGiver idea: I tie the Venetian blind cord to the zipper and get on the floor and crawl away backward. Well, now the zipper is halfway up, but the blinds have come crashing down.

Now, I'm lying on the floor staring at the ceiling of my apartment. I spy a half-eaten sandwich under a bookshelf, which must be from the Paleozoic era of my life here. *God, I'm a slob.* Oh, well, I don't care — I'll be moving soon. I'm getting married in three weeks. The rest of my life will be perfectly packaged in a neat little Tiffany's box. I'm to marry Arthur J. Higginbottom – International Lawyer. Then, I'll never go hungry again. *God, I sound like Scarlet O'Hara.*

I'm disrupted by a fervent knock on the door, so I schlep out to the entry, dragging the Venetian blinds in my wake. It's my friend David Etherington, all hunched over and wearing a safari suit. I am reminded of the day I met him. He was subletting the apartment next door, and had gotten his toe caught in the bathtub faucet and cried through the wall — which was our bonding moment.

I can't help but ask, "How was the Dendrologist Convention?"

His freckled face musters some glee. "So exciting!"

With his elegant British accent, he adds, "But the next time I decide to fly coach from New Zealand to Boston –shoot me."

"Okay. How many times?"

As he follows me to the kitchen, I see him scanning my living room, which is now scattered with papers and books. To distract him, I pop open a bottle of Veuve Clicquot and pour two glasses. I can see the gears in his 48-year-old head jam-up trying to find something nice to say about the décor.

"It looks like my favorite writer has been focused on her book deadline."

"I thought my novel was finished, but now my editor says it needs a new beginning, a new middle, and a new ending."

I turn to look at my cake and find my dog licking the bottom tier with her aardvark-esque tongue.

David examines my creation. "Camille, I've never seen such an exact replica of the Leaning Tower of Pisa."

"Thank goodness it was just a practice one."

I cut two slices for us and ask, "So, how was your layover in London?"

David looks at my face as I shove in a massive piece of cake. "Oh my god! What are you doing eating food three weeks before your wedding?"

I look down in shame.

He runs his hands through his ginger hair and a look of worry and pity connects his eyebrows. "Don't tell me you found out about Arthur?"

"What about Arthur? Is he dead?"

David speaks rapidly. "Nooo, but you'll wish he was. Remember when I asked you if he had an identical twin brother in London?"

I'm now licking the frosting off the candy bride and groom. "Vaguely."

"Well, it *was* Arthur that night at The Dorchester Hotel."

"He goes to London a lot on business."

David begins a jet-lagged prattle. "Well, my mother and I were there for tea —well, it was technically gin—and we saw him and that blonde secretary go up to a hotel room. My mother naturally volunteered to listen at their door. You don't ever want to hear one's mother mimic *those* sounds."

"Were you not going to tell me this?"

"I was worried you'd cancel the wedding."

"Don't you think I should?" I say, biting the head off the groom.

Chapter 3

Despite massive protests —well, mostly from my Mom — I call off the wedding and go into seclusion. Frankly, staying in bed with my dog *is* how I'd like to live out the rest of my life.

After a week, I peek out from the comfort zone and find David still in my living room. At least I think it's my living room; it's now so neat I think I'm in the wrong apartment. I march out, still in the wedding dress, which is now ripped and soiled. I've become a Dickensian character: Mrs. Havisham. I'm carrying the remains of the cake, so David quickly wrestles it from me and tosses it out the window. I gasp as Stella nearly goes out after it and look down at the street. "Oh, great, that was my landlord's head."

David pats my hand. "Camille, it's time to move on. You need a new man."

"But it's only been a week!" I peel off the old wedding dress and leave it crumpled on the floor.

Maybe he's right. Perhaps the best way to get over a man is to get some new ones. I'll start all over. I'll create a fresh new mess!

He's back at his laptop typing. "I've taken the liberty of signing you up for a dating site." He pulls out a paint chart and chases me around. "Just as I thought: your eyes are Pantone #337." He types a parenthetical (pale turquoise) on my bio page.

I pull on an old bathrobe and grab a cup of coffee and sit next to him. On his screen, I can't help but notice a photo of me —standing on my head.

10

"It takes 10 years off," he says, typing like a hyper rabbit. "Okay, Camille, I filled out some of your bio but wasn't sure what to put for your occupation."

"Did you put food blogger and flute player at second weddings?"

"Heavens, no." David types rapidly. "How about, 'Up and coming novelist, wine critic and symphony flutist?'"

"Wine critic?"

"I distinctly remember you complaining about my Pouilly-Fuisse last summer."

David straightens his glasses. "Just a few more details until your profile is complete. Now, please describe your perfect man."

I pour more coffee. "Well, let's see... he'd have a voice like butterscotch and violins. He'd eat toast and marmalade every morning and read the paper to his dog." Getting into the spirit, I add, "If he has a pirate ship full of pug puppies, he is to write straight away."

David stops typing and looks up at me. "Good luck with that, Dear."

The bios are fascinating, so I read one aloud. "*Rope & Hatchets, 57*. He must be some sort of ax-murder."

"No, he's a fireman."

"He sounds sweet." I read aloud, "'*Been looking for love ever since Mum left me on a doorstep wearing only a mitten.*'"

David says, "Never mind; that one is going to have issues."

I see a face and gasp. "What about that one?"

David nods his head and reads aloud. "'*Agape 44*'. That's the sign of unconditional love, which you'll need if you keep eating cake."

When I look at Agape's eyes, my heart starts to pound. He's so handsome in a soulful kind of way. His face looks a little Slavic, with brown hair, green eyes, and charming dimples.

"He's 44 and looking for a woman who doesn't smoke."

"Oh good. He doesn't sound too picky."

David goes on. "Yes, some of the other men have long lists of disqualifiers such as *'drunken, cheating, liars with cats need not apply.'*"

"I suppose one would put up with such a woman if she had dogs."

David says, "He sounds perfect for you! It says he's newly separated from his wife, which is a plus as he's in that sweet spot between happily married and bitterly divorced."

I gaze at Agape's dimples again. "Okay, let's wink at him."

After David presses the wink key, he cries, "Oh no. He's from Ipswich!"

"What's wrong with that? I love Cape Cod, and they have those yummy fried clams."

"Ipswich, England. I logged in on mother's account."

"Your old mother is on a dating site?"

Right then, David's mobile phone rings, and he cowers. "Oh, no. It's my pesky wife." Then he answers and utters a series of, "Yes, Dears."

He hangs up and looks down. "She says I have to come home."

Chapter 4

After David flies back to Auckland, I feel a little lonely. Then I notice an alert from the dating site. *I have a message!* Probably one of the ax murderers has been released from prison. It is from Agape 44. *Yay!* I learn his real name is Oliver, and he's a poet. He writes that while he does not have a pirate ship of pugs, he does have a cat named Captain Hook and lives by the sea and loves orange marmalade. He asks if he's a match. *Close enough, with those dimples.*

He's also a professor of Ancient History and has six-year-old twin boys. I'll bet they have adorable English accents and wear little uniforms and say things like, *'Mum, might I have another Hobnob?'*

As we go from winking to writing, I find out more. While this new Oliver and I have many things in common, we also have many differences: He has been married his entire adult life and living in a small English village. I have been single my whole adult life and living in a large American city. He asks if I have children. I type back: *'Not that I know of.'*

We start writing to each other every week. He says he wants to bring me flowers; I tell him that I hate gifts that die. He asks what I *do* like, so I say chocolate —chocolate doesn't die. In another letter, I go on about licking melted chocolate from his lips. This prompts tech support to send notifications stating that they "occasionally" read private messages, which really means "continuously." I'm sure our steamy letters are read aloud in the tech support lunch room.

There is something about Oliver. It's a knowing. Oh, why do I live an ocean away from him? We could do video calls, but I dread having him see me from that unflattering perspective, i.e., with a camera up my nose. No, I want the mystery to continue until we meet in person. We begin sending handwritten letters on parchment paper — sealed with cinnabar-colored wax. *Ah, it's all so romantic.*

Oliver and I carry on our long-distance romance for nearly three months. During this time, my friend David subscribes to regular updates. He says I *have* to meet this man —or I will regret it for the rest of my life.

I tell David the problem is Oliver can't just up and fly to America, what with all his baggage. And I can't fly to England because I've spent my last dime on the stupid non-wedding. The other problem is that I don't dare leave my dog Stella in her delicate geriatric state.

The next morning, Stella is sitting on the back of the sofa, minding her own business. She's near the opened window on account of her non-stop farting. Then it happens. She jumps out!

She lands on my landlord's head. He survives, but sadly, she doesn't.

David calls to console me. "I'm so sorry, Camille. She was sixteen, after all, so I hope it wasn't a huge surprise."

"Well, I knew she was deaf, blind, paralyzed, and incontinent —but I didn't know suicidal. She must have heard me say she was keeping me from Oliver."

"Maybe she wasn't so deaf, after all."

14

Chapter 5

A week later, David calls frantically, which is his usual tone. "My mother fell down the stairs!" He takes a breath. "She was fencing like Erol Flynn, after we specifically told her no swords after she's gotten into the sherry."

"Oh, no! Is she going to be alright?"

"She broke her hip and is in the hospital."

"For how long?"

"Who knows? Say, I just thought of something. How would you like to cook for Robert Palmer?"

"The 'Addicted to Love' singer? Didn't he *already* die?"

"Yes, no. I mean, my mother's dog. She needs someone to watch him."

"A dog sitter? But I'm about to become a famous novelist."

"It's just for two weeks. That is if you can manage to peel yourself away from La-La land."

"Sure, but shouldn't *you* go and see her?"

"My wife won't let me leave the country. She's in the house ovulating."

"Okay, when do I start?"

"Is Tuesday too soon? I'll get you a flight."

"Oh, that will be nice; I'm a little low on funds."

"Just think — now you can finally meet your soul mate."

Chapter 6

London, England

I arrive in London with a small suitcase and great expectations. As planned, I take a taxi from Heathrow airport to St. John's Wood —one of London's most exclusive neighborhoods.

Mrs. Etherington has a stately three-story home on the very upscale Acacia Road. I read my scavenger list and find a key hidden under a kissing frog statue near the front door. When I open the door, I survey a vast marble entry and a grand curving staircase. The house smells of old books and fond memories.

Next on my list is to call the pet taxi service called *'London Woof.'* As I wait for the dog to be delivered, I explore the mystical old house. There is a charming mahogany library just off the foyer. Archaic books line the walls, while velvet Empire sofas and brown leather chairs sit in an audience of the revered limestone fireplace. A rolling art-deco liquor cart, stocked with sherries and port, is the court jester. *Yes, I'm going to like it here.*

I venture upstairs with my suitcase and find five large bedrooms, chocked with worn antique furniture. It feels like a museum. I'm to stay in any of the guest rooms and have been forewarned that the dog will find me no matter where I sleep.

The doorbell rings, and I'm greeted by a furry blur. When I catch up with him, I see that Robert is a classic Welsh Terrier: a medium-sized dog, with wide eyes, curly tan hair, and a black saddle. Too bad that pesky Robert keeps howling all night. Howling bed hog. This house has

4,999 other square feet for him to sleep in, but he insists on using the middle of my bed. However, I suppose it's worth putting up with him to stay in a grand house in a posh suburb of London. Besides cooking, I've been given the lead role in a covert operation: I'm to smuggle a bottle of Boodle's gin into the hospital —along with the dog.

Chapter 7

After much debate and five run-throughs, I settle on the #102. This is no trifling matter, since I'll finally be meeting Oliver, and having just the right shade of lipstick— Chanel #102—could make all the difference. Of course, men would say that this was rubbish, but I happen to know that millions of dollars are spent each year on lipstick—and not just by me.

I write in my little journal so I can remember what to tell my mother later.

11:45 Getting into English spirit by making little cheese sandwiches smeared with Branston pickle.

11:48 Dog steals my sandwich!

1:30 I take a relaxing bubble bath but dog insists on watching. Seems a bit pervy if you ask me. Only been here one day, and already saying British things like "bit pervy." Then the dog jumps in! Oh great, my mobile phone is now at the bottom of the bathtub.

2:20 Figured out what to wear: fishnets and a sexy Hermes-shade orange dress. That and my button-up high-heeled boots. Okay, now I look like a hooker. I decide to start again with a different concept for Professor Oliver Ogilvie. I find a school-girl pleated skirt and a periwinkle sweater with a Peter Pan collar.

3:05 Not sure how to get to the Claridge's, and it's already getting a little dark from the rainstorm. Wouldn't want to end up murdered before I get there. Mrs. Etherington calls to say she will send her driver to take me to the hotel. Wonder how this day will turn out.

Chapter 8

For twenty-two minutes of my precious life, I have to listen to the driver argue with his girlfriend on his mobile. Finally, I am deposited at the hotel's side door. I make a mad dash through the rain to the foyer, and now I'm cold and sopping wet. I settle in the clubby lounge with its orange and purple velvet wing chairs. I'm the only one here for now, so I try out a few different seats to get just the right one.

4:10 I order tea and scones and sit, wondering what our kids will look like when I marry Oliver.

4:54 I order a Malbec from the lethargic Penguin posing as my waiter. I've been waiting nearly an hour; I wonder what's happened. Oliver has probably tried to call a hundred times, but there's no cell service at the bottom of the tub.

5:42 I order another Malbec. What was I thinking flying all the way to England to meet someone who surely must be an ax-murderer? I'll bet the little boys are both fictitious and ill-behaved.

5:58 Not wanting to leave my post, I carefully apply more Chanel #102 using the reflection in the tiny jam knife.

6:07 Did I just fly 3000 miles to meet a stranger? Why can't God deliver a soul mate to my zip code? I can only conclude that God wants people to travel.

Suddenly, I am dislodged by a strong perfume — *My Sin* —I'd know it anywhere. Then a beautiful brunette storms in – and comically trips over a little velvet tuffet. She apparently doesn't find this as amusing as the waiter, and I do. He even laughs the way a penguin would with flapping arms. After a signal from her, he opens a bottle of Louis Roederer Cristal and starts pouring. With nothing else to do, I study her supermodel features: thin frame, kitten eyes, and a tiny nose. I watch as she makes hyper movements to scan the room and drink her champagne. *It's smart of her to get a whole bottle at the rate she's downing it.*

Maybe we can be friends—the two stood-up girls at Claridge's.

Right then, a strikingly handsome man with angled black temples and high cheekbones enters the scene.

"Maryel!" He takes her bejeweled hand. "*Je suis désolé je suis en retard.*"

The penguin waiter curtails wiping up my scone crumbs for a moment to take in the dramatic scene with me. He says, "Did he just call himself a politically incorrect name?"

I remember some of my high school French and translate for him. "No, he just apologized for being late."

Thankfully, the handsome man reverts to English and says, "Sorry, I was caught in traffic."

"You live a block away."

"I had a meeting with Clover. Er. Um. Clover's mother."

The fat, balding Penguin, trudges over to pour more bubbly, blocking my view. Suddenly, the Maryel girl flings her Champagne at the handsome late-comer's face! In my book, £400 champagne is not to be flung.

The Maryel woman seethes. "Je pars cet instant!"

Penguin, who is now sitting on the sofa with me, turns his head to me for the translation. I say, "I'm leaving this instant."

He points to me. "Not without paying, Missy!"

The red soles of Maryel's shoes flick rapidly out of the room. The sexy man sits back in defeat and catches me gaping at him. So, I hide behind the wine menu, thinking I'm safe until I realize it's upside down. From his vicinity, I hear words in perfect Oxford English: "I am sorry you had to witness that spectacle."

"If it featured a woman wearing Christian Louboutin shoes splashing Cristal in your face...no, sorry, I missed it."

As Penguin wipes up the wet sofa, the handsome man says, "I'm just glad she didn't order a Balthazar of champagne."

I pat the dry chair near me.

He laughs and saunters over. "Thank you. I'm Julian."

"I'm Camille, and I won't ask what that was all about." This would be my polite way of asking *what* that was about.

He shakes his head. "I suppose when it's not right, you fight."

"At least you have someone to fight with."

"Aren't you waiting for someone?" He looks at my prim outfit and adds, "Your father perhaps?" Without waiting for an answer, he nods to the waiter for another bottle.

"I'm waiting for a blind date. He probably saw me and ran."

With his elegant accent, Julian says, "I am sure that's not the case."

Penguin fills him in. "Pity, she flew all the way from Boston to meet him."

Julian's face makes an amalgamated look of pity and empathy. He's probably wondering if he can cancel that bottle and back out of the room.

"Cheers," he says, executing the most alluring wink as we salute. Then he says, "Please tell me you didn't find him on the Internet." He looks at my forlorn face and finds the answer. "Oh, I see."

21

"Well, he seemed genuine and kind. We wrote to each other for three months—we even used parchment envelopes and sealing wax."

His eyebrow arcs. "Really? Like in a Bronte novel."

I continue. "Yes, I thought he was my soul mate."

Julian leaps to a happier topic. "How long are you here for Camille?"

Penguin opens the new Champagne and answers for me. "She's here for two weeks."

I say, "Yes, I'm dog sitting in St. John's Wood."

"Oh, fantastic!" Then Julian's face sinks. "Sorry, you're a dog sitter?"

"Well, just for now. I'm actually a writer."

I can tell I've regained some footing when he says, "Oh, fascinating. What do you write?"

"I have been writing a food blog, but now I'm working on a novel."

"Oh, what's it about?"

"Well, *now* it's about a woman who poisons her unfaithful fiancé with wedding cake."

Both Julian and Penguin look at each other and go about their respective tasks of drinking and eavesdropping. I ask Julian what he does, and he replies in that vague British manner. "Err... Um. I work for our family pharmaceutical business."

I laugh. "Oh, for a moment, I thought you were a spy."

Hesitantly, he offers me his card. It says: Julian Zarr, CEO of Zarr Pharmaceuticals. I find myself distracted by his uncommonly colored eyes. They are very light blue, like those Husky dogs.

I think of a sentence to describe them. *'He had the kind eyes that bore through you — on your way to find his soul.'*

Julian sips his drink. "So how far was this poet venturing—just across town?"

"No, he's coming in from a place called Ipswich."

"Dreadful place —and it's nearly two hours away."

"Yes, I would have gone there, but he's separated and has kids."

"Separated? For how long—two hours? Sorry, I know how men can be."

"He seemed trustworthy. Writer types usually aren't too dangerous."

"So, I'm safe here with you and that tiny jam knife?"

I attempt a wink. "For now."

"Say, Camille, would you care for a bite to eat? The foie gras is fantastic."

"Yes, I'm starving! That sneaky Robert stole my sandwich, and then knocked my phone into my bubble bath after ogling me…"

Julian pours more Champagne. "Go on, especially the bubble bath part."

"So, Oliver may have tried to call me…"

"Say…if he remembered he was married?"

"But I'll never know. His number is in my wet phone. I suppose he could have called Claridge's and asked for the pathetic woman drinking all alone."

"Sorry, did you say Claridge's?"

"Yes, we had specific plans to meet at Claridge's at 4:00 p.m. on April 8th. It is April 8th isn't it? "

Julian gets a smile on his face, like a slow revealing of ivory piano keys. Then he takes my hand and says, "My dear, yes, it is April 8th—but this is the Connaught Hotel."

Penguin throws his arms up. "Silly! You've been waiting in the wrong hotel!"

Chapter 9

Thoughts swirl in my head. *Oh no!* The wrong hotel? I distinctly remember telling Mrs. Etherington's driver to take me to Claridge's. But then again, he was quite distracted. Julian silently holds up a cocktail napkin embossed with the words, *'Connaught Bar,'* complete with logo.

"Yes, I noticed that, but thought that was just the name of the bar inside Claridge's Hotel."

Apparently, this is a reasonable mistake to have made, for he nods his head. "Claridge's is not far; I'll show you the way."

Julian and I race out the door in the rain. Soon, I hear wheezing and see the penguin waiter trailing us.

Julian yells, "Not to worry, I'll come back and pay the bill."

Penguin says breathlessly, "I know Mr. Zarr. I just want to come and see what the poet looks like."

When the three of us reach Claridge's, we scan all the public rooms — only to discover that there is no Oliver. I ask the maître d' if he saw a man with poet's eyes and dimples. He asks if the man would have happened to be 5'10" and mid-forties with a box of chocolates.

I answer, "Yes, he would."

"No, haven't seen him." Then he doubles over laughing and says a man matching that description sat for three hours looking sad. "He didn't eat a single chocolate. Not a one."

Oh my god. I feel awful. Like I missed the last boat of my life.

Julian says sweetly, "How about I take you to dinner. There's a lovely place nearby called Scott's."

Penguin says, "Sure! My shift ends at eight."

Julian laughs, "Um. Sorry, I meant Camille."

I notice Julian's laugh: It's a repressed series of lower case, "hmm, hum hums."

I say, "Thank you, Julian, but I'd better be getting back."

He asks for my number, so the dejected Penguin pulls out a cocktail napkin for me to write on. Julian hails a taxi and says goodbye. As I pull away, I wonder if I've just made another colossal blunder.

Chapter 10

Now back in St. John's Wood, I open the door, but there is no one greeting me in the servile manner of a dog. Then, I hear commotion upstairs, and I run up to find Robert in my bed with my fancy button up boots. He's coughing. All 18 of the buttons are gone, making me speculate that they are now in his stomach. *What should I do?* I don't want to alarm Mrs. Etherington or—more importantly—get fired on day two of my international posting. I use the house phone to call my only friend in London: Julian Zarr. After I explain the issue, he tells me to hurry to The Primrose Veterinary Clinic.

I call a taxi, stressing the urgency. When the driver arrives, he says, "Sorry, no pets."

It's too late to call London Woolf, so I start to cry, which works like a charm.

When I run into the vet's office carrying the dog, I'm still crying. I spot Julian, who appears deep into an article titled, "So You Want to Become a Vet?"

Rushing into the brightly-lit waiting room, I say, "This is so sweet of you."

He wipes my tears. "After the day you've had, I couldn't leave all alone."

Ah. Maybe the dog is my lucky angel. They say that dogs are miracles with paws. Not so sure about cats, as one comes in with his head stuck in a jar —which preempts our turn in the queue.

While we wait, I discover a little bit more about this Julian fellow. I learn he went to Oxford and was raised by a Swiss-German father and a British mother. *What a cheery combo.* He peruses my features and guesses I'm of Irish ancestry.

"I had my DNA tested. I'm Irish, English, Scottish, Lithuanian, Austrian, and Norwegian."

He tells me that he's never heard of such a mixture, and says my parents sure got around.

I tell him I'm adopted.

After a while, the miracle paw workers pump Robert's stomach and find seventeen buttons. While easing my mind, I worry that there is still a button left in the dog. This chronic state of worry partially explains why I do not have children. Other reasons shall become apparent.

When I ask for the bill, the receptionist tells me it has been taken care of. Thinking Mrs. Etherington has a running tab for such fiascos, the receptionist points to Julian and says, "Good that you have a Black Am Ex card, Mr. Zarr."

"No. This is not yours to pay. I'm sure Mrs. Etherington will give me the money back. Well, maybe."

Julian smiles and opens the door. "Too late."

"Thank you, Julian."

He offers us a ride home in his blue sports car. I'm so tired I just look out the windows at the houses, replying the day.

Upon reaching Mrs. Etherington's house, Julian says, "Nice little situation you have here."

"Yes, it's worth all of the cooking and smuggling I have to do."

"Camille, how about dinner tomorrow night?"

How can I say no?

27

Chapter 11

I muster the courage to call my new boss, Mrs. Etherington, to mention the hijinks o' Robert. After assigning total blame where due, I strain to hear what is merely a long pause. Finally, a voice befitting an Edwardian-era queen says, "Oh dear, not again. He always ate the buttons off the butler's suits."

Whew! I thought my dog-sitting skills were to blame. Mrs. E. says, "There's a checkbook in the biscuit bin adjacent to the refrigerator. Please bring it, and I'll reimburse this Julian fellow. And do bring Robert."

Just as I'm picturing Robert in a taxi with the checkbook in his mouth, Mrs. E. provides me with the details of my after-lunch task.

"Go ahead and take the Jaguar as the Vauxhall is low on petrol. Now they do not permit pets, so you'll have to come up with something to get him into the hospital." She glosses over this bit of detail.

I decide to take a taxi to meet Oliver, as I'm afraid to drive Mrs. Etherington's car in the city. I stop to get a new phone with London service, so I will no longer be in tech exile.

Okay, so now—after all this time—I am finally meeting Oliver. I'm not as nervous as I was yesterday. I guess my nerves are too shot to pulse. What do I wear? As yesterday's school-girl outfit so successful, I decide to wear it again, but with a different periwinkle sweater. Periwinkle is the universal flatterer, so I have many garments in that color.

I manage to get to the Connaught early and somehow wind up with the same penguin waiter. He probably thinks I never made it home last night. Frankly, he's wearing the same outfit and shouldn't talk. He probably thinks I slept with Julian, so I hope he's not a blabbermouth.

Suddenly, my heart starts to pound. *Oh, brother, what a time to have a heart attack.* Well, if I'm going to die, at least it will happen in a five-star hotel. When I tell Penguin of my heart condition, he says, "Not here you don't, Missy. Not on my shift."

My chest feels like one of those gigantic throbbing cartoon character hearts. It is difficult to tell the difference between love and a heart attack. There he is, my Oliver. He looks worried, then he sees me. His face melts to a smile —a nervous smile.

As he approaches, I see his dimples that make spontaneous genuflections on his cheeks.

In a soft voice, one that could only be played by a woodwind instrument, he says, "Well. Well."

Thoughts ping against the sides of my head. Does he think I'm a stupid cow for going to the wrong hotel? Who takes a bath with their dog? It's not even my dog. My face must look apologetic, for he kisses me. Just like in the photos, Oliver has incredible lips. Men's lips generally go unnoticed with some having a mere buttonhole; but not Oliver, his lips are full and curvy, with a third dimension of sensuality.

Presenting menus, Penguin disrupts me from my lip haze to ask if I'd like a drink. Then he mentions that they have Cristal Champagne by the glass— that is unless I want to order a bottle like last night. I give him a look that says, *'Say another word, and I will pummel your dorsum with this menu.'*

After we order lunch, my mind drifts back to the attractive man sitting across from me. I must keep track. My shrunken brain is now making a rattling sound. Did he say he came from Ipswich or Felixstowe? How do playboys keep track of their women's details? Now, I worry that I'll call Oliver —Julian and vice versa. This is probably why playboys call everyone 'Love.' It's pet-like and never wrong.

Oliver sighs. "Well, I must say you are even prettier in person than in your photos."

Whew! What a relief. That was a long wait for the refrain to his ancient, "Well. Well."

He says, in the most enchanting voice, "What a pity we missed each other last night."

"Yes. What a crazy night."

He goes on. "I ended up having dinner at a place called Scott's. It was first-rate, but a bit much for my humble tastes."

Thank goodness I didn't go there with Julian last night!

As he speaks, my mind wanders to thoughts of honey and kittens.

Oliver asks, "So, how do you propose to sneak the dog into the hospital?"

"Um…I was thinking of dressing him up like a baby, or else pretending he's a service dog. I haven't made my mind up yet."

Oliver smiles. "How do you get yourself into these things?"

I was wondering the same thing myself. "I think I'll wear a trench coat. Maybe I'll pretend I'm pregnant and put the dog under the coat."

Oliver laughs. "Oh, very clever. That is until it starts barking."

"Babies bark sometimes. My hairdresser's niece had a baby that howled like a coyote."

Oliver pours his tea, and our eyes meet. Instead of boring through you, his eyes pull you back into his deep warm soul.

The strange thing about our correspondence is that I already know everything about him. At least on the outside.

Then he blurts out, "Have you ever wanted a baby, Camille?"

Whoa! That's very intimate. It makes me want to get a room upstairs and make a baby. "Well, yes, but not one that would bark."

Oliver touches my knee. "I love children."

"I can't wait to meet yours."

"You should come up sometime. How long are you here for?"

"Until Mrs. Etherington's hip heals."

"I'll mark my calendar."

"I know, isn't it strange that my fate is dependent on a seventy-four-year-old hip? I hope she's a slow healer."

He looks nervous, yet hopeful. "It sounds like we will have more time to get together."

"Yes, maybe Mrs. Etherington will let me take the car up. She has an old Jaguar."

"Is it an MK2? My wife's parents had one, but it never started."

Penguin's eyebrows rise whenever Oliver mentions his wife. After scuffing away, Penguin returns with our food. Oliver shakes vinegar on his fish and chips, saying he can't afford hotels like this. He prefers camping and takes the lads up to Scotland's Speyside area from time to time. Then he asks if I like camping. Thankfully, I'm busy catching a stray grape that has escaped from my chicken salad, which gives me time to think up an answer. Something that will not kill the relationship before I secure the grape, but also something that will not catapult me into a tent with two little boys on a chilled bog.

31

"Camping?" Suddenly I have a vision of Oliver in a cable-knit sweater singing, "Puff the Magic Dragon," to the boys while I stir a pot of stew over a campfire. "I love camping!" I instantly bewail my comment —especially the exclamation point.

Oliver slaps his corduroyed thighs. "Then it's settled. We'll go camping. I'll bet you look lovely without makeup."

This man is a dreamer. What have I done? Thoughts of elegant hotels and Chanel #102 fly out the door—while the smell of tent canvas and kerosene marches in.

When lunch is over, Oliver hands me the box of chocolates. It has melted into one colossal chocolate blob, so I break a piece off and put it in his mouth. He does the same for me, and I make a deep, moaning sound. We look up to see Penguin with hands in prayer, watching our little soap opera.

Oliver says he'll drive me back to St. John's Wood. Together we walk silently out of the hotel past a reflecting fountain; I glance down to see our faces —muddled and wavy like we had grown old together.

Oliver has an old green Jeep, full of footballs, and coated in dog hair. He finds Acacia Road without GPS or a map. I love men with natural navigational skills. When he pulls into the driveway, he whistles at the house.

He silently turns to kiss me goodbye. It's hard to kiss sideways in a car. I am worried that it will go out of gear, and we will coast into Mrs. Etherington's rose bushes, and her kissing frog statue. It's hard to kiss when you're worried about kissing frogs. Oliver has a comforting kiss: like warm cream and vanilla, stirred with a wooden spoon. Ah.

He pulls the spoon out. "I'll let you get to your dog smuggling. I'll ring you tomorrow, Camille."

And he's off. It was all so fast. It was a three-month relationship of planning and dreaming. And now he's gone again. I spend the afternoon replaying the tape-in-my-mind of our lunch, mostly his voice and his kiss.

Chapter 12

How am I going to sneak this dog into the hospital? I'm sure the service dog scheme has been overplayed.

2:04 I mull over my repertoire of subterfuges. I love the word "conniption" and will use it in my defense if caught. Think I shall put the dog in a pram, with a pillow under my belly, and then have an Academy Award-fitting conniption fit.

2:34 I'm late. I have come to learn in my three-day international posting that Mrs. Etherington has her tea and sticky pudding promptly at 3:15. So I must hurry. It's raining again, so I decide to drive her 1967 car.

2:48 When Robert sees me behind the wheel, he hides under a cardboard box. Then I see the box hover across the back of the garage in pursuit of an exit. That's it! I'll cut a hole for his head and tail with the garden shears. I'll just walk the box into the unwitting hospital. If anyone says anything, I'll just ignore and say I work for MI5 and not breathe a word. The trench coat will help.

It doesn't exactly go well, but the nurses manage to peel themselves off the floor when their laughter subsides. The box and I are led down a red stripe on the floor. Soon I find a delicate woman propped up on a bed —it is unmistakably, David's mother, Mrs. Etherington. She has short grey hair and lively green eyes, the same color as David's. Like him, she looks very Scottish. She has a face that tells you she was once beautiful.

With her Edwardian accent, she gushes, "You must be Camille."

"Oh, Mrs. Etherington, it is so nice to finally meet you."

She gives me a long hug. Then eyes the box hovering on the linoleum. "Oh, you remembered to bring my nondescript parcel."

The nurse shakes her head. "Pitiful attempt, I tell you."

Mrs. Etherington quips, "Yes, but that's the beauty of it all. She didn't even try."

Actually, I did. Mrs. Etherington is all dressed up, wearing a boiled wool sweater, plaid skirt, and pantyhose. Who breaks her hip and puts on pantyhose? Maybe they hold it all together. As we have tea, she details matters of the household. She tells me she had a Chinese housekeeper who ran off with the butler and that I'll just have to do without help until she can bring someone in.

I learn that her late husband was a UK Ambassador posted in Shanghai. When I ask further questions, she quickly gets off the subject by asking about my lunch with Oliver. When I tell her I've been hoodwinked into camping, her eyes go wide.

"Camping? Do you mean actual camping, or are you referring to a three-star hotel?"

"No, actual camping outdoors—with little boys."

"Dear God!"

I get carried away and tell her that Oliver's kiss made my heart pound and, "He has these dimples and these beefy man hands..."

A pair of busybody nurses is hovering in the room, listening in on my romantic tale. They want to see the photos of Oliver.

The skinny nurse says, "Whoa. Look at that hair."

"Marry him if he makes your heart flutter," comes from the portly one's mouth.

Tempting as that is, I feel the need to clarify. "Well, the thing is, he's still technically married, but…"

The nurses look aghast and depart in a huff.

Mrs. Etherington leans into me, "Can you get out of it? I can help you make something up — like a sudden allergy to trees?"

"It's too late."

She shakes her head and asks for the check book and writes out a check to Julian Zarr. "Don't let the Swiss one slip through your fingers."

Chapter 13

I sit and wait in the clearly designated meeting point —Mrs. Etherington's house — but my date is an hour late. Finally, the doorbell rings.

"Sorry I'm a bit late," Julian says with his posh accent.

"That's okay; I had some of the dog's dinner."

"Ewe."

"No. I made him rack of lamb with a truffle and fennel compote."

A crease parts Julian's forehead. "Are you serious?"

"Yes. Page 124 of the Daniel Boulud cookbook."

"Maybe I should fire my cook and hire you."

I hesitantly leave Robert with the run of the house as I hop into the co-pilot seat of Julian's Aston Martin.

On the way to dinner, I cheerfully ask Julian how his day was. He replies. "Oh, had meetings and then dropped by the club."

"Which club?"

"The Royal Automobile Club. Sometimes after work, I play billiards. It helps to relieve stress."

When I ask him what is causing his stress, he tells me there's a problem with the Zarr cancer drug, and it's been recalled. When I ask more questions, he says he doesn't want to talk about it tonight. Hm.

We head to Knightsbridge and enter the Mandarin Oriental Hotel. What a pleasant surprise: It is Bar Boulud, run by Mrs. Etherington's favorite chef. The restaurant is a

French bistro with a sleek modern decor. As we read the fascinating menu, Julian asks me my favorite food.

"Butter."

"If the chef only knew."

Julian says this as he's feeding me foie gras with apricot coulis sumac. Naturally, it ends up on my dress, making me glad I'm wearing an apricot colored dress. I make a note of the sauce in my little book, so I know what to tell the drycleaner. Ah, I sip my wine and ponder this new Julian fellow.

After dinner, he asks if I'd like to stop by his place in Mayfair for a drop of vintage port. He asks this with his fingers up my dress. Hm? Is this our first date? I say it's a bit early for that. He looks at his watch and says, "Alright, shall we wait until midnight?"

When I send his fingers marching in the other direction, he says, "I'm having a party Saturday night. Will you come by then?"

"Is this going to be one of those parties where I'm the only guest?"

He winks at me. "No, but I should add that to my repertoire of bachelor tricks."

After he drops me off at home, I see a text from Oliver. He has invited me to a picnic in Ipswich on Sunday. How exciting to have two dates on the same weekend; this would never happen back in Boston. I realize it was an excellent decision to have come to England.

Chapter 14

Upon Mrs. Etherington's advice, I head to Harvey Nichols department store in Knightsbridge for a cut, color and makeover. This takes all day, so I have to head straight to Julian's after a stop at the drycleaners. Thank goodness, I've left the terrace door open for Robert. *Really, who has time to walk a dog?*

Julian has a grand townhouse in Mayfair — one of the most expensive neighborhoods of London. After a long wait at the door, an old lady lets me in. With a thick French accent, she introduces herself as something that sounds like 'Mrs. Coquin.' As she guides me through the stark white modern house, I take a glass of Pouilly Fuisse from a passing waiter, who scoffs and grabs it back. I land in the über-sleek kitchen and she hands me an apron. *Okay. I'm happy to pitch in, given the surly help.* Mrs. Coquin points into the oven and says, "See the duck canapés? Garnish them when they're done."

She talks so fast, I can't tell if she says 4-5 minutes, or else 45 minutes. I decide on the shorter time and start making little faces on the hors-d'oeuvres using pistachio nuts for eyes.

When I offer one to her, she shrieks, "Are you trying to kill me? I'm allergic to nuts!"

"Sorry, I'll take the eyes off."

"Don't bother. I had some earlier when that sweet Maryel dropped them off."

Wanting to get intel, I say, "Oh, you know, Maryel?"

"Of course! I was her cook too."

"She eats?"

"Not like you appear to, but yes." Mrs. Coquin arranges the canapés on a plate and says, "I'm going to help her get Julian back tonight."

"Um. You know I'm dating him."

She falls on the floor, laughing. "You!"

Julian appears in the kitchen. "What are you doing, Camille?"

"Um. Helping Mrs. Coquin out in the kitchen."

"Her name is not Coquin. That's French for naughty. It's Couquin."

I fail to hear any difference and decide to stick with my descriptive spelling and pronunciation.

He looks at my black pants and a white shirt and laughs. "I suppose this is what happens when you arrive early, dressed like the catering staff. I hope you brought something nice to wear."

When I point to my dry-cleaning bag, Julian says in a deep voice, "Come with me."

Mrs. Naughty trails us and yells, "She still has to devein the shrimp!"

Julian leads me upstairs, where I find the decor is also the same stark white, but now there are a few black accents. It has all the warmth of a German operating room. He presses a button that opens another door that leads to another bedroom –like in a James Bond set. "You can get ready here. Take all the time you need."

"All I have to do is put the dress over my head. It doesn't even have a zipper."

He smiles and turns on his heel. "I'll be in my room if you need anything."

When I open my dry-cleaning bag, I see an unwelcome surprise. It is not my sexy orange dress. It is a gigantic blue dress. Oh no! I press buttons on the wall frantically until I find Julian and hold up the dress. We both see the tag: 'A Pea in the Pod.' Oh no —it's a maternity dress!

"Camille Carano, I love a woman who likes to play dress-up. First school-girl, then a caterer, next naughty pregnant lady."

"It's not mine. The dry cleaner gave me the wrong dress—and now they're closed."

He sends a text and says, "I've asked Mrs. *Couquin* to bring you a scarf."

We hear her huffing up the stairs, and soon she's tying some sort of burlap coffee bag around my neck. Julian says something in French, and she quickly departs. *I must learn this useful phrase.*

Once we are alone, Julian kisses me long and deep in the closet, and I can tell he is 'enthused.'

He rubs my hand on 'him' and laughs. "Looks like all the guests are arriving early."

I whisper to Julian, "Let's pretend I'm the wayward caterer, and we just had sex upstairs."

Julian laughs. "That's what I love about you, Camille; you're very playful." *Did he just say he loved me?*

Mrs. Coquin reappears and catches us kissing. She then throws an elegant Chanel scarf at me, something she was apparently holding back on. The doorbell rings, and she tells me to follow her down the stairs; here, she hands me the plate of duck canapés to serve. The doorbell rings again, and I'm so startled, I drop them on the floor. She shakes her fist at me and I learn some new French words. The she yells, "Oeuvre la porte!"

When I peel back the massive front door, I find four tall thin women who must be models: a blonde, brunette, redhead, and a pink. I recognize the beautiful brunette Maryel, Julian's ex-fiancé. They throw their raincoats on my arm as they gallop past to the living room. When the doorbell rings again, Mrs. Coquin says she's not feeling well, and I'm to be in charge of the door.

Next, a stout forty-something man abruptly hands me his coat and umbrella. Julian appears and introduces me to Simon, his brother. I nearly burst out laughing —a gesture I picked up from Mrs. Coquin —until I see a familial look about the earlobes. While Julian has Arctic eyes and chiseled features —his brother has muddy eyes and potato-y features.

Julian must see the doubtful look on my face and adds, "He's my half-brother. We have the same father, but different mothers."

I'm glad that mystery has been solved.

Then the door flies open. My ears are assaulted by a voice that evokes the feeling of fingernails on a blackboard. "Why didn't you wait for me, Simon?"

Julian introduces me to Simon's American wife. She's a roly-poly mid-thirties "blonde," with telltale black roots. He uses the hideous initials B.M. instead of a name.

After the hurricane passes, I whisper to Julian, "What, dare I ask, does B.M. stand for?"

Julian replies, "Her name is Beth Marie, but we call her B.M. Short for Blabber Mouth."

"She must have some endearing qualities for your brother to have married her."

"Pregnancy can be endearing. I don't know how, but somehow it happened the weekend they met."

I pull his lips in. "You don't know how?"

Julian introduces me to his friends, but they all seem to think I'm a caterer. One of them even wants to hire me until Mrs. Coquin scoffs, "Elle mange tous les amuse gueules et en plus elle est paresseuse."

Not a glowing recommendation as I believe she said I'm lazy and I eat all the food. Who cares? I am starving and grateful for the waiter who is now passing hors d'oeuvres. However, every time I reach for one, he says they are not for staff and retracts his silver tray.

More supermodels arrive. Like a tower of giraffes, they horn their way into Julian's home—and possibly into his heart. Pretending not to care, I watch as Julian is hugged by one beauty after another. He introduces me to a stunning six-foot-tall blonde named Clover. He quickly adds that she's his new step-sister. Her mother is the father's latest wife. *Oh great, that means she'll always be around.* Clover pulls at my new Chanel scarf, nearly strangling me. "Did you steal this from Maryel?"

"Um. No. Mrs. Coquin loaned it to me." Clover yanks it from my neck it, leaving me with the uniform of a lowly caterer.

After more angst-ridden moments, I elect to hide in the kitchen with Julian's pregnant sister-in-law, B.M.

She's the only other American at the party—and the only one who is not model thin. B.M. tells me she was even fatter before she got pregnant and lost weight thanks to morning sickness. *Not sure that will make a popular diet fad.*

Every time the kitchen door opens, I can see her husband Simon chatting up Clover, so I try to block the view to spare B.M.'s feelings. She tells me that this Clover girl is Maryel's best friend and flat-mate in Paris. Okay, B.M. will helpful at gathering info. Too bad about her accent, which I can only describe as cat-twang Southern. B.M. reverses her data dump and begins to interrogate me. "So let me see if I have this straight, Camille. You cook for an old lady's dog. Are you some sort of pet chef?"

There go my food critic credentials.

Julian comes into the kitchen. "There you are, Camille! I'm going to open up a bottle of Domaine Ramonet Montrachet, so come out for a glass." As he silently searches through the kitchen wine chiller, B.M. continues her chat.

She says to me. "You must love dogs to cook for one every night."

"I do. I had a pug who just died…"

B.M. blurts out: "We had a pug once! Well, it wasn't a real pug—at least not anymore. My Daddy is a taxidermist, so Mr. Pugsley was stuffed and had these little wheels under his paws…"

Julian rolls his eyes and leads me to the living room. The guests are now playing Charades by acting out movie titles. We see the back of his brother Simon —now in drag —wearing an emerald green dress and a reddish-brown bouffant wig.

I look at Julian. "No worries, every family has a cross-dresser or two."

The supermodels have trouble guessing the movie title, and Simon throws his hands up and turns around. I see it is not he, but a squatty 60ish female version of him. She sounds a little Eastern European when she yells, "No. Love is a Many Blundered Thing."

Julian whispers, "And *that* is Simon's mother. My father's second wife."

Simon pulls Julian aside for a private chat, so I grab a tray of martinis and pretend to serve, so I can eavesdrop more easily.

I hear Simon whisper to Julian. "We've got trouble in the Zurich lab."

Unruffled, Julian asks, "What sort of trouble?"

"Five people died."

Maryel drops a series of queen-sized olives in my path, which sends me careening down the stairs, and my tray of drinks flying in the air. This prompts the mean girls, Clover and Maryel, to burst out laughing.

Mrs. Coquin takes this opportunity to yell at me in front of everyone. "Fille maladroit stupide!"

Julian helps me up and gives Mrs. Coquin a look that could kill, so she spends the rest of the night hogging the first floor powder room.

Maryel knocks on the door and tells Mrs. Coquin it's her turn for charades, so she ventures and climbs on the coffee table which has become the stage. Then she clutches her chest and makes a dramatic fainting scene in the middle of the living room.

Maryel yells out, "Cleopatra!"

Simon's mother calls out, "No, no. It's Death by Pipe Cleaner Spider."

What?

Simon cries, "That's not the name of a movie. That's a murder method."

Everyone stands around the collapsed Mrs. Coquin in the middle of the carpeting while trying to guess the movie's name.

She even has special effects, making it look like blood is coming from her mouth —accenting the neutral white carpeting. Clover steps over her to get another drink, as others call out movie titles.

This looks like it will take a long time to figure out, and I need to get back home to tend to the dog.

After retrieving my maternity dress, I come back down and stand in the entry, awaiting a taxi. I turn back to see everyone now standing around Mrs. Coquin. Then Simon picks up her wrist and announces: "She's dead."

Ah, there's my taxi now.

45

Chapter 15

Ipswich, England

Whew! I leapt into the taxi without looking back. If I had lingered, I knew I would have been blamed for something —or made to clean the kitchen.

Today, my barking travel mate and I are venturing to Ipswich for the day. It takes over two hours, making me realize that Oliver and I are not geographically compatible. Thanks to GPS, I find the school and see Oliver in the distance. He is coaching a group of boys, including two smaller versions of himself —presumably, his sons Trevor and Tristan. From this distance, they do not appear to be fictitious or ill-behaved. And when I finally meet them, I discover that they do indeed have adorable accents.

We bundle up to share a tailgate lunch of pea soup, with cheese and pickle sandwiches. One of the boys brings me flowers; the other brings me weeds. One of the boys kisses me; the other bites me. *I wish I could tell them apart.*

One of the boys has walloped a chipmunk with a football. The other boy is crying and holding the limp creature. Oliver must be used to this, for he calmly pets the creature back to life. *Could he be more adorable?*

A rainstorm abruptly ends the picnic before the boys' mother comes to retrieve them. Oliver and the wife alternate times in the flat when it's not their turn to stay at the house with the boys. I imagine marital separations with children are logistical challenges.

While Oliver drops the kids at the house, I'm left alone in the tiny one-bedroom apartment. It has a certain charm due to high ceilings, old books, and antique furniture. It's the antithesis of Julian's place.

Frankly, I'm happy to have a bit of time to myself to process the past few days. Oliver couldn't be more different from Julian. The question is — who is meant for me?

I make a cup of tea and look around the charmingly rustic flat. It was trusting of Oliver to leave a busybody like me here alone. Even though I'm dying to snoop around, I honor his trust.

Robert, the dog, has other ideas. I have to make frequent trips to the bedroom to get him out of the dirty laundry basket. He unearths a pair of women's cotton underpants, and I have to chase him around the flat to retrieve them, praying that the rightful owner does not return in mid-chase.

I check out the bedroom that he and his wife share. While not at the same time, it still must be odd. I can't help but sniff the pillow on the man's side of the bed. It has Oliver's scent of melted butter and oats. I wonder how the wife can sleep here without wanting him back.

Suddenly there is a crash. I run to the kitchen to catch Robert on a journey to the bottom of the trash. On the linoleum, I find coffee grounds and eggshells, and bills—remnants of their shattered marriage. I also see a tea-stained poem.

The girl beyond the sea

After a lifetime, she came

Deeper than my dreams

Swirling moons and mermaids

When I looked into her eyes

Past the turquoise waters

that arouse distant tides

It all came back to me

Thoughts and memories.

I had known her soul

A thousand years ago

Will she save me?

I am drowning under her sea

She is the past

She was the future

She will never be.

I wonder if his wife also has turquoise eyes—or is that poem about me? I can't very well ask, or he'll know I've been snooping through the trash. I guess he liked me better when I was imaginary. Does he only love in his head? If so, he and I are as one. Oh great—I finally find my soul mate, but his poet soul is unavailable, out of stock.

Re-crumpling the poem, I put it back with the broken eggshells and try to reconstruct his life's debris.

After two hours, I start to wonder where Oliver is. *Perhaps something happened to one of the boys or both? They have pummeled each other with bats, most likely. I can picture my poor lover pacing the floor at the hospital—torn between coming back to see me, or waiting out their brain reconstruction surgeries.*

As the dog runs about with ladies underpants in his mouth, I suddenly hear a key in the lock. Instead of Oliver, I see a strange woman standing in the kitchen. She screams. I scream. Except for the deranged look on her face and the cricket bat in her hand, she looks harmless. She is thin and beige, so I assume that she is Oliver's wife. She has an old yellow suitcase, like the ones people used to run away from home with.

With a Scottish accent, she says she left a message for Oliver. The heat is broken at the house, so they will all have to stay here tonight.

In a minute, Oliver returns with the twins. He walks me to the car, saying he was hoping I could have stayed over. When he studies my face, he says not to worry; he's not intimate with his wife anymore. The relationship has been on an 'amicable fade.' I suppose that's better than a plate-throwing split.

Then he invites me to come up again next weekend. Hm?

Chapter 16

After a few idyllically quiet days alone in St. John's Wood, I feel happy. Despite a few unsuccessful attempts, I make gourmet dinners for Mrs. Etherington and Robert. In the evenings, I play my flute to the howling dog and write in my journal.

On Wednesday, I get a call from Julian.

I can't help but ask, "Did they figure out what Mrs. Coquin died of?"

"Foie gras. It was probably a heart attack. She was 74 after all."

Then I notice that his eyebrows are bookending a deep furrow. "We may never know. They didn't do any autopsy in London, and her son had her body sent back to France."

Hm. Remind me not to get fat and old. No one thinks it's suspicious if you die.

Then he says, "I'm headed to Paris for a long weekend, and I was wondering if you'd like to come along." He tells me we'll be flying on his jet.

"Will you be the one flying it?"

He laughs and says, "God, no! And, yes, that should have been your first question."

I tell him that I've got plans for the weekend, leaving out the camping and Ipswich part. "Besides, I'd have to figure out what to do with the dog."

"If you don't want to go, just say so."

"But I do."

He tells me to let him know by tomorrow. Later, I take the dog along to solicit advice from my romance counselor, Mrs. Etherington.

She sips her tea and says, "Let's see…we've got Oliver in a tiny flat with no heat, who is still technically married. Then we have the rich, handsome, single Julian asking you to go on a private jet to Paris. Quite a dilemma you have, my dear."

"I know. But I've already told Oliver that I'd bring the dog up. You don't mind when I take Robert up?"

"Not at all. He tells me he loves it there."

I look out the window. "Well, I am sure there will be other trips to Paris with Julian."

"Right. That is until some supermodel steals him away from you." She pets her dog and bursts out with enthusiasm. "I've got an idea! Why don't you drive up to Oliver's, then feign a lady problem, get him to watch Robert, then fly off to Paris with Julian?"

"That sounds a little sneaky."

I wonder how to delicately bring up the real dilemma: Sex. If I go to Paris with Julian, surely he'd expect some sort of matriculation. I have been saving myself for Oliver, so this could be tricky. Then, like she can read my mind, Mrs. Etherington says in her genteel manner, "Which one would you want to know your quaint honor?"

I look at her.

"You can't do them both."

Right then, Oliver calls to say that his wife has taken ill, and could we postpone for another weekend. Mrs. E. hears the conversation and waves her arms and shouts, "Hallelujah." She gets out of her bed and starts marching around, giving orders. "Now hurry up and accept Julian's invitation." As I'm texting him, she hands me a piece of paper and starts dictating things to bring her from Paris.

51

I tell Oliver that Mrs. E. is sending me to there for shopping, and ask if could he watch the dog for a few days. It's kind of true. *I'm a terrible liar but a masterful omitter.*

We agree to meet in Chelmsford —the perfect halfway point for a dog drop off. I drive the old Jaguar and play the outdated car radio, which, for some reason, seems to only play songs from the 1960's. Robert howls along to Cilla Black singing "Alfie," and LuLu singing "To Sir with Love."

This makes me think of my professor Oliver Ogilvie. He suggests we meet at a place called *The Pig and Whistle*, so I drive down hedge-rowed country lanes and stop at an old Wedgewood-blue colored restaurant. The interior is warm and enchanting with linen tablecloths and tall candles.

When I walk in with the dog, I spot Oliver at a corner table in the dining room. I get a tap on the shoulder from the manager, who suggests the wet, smelly dog dine in the parking lot. This will now be a short visit.

When I get closer, I see Oliver reading a hard-cover book and sipping a Guinness. When he jumps up to greet me, his eyes evoke images of a drizzly day in a seaside village. He's reading a Graham Greene novel, something his brother gave him. It's "The End of the Affair." I hope it's not an omen. God, he looks so handsome that I want his mouth and hands on me. He could perhaps be talked into joining me, but our lover's lair would have to be in the car with an ogling dog.

We dine on divinely crunchy battered cod, with chips and mushy peas and sip chardonnay. I decide this is one of my favorite places.

Oliver tells me that the lads are keen to see Robert again. He had promised the twins a new dog when their sheepdog, Kipling, died. Oliver looks down and says, "Then this came up." I realize he probably means his separation. I want to ask who and what caused it, but think it rude to pry.

Oliver exhales. "Watch what you hope for."

I say I have no idea what marriage is like. "I imagine it's like a roller coaster ride."

He pauses, takes a sip of his dark beer, and then says, "I would love a roller coaster ride, then I'd know I was still alive. No, marriage is like a slow, flat train ride across Siberia."

I silently ponder the benefits of singlehood. The waitress comes over to alert us that there is a howling animal in an old Jaguar, and do we know anything about this.

Our rendezvous has now come to an end. We kiss goodbye to a Dusty Springfield song. Then Oliver takes Robert and his little 1950's train case full of dog toys and puts them in his jeep. He drives away with his co-pilot, off on their own adventure.

All of a sudden, I feel a concrete wall of regret come crashing down on me. Why did I so quickly agree to go to Paris with Julian? When all this time, I've been waiting for Oliver. Now the die has been cast.

Chapter 17

London, England

Julian calls to ask if I can be ready by four p.m. on Friday. I tell him yes, as I have nothing to pack. I had planned on wearing wool in Ipswich, not silk in Paris. He quickly replies. "Say no more. I have a personal shopper at Harrods."

Oh, how I want to dress smartly, like Maryel. A woman rarely gets to meet the other woman ahead of time, but quite handy. Unfortunately, I won't have time to lose ten pounds and grow four inches in the next 24 hours, so I'll have to buy Spanx and high heels.

I'm to meet his personal shopper, Paulina Krakowski, in lingerie. She's easy to find: a sturdy woman in her mid-fifties with short magenta hair. She greets me with her pronoun-free accent. She's an efficient Polish woman —not to be redundant —who wastes no time taking my measurements. Frankly, she gets a little friendly with the tape measure. She shakes her head and says she's glad we started with lingerie. She's used to Julian's thin models coming in at the last minute, "but not…this. You are an hour-glass type, but the dresses are all shaped like... how you say, test tubes."

I knew this was too good to be true. Now I'm depressed.

"And no time for alterations." Then she sees my face and says, "Don't worry, we go stretchy."

She pulls out all sorts of lacey brassieres and see-through nightgowns and asks what color I like. When I think I have died and gone to heaven, it gets even better: there's a sale! She catches me looking at the price tags. "Julian says not let you see prices. You get what you like."

Paulina hands me the most beautiful work of art and engineering: a pale pink brassiere with lacey understruts and seamless sheer cups. From Agent Provocateur: £290 and £87 for the tiny matching thong.

Over the year, I've found expensive lingerie is quite practical as it often pays for itself in free drinks. My new best friend suggests I buy the pale pink baby doll nightie. Then she proposes I get the same bra, panty, and baby doll ensemble in every color. This way, she explains, "We don't have to go through all that again."

She's pushy, maroon, and brash, like a high school marching band as she leads me through the massive store.

"You'll need a better coat," she says, looking down at my rumpled raincoat. She finds a glorious Alexander McQueen white crepe masterpiece.

I catch a peek at the price tag. Whoa! "Okay, this might be a little bit pricey."

"This is on the Zarr account. It is a drop-in zee bucket for him." She holds her hands up in the air. "Don't you know how rich he is?"

I shrug my shoulders. "I gather Julian is doing alright for himself. But I wouldn't want to take advantage of him." *Or become beholden to him.*

Paulina makes an exaggerated sad clown face. "Julian doesn't care. But I do! I only get paid on commission. That's why it's better to shop with me instead of in Paris."

Well, when you put it that way. "Okay, the coat is divine, and I like that Victoria Beckham bag."

She drags me to couture dresses, holding one up with gusto. "Look, Balmain, and it just might fit if you don't

55

eat so much." This is so exciting that I feel like I'm on a game show.

When it all gets rung up, she blocks me from viewing the final bill. "All set. Everything will be sent to Julian's." Then she gets a tormented look. "Oh, no. Mrs. Coquin won't be there for the delivery!"

"I know. How sad about her heart attack."

"What? No. She was poisoned."

Chapter 18

The next day, I see a big black Maybach pull into the driveway. As Julian approaches the front door, it hits me that I'm really doing this. To comfort myself, I bring a suitcase filled with ugly stuff from my previous life.

Julian opens the trunk, and I see it's full of bags from Harrods. I say, "I hope I didn't go overboard."

"Not to worry; it will be a pleasure to see you dressed."

"You mean, undressed." I try to wink provocatively, but it probably looks like I have a tic.

After a quick drive to London City Airport, we board a small, four-seat Embraer jet. Julian says it's the only way to travel these days. He pulls out a half bottle of Pol Roger brut for me, then pours himself a glass of Lagavulin.

I say, "Did you hear? Mrs. Coquin was poisoned!"

"I see I'm going to have to have a word with Paulina about discretion."

Not wanting Paulina on my bad side, I say, "It's not her fault; I wheedled it out of her."

"Yes, it was food poisoning, according to the Lyon coroner."

"Just think, we've all could have been killed."

"Life, my dear, is dangerous — if well-lived."

Hmm. Not the kind of platitude one wants to hear 1500 feet in the air.

I look at Julian who is nose deep in MO Magazine; then it occurs to me: maybe he's gay! Never married and well dressed. Hmm.

He closes the magazine and says, "I'll set you up at the spa. I've booked a suite at the Mandarin Oriental— MO."

"But don't you have an apartment in Paris?"

"Err...um. It's being painted. Yes, they are repainting or papering. The hotel will be better."

"Why do you have an apartment there anyway?"

"Have you seen the women in..." Then he stops short, "We used to have a lab there, but sold it and set one up in Vienna."

He leans over and gives me the most provocative French kiss. *Definitely not gay.* So, I guess I've set myself up to do "it" with him. I suppose I could say I'm not ready, or contract hives like in some Doris Day movie.

I should have looked both ways before crossing.

Chapter 19

Paris, France

After a quick ride through Paris, we are at the hotel in no time. Here we are ushered to a sleek off-white suite with a stunning view of the lights of Paris. The minute we enter, a bottle of Dom Pérignon Rosé and Beluga caviar are delivered and served. *I could get used to this.*

Julian pretends to cover his eyes while I try on the new pink dress and white coat. "Yes, pretty," he says, "love the dresses, but what about all the lingerie?"

I happen to know that it is never a good idea to model lingerie before going out to dinner, as one never gets out of the room. "Okay, after I have a bath."

Venturing toward the spacious marble bathroom, I spot a long, deep bathtub near a window overlooking the Jardin d' Tuileries.

He peeks his head in, "I'll be back in a bit. If you give me Mrs. Etherington's list, I'll have the concierge do the shopping for you."

Could he be any more perfect? Julian refills my glass while I wait for the tub to fill. He jokes, "I don't want the room service guy jumping in with you."

"Yes, I've seen him."

Julian disappears, and I play vintage French singer Édith Piaf's song, "The Blonde and the Brunette" on my new phone, careful not to knock it in the tub. Boy, if I hadn't signed up for that dating site, I wouldn't be here. I'd be all alone in Boston.

As I pour in coconut salts, I fall deep into the white waters of the bath. My thoughts run to Robert, the dog, and how he is faring with Oliver and the boys. I really thought Oliver was the one. Now, I'm confused by this fascinating man, Julian. This perfect on paper, Julian.

After a while, he returns with a gentle knock on the bathroom door. "Camille, may I come in?"

"Okay, but I must advise you that I have nothing on."

He bursts in the door and gets a good eyeful of my blurred nakedness in the water. He arches a dark eyebrow. "You've got lipstick on."

His sweater comes off, and he perches his bum on the edge of the tub.

"Camille, I hope you don't mind, but I made a reservation for us at Thierry Marx downstairs at half eight. It's going to rain all night, so I thought we'd stay in the hotel. I've also gone ahead and booked you a morning at the spa downstairs. I'm assuming women like that sort of thing."

"To be gently rubbed with warm lotions in a quiet setting? No, I'd rather go camping," I joke, then realize the horror that I have narrowly escaped.

Julian reads the spa menu: "Let's see; you have a flower petal facial at 9:30, then something called a cocoon wrap. Afterward, I thought we'd have a long leisurely lunch near the Louvre. Then do a little shopping and then have dinner at The George V. What do you say to that, my dear?"

"What can I say? This is every girl's fantasy."

As he takes off his pants and reveals his long, lean body, I somehow, I can't help but utter, "What was that Maryel thinking?"

A scowl parts his forehead. "What do you mean?"

"Breaking up with you."

He carefully hangs his pants on the towel rack. "But I broke up with her. She's a pathological liar for starters."

"But, she stormed out on you."

"Camille, my dear, do you think I have learned nothing? You have to let the crazy ones think they are breaking up with you."

"How do you do that?"

"It's easy and quite fun." He lets out a devilish giggle. "Now, why am I telling you my man secrets?"

He leans over to kiss me, but my slippery weight pulls him in the water. It's a large tub, and his face somehow lands right where my legs part.

"Now you've done it, Ms. Carano."

He takes a deep breath and submerges his face underwater. His protruding tongue has found me. I conclude that only a properly trained Navy Seal type could do this maneuver —or a playboy.

God, who is this sexy man? He stands up, leaning on the towel rack, so I yank down his wet Williams. He springs to a Royal Mountie. Now he's only wearing his wet, white tee shirt. He lifts it over his head, and I grab it and put it on myself.

He smiles. "Ah, I just can't compete with you in a wet tee-shirt contest, Camille." He pulls on my feet, so I am floating on my back in the warm water. Julian is licking me so gently that I manage to stay afloat. It takes a while due to the light pressure, but eventually, I arrive, as they say. The subtle buildup makes it even more intense. *This guy is good!*

He glances at the clock and says, "I could spend all night here, but we are about to lose our dinner reservation."

He helps me out of the tub, and I stand there, dripping wet, while he gets one of the heated towels. Oh, how I adore a 5-star hotel! He turns on the shower to rinse the salt and oil off. Through the steamed glass, I can make out his finely chiseled body, like an enhanced statue of David. How can I possibly focus on my makeup with this work of art nearby? I decide to join him in the shower. He welcomes me by saying, "The more, the merrier."

We are under the sunflower showerhead of cascading water, and he bends down to put his mouth on my breast. Then he pushes my arms up against the frosted glass and kisses my other nipple.

I kneel down with my line of sight just below his waist. He's so clean, wet, and ready. Ah. The warm water is pounding on our bodies. I feel him getting even harder. I wonder how he keeps from falling; there must be no blood left in his legs because it's all been relocated.

Finally, he lets go without any verbal warning; a warm whiteness hails the occasion, like a fireworks finale. He falls back against the fogged glass, and we sit together in the hot rain.

When we finally emerge, he wraps a warm towel around me. "Prefer to skip dinner?"

When will I ever learn not to start what I can't finish? "No, I'm starving. I can dress fast."

Julian catches me in mid-gaze. "I'll go down and try to hold our reservation."

Pretending I'm on a game show, I challenge myself to get ready in ten minutes. Despite having Einstein hair, I grab my shoes and run to the elevator with my dress unzipped. Why the mad rush? Yes, there's food involved, but it's also because Julian strikes me as the type who would make another female company in no time.

Mustn't let the good ones out of our sight for too long, according to Mrs. Etherington.

Chapter 20

When I get to the bar, I see Julian looking serious while typing on his phone. Fortunately, he's alone. He smiles when I appear, but I realize he is probably laughing at my hair. His frown returns, so I ask him what's wrong.

He sighs and says he just received a report from his father. "Oh, it's nothing. Just ten more deaths due to our drug."

"Oh, no. I'm sorry."

"There is a bright side."

"What — reducing overpopulation?"

"No. Our stock price is lower and my father is trying to buy back shares to regain a controlling interest."

"I thought he owned it."

"He lost it when we went public. Now he's trying to donate the patent, but the board of directors won't let him."

"Interesting. I want to hear all about it."

Julian pats my head. "Not tonight, dear."

In French, Julian orders a bottle of Chateau Palmer Margaux. I think of a line for my novel and pull out my little book to write it down.

"When he spoke French, it was like dancers in pink dresses pirouetting across my heart."

When the bottle arrives, I can see that it has red sealing wax on the label, and I think of Oliver and our parchment paper letters.

Julian orders the eight-course tasting dinner, starting with structured and de-structured carrot, which frankly sounds like someone went to a lot of trouble for a carrot. After the first course, I ask Julian about his family. He reminds me of his younger brother Simon, whom I met in London. He tells me his father lives in Zurich and Lugano, Switzerland. I learn that Zarr Pharmaceuticals has labs in London, Zurich, and Vienna where they make cancer drugs.

He asks if I have siblings. I say no, adding that my dad died three years ago, so it's just my mother and me. Thankfully, the waiter arrives right in time with the next course, making for easy topic changing.

Julian sips his wine and studies my face. "I can't believe you've never married."

"No. They all got away."

A tiny plate of soy and oyster Risotto with Black Truffle arrives.

"What about you —have you ever been married?" I ask Julian.

He takes a tiny bite, continental style. "I am afraid—"

The waiter interrupts him to pour more wine. *Go away.* I look at Julian. "Afraid? What about love? Doesn't that conquer all?"

"You tell me."

He's got me there. Finally, I say, "I guess I'm afraid too; afraid of being trapped, smothered…murdered."

He puts down his knife. "My thoughts exactly."

Boy, you can't win. A man is either tied up in a marriage or afraid of commitment.

"Besides, Camille Carano, you will be back in the states as soon as Mrs. Etherington is up and about."

"Don't worry; I'm sure it's just a matter of time before the dog trips her again."

I try to feed Julian a scallop, but it falls on the napkin on his lap. He smiles and looks around. "I dare you to pick it up with your mouth."

I wink. "Laps are a daring adventure or nothing at all."

We are alone in the dining room, except for a man reading a book on Marx. I'm glad there are no children within viewing distance. I bend down and eat the scallop without using my hands. It's easy— but looks naughty.

He laughs. "I love adventurous women."

"Plural?"

When I come back up, the waiter is standing next to us, clearing his throat. He brings the next course and quickly confiscates the remaining scallops.

Now we have a little game going on. Julian attempts to feed me Ricotta cheese ravioli. I close my eyes, but it never comes. Then I feel warm dampness on my chest. My eyes glance down to see a small ravioli resting on my cleavage.

"Now look what you've done, Mr. Zarr."

"Slippery devils, aren't they?"

His eyes crinkle as he scans the dining room, then he positions his lips on the errant ravioli. I look down to see it disappear into his mouth.

This time the waiter heralds his approach with a loud dropping of a metal lid before announcing the arrival of smoked beef with chestnuts, olives, and capers.

Julian looks on in delight. "Ah, tiny rolling foods."

The waiter pours the rest of our wine. It has barely had a chance to breathe. Nor have we. To get us to the finale, the waiter reels off a detailed list of desserts and then asks which we'd prefer. Julian looks up and says, "The one with the most whipped cream."

I am sure the waiter regrets this offering, as he suggests we have dessert in our room.

Julian laughs and calls out, "L'addition, s'il vous plait."

The waiter practically gallops across the dining room with the bill.

Back in the room, Julian unzips my somehow unscathed dress. I sneak to the bath to put on my little pink nightie. When finally I make my boudoir debut, I come back out to find Julian is fast asleep. I suppose that's what eight courses, scotch, and wine will do. Maybe we should have gone A'la carte.

Chapter 21

In the morning, I am poked awake with that familiar sensation of something soft, yet hard at the base of my spine. Julian disappears into the bath and returns wearing nothing but a playful grin.

He silently takes my hand and puts it on him, and he gets longer and thicker in my fist. Now his lips are kissing right through my sheer pink nightie. He is on his knees, yanking the little pink bottoms down, which he tosses across the room. "Won't be needing these."

His hand is on my slipperiness. Ah. Right then, the doorbell rings. *Rats!* A Frenchy-sounding "Room service" emanates through the door.

Julian takes a towel and covers himself, though frankly, the jig would be up with one downward glance. I retreat under the covers as the room service man wheels a cart into the sitting area. He says someone had put out the room service card last night, requesting coffee and toast at 9:15. *Oh, that would be me.*

Julian sighs. "I am bemoaning my own planning. You have 15 minutes before your first spa appointment. I am afraid that even I cannot pull that off."

The room service man is standing by the door, pretending he has no interest in our conversation. With a peck on each cheek, I am dressed and dispatched to the spa.

Here I find a tranquil turquoise lap pool, dark zen wood, and sumptuous furnishings. My first treatment is something called an Orchid Imperial facial, then a deep tissue massage, and finally a cocoon wrap. The whole time,

I'm thinking of cozy corduroy Oliver wrapping me in a blanket. *Oh no! I've got him out of my head.*

After four hours, I'm relaxed but starving. I head back to the suite, expecting to find Julian with a lingering display of excitement, but only find flat empty sheets. At least his stuff is still there, all neatly folded; mine is in a messy pink pile.

Maybe he realized I'm a hopeless slob and ran off, abandoning a subset of his possessions. I text him, saying I'm in the room, but do not hear back.

Paris is all around me, but I have not left the hotel since I arrived. Thanks to Julian, I'm becoming accustomed to fine epicurean delights and think a bit of brioche or Steak tartare might be in order. As much as I try to be a vegetarian Buddhist, the universe and chefs conspire to keep me from my path.

Venturing out, I walk about three blocks before I notice large raindrops in my path. Bailing on brioche, I start heading back to the hotel. Then, in a cafe window, I see a tall man with dark hair and chiseled features hugging a beautiful woman. It is Julian —and he's with Maryel.

I should have known that one of the supermodels would appear, but not *the* supermodel.

Julian sees me and runs out to catch me. "Camille!"

I huff, "What is *she* doing here?"

He looks at me with earnest eyes. "She called *me*! It seems her Peteaux has come to a sticky end."

"What are you talking about?"

"Her little pussy. It's not really so sad. What with being over nineteen."

I give him a look.

Then he smiles. "I'm talking about Maryel's cat. It died of feline leukemia."

I look in and see her crying—or simulating a pathological liar crying.

Not wanting to engage myself in a woman's cat tragedy, I say, "I'll be back at the hotel."

Now I'm glad I didn't do *it* with him and shall gratefully acknowledge the timely room service guy. Had we been fully intimate, it would have hurt to see him with his ex, crazy bitch, and all.

When I get back to the suite, I take off my wet clothes and climb in bed. Pandora plays the apropos Damian Rice song *"Gray Room."*

A little while later, Julian returns, searching my face for clues as to my mood. Having no doubt suffered from a bout of amnesia, he chirps, "I'm famished. Do you want to order room service?"

He hands me an offering from La Maison du Chocolat. "I brought these for you, and a box for Mrs. Etherington."

"Thank you. That was a wise move," I say, opening the beautiful ribbon-wrapped box. "How did you know I love candied orange peel?"

"They were on Mrs. E's list." He smiles, probably thinking he's out of jail.

"How is it that Maryel happened to be three blocks away?"

He opens the room service menu while trying to collect his thoughts. "Err. Um. You see...the thing is, it seems that B.M., well, she's still friendly with Maryel and must have mentioned that I was staying here instead of in Neuilly... how about lobster for lunch?"

"Neuilly? That's where you have a place."

He looks down at the menu again. "Maryel lives in Neuilly. Actually, right next door to my apartment. That's why I wasn't too keen on staying there."

"I thought it was being repapered?"

"Yes, well that too. Many reasons not to stay in Neuilly." He takes off his wet shoes. "I have no interest in Maryel anymore."

"Then why is she still in your life?"

"We're friends. And while I still find her beguiling, she makes me want to strangle her with my bare hands."

"There are so many things I don't like about that sentence."

He takes a chocolate and puts it in my mouth. "Are you angry with me, Kitten? If so, I can give you Mrs. Etherington's box as well."

I laugh. "No, Julian. I'm still friends with all of my ex-boyfriends, and I would do the same if one of their cats succumbed to feline leukemia."

Julian looks up. "All of them?"

He innocently takes off his wet jeans and puts on a robe. I can predict the future, and I think it will involve licking melted chocolate from his lips.

"You were engaged to Maryel. Do you still love her?"

A reply comes from the closet. "It was never a burning love; it's more of a...chilled like."

Noting the present tense in his chilled like, I ask, "Like a Vichyssoise?"

"That sounds yummy; say, shall I have them take their time bringing up lunch?"

My mouth is full of chocolate. "Sure."

He's running his fingers under the covers and says,

"Why don't you put on that little pink thing, and we'll warm up in bed?"

I pull on the tiny nighty, knowing it won't be on for long.

Right then, I hear a harpsichord on my phone. It's a text from Oliver in Ipswich: *Dog Gone! Please call.*

Confused by the text, I call Oliver back, trying to sound businesslike despite wearing a diaphanous nightie in a Parisian hotel with a handsome man running his fingers up my panties. When I hear the sound of Oliver's voice, my heart starts to pound — like a hummingbird trying to escape from a bass drum. I then notice his voice is slightly higher, like lemon curd and balsa wood, and a bit breathless.

He says rapidly, "Not to worry. I've got my mates on it."

"On what?"

"The lookout for Robert. He's lost! The lads were about to give him a bath and had just taken off his collar when he ran away."

As I convey the situation to Julian, I realize he heard the whole thing when he and his finger were connected to me. He turns away to send a text.

After I hang up, I ask, "Are you texting Maryel?"

"No. My pilot. He can take you to Ipswich airport—that is, if they have one."

"Thank you, Sweetie. You're coming too?"

He says he can't join me because he has to go to a meeting in Basel now.

Now, I'm sorry to leave him—and just as we were getting well acquainted. Leaving Julian in the same town as Maryel could be regrettable.

Julian breathes in my ear. "I'm probably making a huge mistake sending you to him. And I was all ready to take you gently."

Chapter 22

Ipswich, England

The pilot lands at a private airport nearest the thriving metropolis of Ipswich. Here, I find Oliver pacing by the window. He sees me get off the sleek private jet wearing my elegant white coat. He stares for a moment, then finally says, "Who do we have here? The Duchess of Suffolk?"

I laugh. "That jet sure came in handy."

Oliver takes my bag. "I didn't know pet sitting paid so well."

"A friend of mine has a plane that was going this way."

Oliver shakes his head. "If you like that sort of lifestyle, you are looking at the wrong chap. I can barely afford EasyJet."

After about twenty minutes of Oliver-o-apologies, we arrive in the quaint coastal town of Felixstowe. Oliver takes me to an old stone cottage surrounded by birch trees that overlook a tiny pond. It is so romantic that I wonder how anyone could fall *out* of love here. His wife hesitantly opens the door to their family home. I didn't get a good look at her before. While some people shine, she has an absorbency about her.

Oliver grabs the pile of handwritten 'Lost dog' posters, and we venture out while Enfys holds down the fort. As we walk around, I find it disconcerting to have been wrapped up in a warm spa a few hours ago and now be in the cold, damp night calling for a lost dog. I have decided not to upset Mrs. Etherington with the news until tomorrow—or maybe the day after that. Oliver holds my hand as we walk. Except for the lost dog part, I feel happy.

We call out, "Robert" clap, clap, "Palmer" as we wander the streets. The sound carries in the cold air, causing passersby to join like they have supporting roles in a play. When we get to a park, Oliver stops under a tree and says, "We'd better call it a night." He then kisses me — so gently and thoughtfully. My chest is pulsing, making me wonder what this kind of love does to one's heart.

It is starting to rain, a cold drizzle. If Robert catches pneumonia, I will be to blame. *The headlines will read: Dog Sitter Runs Off to Paris with Playboy: Dog Dies.*

We go back to the house, now adorned with the matching boys. With full-tilted earnestness, the little twins say they are sorry for letting the dog getaway. I find out that Oliver had some of his students form a search party. One cannot help but fall in love with this little milk-and-tea family.

Announcing over the noisy boys, the pale frail Enfys murmurs that supper is ready. It is a thin fish soup. Even her food is pale. After dinner, the boys recite a delightful poem about a goat; then, they are given some sticky pudding and sent off to bed.

Enfys and I sit by the fire while Oliver plays guitar. I melt when he looks up at me with his poignant eyes. Then Enfys grabs the guitar and sings a haunting Sandy Denny folk song, "Who Knows Where the Time Goes?" If I didn't already have shivers, I have them now.

Oliver, fleeing the awkwardness of the situation, goes up to check on the boys. So, I'm left alone with her. I excuse myself to visit the powder room, trying to buy some time to think. But I've walked in a coat closet, so I just hide in there, trying to sort things out like —where I'm going to sleep tonight. Then it's as though she can read my mind. I hear Enfys say to Oliver. "So, where does she plan on sleeping tonight?"

I hear Oliver reply, "Here with us," as he opens the closet door for me to make a sheepish exit.

Enfys announces the sleeping arrangements. "She can sleep up in the study, and you can sleep down on the sofa."

Frankly, I'm so tired I could sleep in the dog's bed. I am put in a tiny, cold room with a thin blanket: no dog, no sex, no pudding for me. I want to sneak down in the middle of the night in my blue baby doll. Not to have sex, but just to snuggle with Oliver and hear him breathing. I say prayers that Robert shows up. It will kill Mrs. Etherington if something happens to him.

The next morning, I hear the raucous boys running down the stairs. Oliver has disappeared from the sofa. Probably run off, never to be found again. Right then, the front door opens, and Oliver bursts in, carrying the dog.

He excitedly reports, "He was at the pub the whole time. I'm just going to run up and tell the lads."

I sit in the living room with the dour Enfys. In her quivering voice, she says something that makes me feel a boulder of guilt in my chest. She says, "Please don't take away the lads' father."

74

Chapter 23

London, England

After fishing the key out from under the kissing frogs, I walk back into Mrs. E.'s empty home. It feels different now. But it's the same. I'm the one who has changed.

I ponder my love life. I had anticipated a future with Oliver, then his wife had to say it: The one thing that would make me walk away from the soulful Oliver.

But, now I've got the Julian factor. He's the wild card.

I visit Mrs. E. at the hospital and report the PG-rated version of the weekend. I include Maryel's appearance in Paris, as well as Enfys' comment in Ipswich — while carefully omitting Robert's disappearance.

Mrs. Etherington purses her bare lips. "Wait a minute. I must have been in one of my juniper comas. How did you end up in Ipswich with Oliver – if you were in Paris with Julian?"

Upon hearing this, the two busybody nurses decide it's time to take her blood pressure, which gives me time to make something up.

"Um. I went there to get Robert, after Paris."

Mrs. Etherington takes my hand and says, "Listen, Julian is a playboy who will break your heart. And Oliver is a married man who will break his wife's heart, if you don't stay away."

She holds my hand. "Keep trying —the right one will come along." She pulls out a lipstick from her pocket — It's Chanel #102.

Chapter 24

When I get back to the house, I see Julian leaning against his car in the driveway. "I've been trying to call you all day."

"Sorry, my phone's dead."

I guide him into the library and pour us crystal glasses of port. The errant dog comes running in.

Julian gives him a pat. "Oh, you found him! That must be a relief."

"Yes, and I see no need to mention it to Mrs. E."

"I'll never tell." He kisses me deeply and looks down at the dog. "It's a good thing dogs can't talk."

Like he can hear us, the dog barks, making Julian nervous. "But they can hear."

Julian asks, "How about dinner?"

The dog barks.

Julian looks at the dog. "I meant Camille. I know a lovely restaurant in South Kensington called Launceston Place."

Julian takes a sip of the port. "Now, I hate to be nosey about Ipswich, but you didn't...?"

I know where he is going with this vague line of questioning, so I feign confusion by asking, "What?"

"Ah. You know, how shall I put this delicately? Did you 'act out sonnets' or anything with the poet?"

"His wife was there the whole time."

"Ah, a manage a trois then?"

"She's so skinny it would be a... Deux et demi."

I ask about the meeting in Basel. "Oh, we've got a bit of an issue."

"What's the problem?"

With his laconic tone, he makes it sound like he's describing a parking ticket. "It seems our patients keep dying."

"So, you're drug is suddenly lethal?"

He waves his hand. "No. The regulators think it was just a bad batch."

"What do *you* think happened?"

"I think it was sabotage."

I can't help but ask, "Sabotage? Who would do that?"

"It's most likely that our competitor sent a saboteur."

God, he's sexy when he says things like "saboteur."

I say, "That's so mean. Don't your competitors realize that you are saving people with cancer?"

He tips back his port. "Saboteurs are usually not the most compassionate of people."

"What a nightmare. Hopefully, it's not that."

I notice that Robert has mysteriously left our company, making me worry that he's choking on buttons somewhere. We discover the dog in the sweet spot of Mrs. E.'s bed. Ah. He misses her. Well, I should have seen this coming, because now I'm in a bedroom with Julian again. He kisses my neck, and I remember Mrs. E.'s advice to stay away from him. I'm not sure whether I want to get so involved with a man who has a lingering ex-fiancé and people dying on his watch.

Hmm. He distracts me. Now, my mind is playing Debussy's Claire d Lune, and Julian's fingers are running down my thigh.

I start to change in front of him while he sits on a little settee and watches. I don't know what has come over me, but I start to do a little striptease by tossing my brassiere at his head.

He gives me an artful wink. "You know, we could stay in."

If we do that, we'll end up right where we left off in Paris, right when we were on the verge of "it." That's often when a woman makes her most profound life choices—on the "verge of it."

Julian gets a call and says, "Sorry, I'm going to have to give you a rain check on dinner. I've got a conference call with my father now."

"Do you want to do that here and stay over?"

"I'd love to, but now I have to fly to Zurich in the morning. And I won't sleep with you flinging lingerie at me."

"Sorry."

He looks into my eyes. "Say, why don't you come to Zurich with me?"

"Tomorrow? What about the dog?"

"You can bring him, or better yet, we can get Paulina to watch him."

Hesitantly, I say, "Okay."

"You could sound more enthusiastic."

I give him a long deep kiss. "I'm in."

Chapter 25

Zurich, Switzerland

As we land in Zurich, I look at Julian's temples and know that we will finally be lovers.

We enter the lobby of the Park Hyatt Hotel Zurich, which has a monochrome beige motif with sounds to match. Even the staff is quiet to avoid rattling the guests—kind of like a sanitarium for business people.

When we get to the suite, Julian raises his eyebrow a tiny bit, and then gives me a Mona Lisa smile. It is a look that tells me to yank his belt off, making his pants fall to the floor. Then I notice that the front of his shirt is lifted by his lustful thoughts. Ah, the mind wanders. Right then, there is a knock on the door.

Julian lets out a pithy, "Damn." I just love it when men swear. Not constant sailor swearing, just the occasional unfiltered manly outburst.

He stifles his 'enthusiasm' with a towel and unlocks the door. I leap under the covers just in time. The uniformed bellman delivers our bags and gleefully announces the upcoming arrival of fine Swiss chocolates and port. Without out asking, Julian issues a curt, "No, that will be all."

"Why did you turn that down? I love chocolates and port."

Julian tries to soothe me in his saxophone voice, "Camille. You know that I'll be approaching—how shall I put it—my zenith, and then there will be another knock on the door."

He comes over to the bed and pets my head, "Don't worry, my dear. I'm sure they are not the last chocolates in Switzerland."

"You'd better be right."

He leaps from the bed to put out the 'Do-not-disturb' sign on the door, and then he locks the bolt and jokingly puts a chair in front of the door. His shirt is off, and he slips off his striped blue boxer briefs. Ah. Here we are. A Glen Hansard song is playing on his phone. As he opens a bottle of Champagne and I think of another line for my journal.

He has such lovely long fingers, the kind that can play the haunting sharps and flats in a Debussy concerto.

His hands are on my now hard nipples. "You know, Camille, I've had to bring you all the way to Switzerland to finally consummate our relationship." He's kissing me from head to toe. Who needs fancy nightgowns?

"We have the whole night to ourselves."

And, sure enough, just as he's getting started, there is a knock on the door.

"Julian, it's me. Why didn't you answer my texts?"

His brother Simon has a voice that is sharp and metallic —making everything seem imperative.

Suddenly, I think the universe must want to keep us from intercourse. Julian puts his finger over my lips and we freeze in stillness. As the knocking continues, Julian walks over to the door and uses the same whisper, "Um. I'm busy at the moment if you catch my drift."

After slow processing this information, Simon says, "I need to talk to you. Come down for dinner, but hurry, they stop serving in a half an hour."

Julian huffs, "Alright."

After the conversation ends, he lifts his arched brow, looks at me, and says, "What can we do in a half an hour Ms. Carano?"

"Well, I'm not sure how long it takes you to do things." I start to think that he may have Swiss efficiency in all areas of life. Sex with Julian will probably be like a well-timed rocket launch, complete with announcements and ticking timepieces. I imagine sex with Oliver would be very different. Slow and gentle like churning cream.

Julian exhales a slow warm, "I'm glad we waited for this."

I babble, "Except your brother will probably be knocking on the door again any minute. Poor thing, he's probably not getting it from Beth Marie. How do people have sex when one is pregnant? I mean, there's a baby at the party."

Julian looks down at the flat sheet. "Now look what you've done. I've gone soft at the mere thought."

Once again, I've babbled my way to oblivion. Perhaps it's a stall on my part as I continue the Julian/Oliver debate in my head. I leap out of bed and say, "Let's wait until after dinner. I've got to get ready."

It's kind of Julian to get me involved in family outings so early on. I wonder if they will start talking about the pharmaceutical disaster. Probably not. With Blabber Mouth there, it will likely be all chit-chat about the upcoming birth.

As Julian hurries into the shower, he gives me a quick smile that shows his white teeth as he combs his jet-black hair. I notice he has the exact coloring of a shiny grand piano.

Metering his words, he says, "Now Camille, just a couple of things."

I begin painting my face as he speaks.

81

Julian continues, "Whatever you say, do not bring up the problem with the company."

"Oh, I would never do that. I'll just wait for Beth Marie to bring it up."

Julian laughs, and then his face contorts into a very edgy look. "I've warned Simon never to tell B.M. a thing. My father and brother and I are totally at odds as to how to handle this."

"Handle what— B.M.'s mouth?"

He pulls out his silver razor. "Yes, that and the investigation of the deaths. We need to be very careful as to how we provide access to the data."

"Isn't that obstructing justice?"

Julian lathers himself up for a shave. "Not if it's done properly."

Oh, how I love to watch a man shave and marvel at the danger of a razor at one's neck.

I finally suggest, "Why not just let them have unfettered access? That way, there can be no cover-up issue."

"That's just what my father has proposed. But my brother thinks we should quickly do a 'purge of excess data.'"

"What do you think?"

"I agree with my father, but worry that Simon knows something we don't know. It would be unwise to hand over damning evidence."

I joke. "Maybe a little office fire would come in handy."

He looks at me in the mirror. "That's what Simon suggested."

I want to delve deep into his temples for more clues. "Do the regulators believe the deaths were the result of sabotage?"

He scrapes another wide swath of the foamy snow on his left cheek with the silver razor. "Not yet. There is not enough evidence. Right now, it's just *my* theory."

He gives me a serious look. "Camille, I'm counting on you to keep all this to yourself."

I feel a wave of love, knowing that he trusts me with family secrets. With high precision, he begins scraping the base of his left sideburn. "It's either a bugger up, a sabotage —or a faux sabotage."

This makes me want to play a girl detective. "Why would someone want to fake a sabotage?"

Instead of merely turning his head, Julian looks at me in the mirror. I see his lips through the shaving cream and hear him whisper, "So they can pin it on someone else."

"Oh, brother."

"Oh, brother is right. I think that idiot Simon might have had his sticky hands in this."

"Sounds like brotherly love."

"He's only my half brother."

"Looks like all the crazy genes came from his mother."

"You have that right!" He glides the blade up to his throat. "Say, Camille, you're a clever girl; perhaps you can help us solve this."

Ah, he thinks I'm smart! This is what all women want to hear.

"I think my brother is being threatened or blackmailed by someone." He looks into my eyes. "Now, not a word to B.M. about this."

I kiss him on his smooth cheek. "Julian, I'm glad you trust me enough to share this."

Without any hesitation, he says, "It's not that. I'm only telling you in case I end up dead!"

Chapter 26

Oh, so he doesn't trust me. I think he can see the disappointment on my face. I must look really dejected, for he finally says, "It's a simple investigation. Could just be a bad batch."

Now I'm really curious about this pharmaceutical business. "What drug was it?"

I follow Julian out to the bedroom, where he is buttoning a crisp striped shirt and pulling on dark trousers.

"It's our new cancer drug: Zarrexifam. My father is an oncologist, and developed a drug to cure brain cancer."

"That's admirable."

"The drug was working so well that they ended the trial early."

"How does it work?"

"It slows the vibration of cancer cells, making them too lazy to replicate. This way, they don't need to be destroyed, which makes it safe for healthy cells."

"That's genius."

"My father holds the patent. But now they've temporarily halted the drug. We've already invested hundreds of millions of francs."

"Your father must be devastated."

"Oh, he doesn't care so much about the money. He's sorry that the drug is not saving lives anymore. All because of possible sabotage."

I've now got Katherine Hepburn and Spencer Tracy in my head. Or maybe Emma Peel and John Steed. I wonder if Julian and I are the team to solve this. "I can see how a competitor would have a motive to sabotage your company."

Julian adeptly folds his French cuffs and inserts silver cuff links. "Our main competitor, Vora-Pharma, has a drug called Faxidam."

"Does it work the same way?"

"Both target cancer cells without destroying them. Their drug, Faxidam, paralyzes the cells, while ours just makes them lethargic."

"So, your drug is safer than um…the other one?"

"It was Camille. It was until people started dying."

Now Julian looks like he has created a monster, and that I'll start getting involved. "Come on, let's head down for dinner."

It's easy to find the table with Simon and B.M, as we hear her sucking down the last of a virgin pina colada. She wastes no time. "Camille, can you believe the mess Julian is in?"

Looking at my menu, I say, "I try to stay out of his business."

She goes on. "Fifteen people died. Don't you want to know what happened?"

"Yes, it's such a tragedy."

Simon says casually, "Actually, they were going to die of cancer anyway, so it's not *terribly* tragic."

Julian exhales, "Simon, your empathy makes me weep."

"I'm just being realistic."

Julian turns back to the wine list and says to the waiter, "a bottle of the Gevrey-Chambertin, three glasses please." Without looking up, he says, "For your information Beth Marie, I'm not the only one in this mess."

Simon speaks urgently from the sides of his fleshy mouth. "This is why I wanted to meet without Number Three around."

As the resident voice-over, B.M. says to me, "That's the father's latest wife. She works in the research lab in Vienna and acts like she invented the drug — well, not now that the drug is killing people."

Julian clears his throat. "Excuse me. Camille doesn't need to know all of this. We don't want her to be served with a subpoena for dessert."

B.M. sulks by trying to cross her arms over her enormous belly, "I was just being po-lite, by trying to keep her in the loop."

The waiter returns with the fine wine and Julian samples and says, "Shall we talk about something else?"

I ask B.M. where she's from, wanting to know, mostly so I can avoid the place. She tells us that she spent her childhood in Texas, and then her family moved to North Carolina, hence the double-layer hillbilly accent. "Daddy started up his taxidermy enterprise, and I was his assistant after school. It was mostly pets, but sometimes farm animals and varmints."

"My, what an interesting profession."

B.M. taps my hand, "Do you want my Daddy to stuff that Robert for you someday?"

Julian says to the waiter, "Before we lose our appetites, we'll have the Loch Fyne salmon and beef short ribs."

As we sip our wine and wait for our dinner, I find out that B.M. was a buyer for a chain of discount stores called The Dollar Store, which is similar to the Pound shop. She met Simon at a wedding in London about seven months ago, and the rest is history.

"Ya wanna get pregnant, Camille? Use Dollar Store rubbers!"

With frozen ventriloquist lips, Simon says, "TMI. B.M. TMI."

86

B.M. looks around, bored. "Have you ever been pregnant, Camille? It sucks."

I answer, "No, not that I recall."

Simon says, "Now that's the kind of reply you need to give tomorrow, Julian."

Julian avoids eye contact with his brother. "I intend to tell the truth."

Simon's voice rises in anger. "So you're going to say this was a lab accident?"

Julian's eyes grow wide. "How can I say that for sure?"

Simon chugs his wine. "We should just get someone to change the records in Zurich to make it look like a few bad batches."

Julian enunciates each syllable. "Are you mad? How can you dare say such a thing? Especially when your wife has a physiological inability to keep anything a secret."

Later, when the food arrives, Julian announces that all conversation must stay off the topics of pharmaceuticals, pregnancy, and taxidermy.

B.M. says, "Then can we talk about the dead French cook?"

Both Simon and Julian say, "No" in unison.

Hm. I think there is more to Mrs. Coquin's demise than meets the eye.

Chapter 27

I wake up around 9:00 a.m. to an empty bed. If asked by a lawyer, Julian would have to plead carnal ignorance of me. He fell asleep the minute he hit the pillow last night, and the poor thing had to get up early for meetings. I decide to lie in and have room service and loll around in bed all day. Then I remember I'm supposed to meet B.M. for breakfast. According to Paulina's clothing schedule, I'm to wear the leaf-green sweater and gray slacks for today's first activity. How did I survive past kindergarten without someone to dress me?

The main dining room is full of elegant executive-looking men. Then I hear B.M.'s voice in the distance. She sees me and—like a stranded sailor—waves across the dining room.

She fills me in with the latest gory details of her pregnancy. "Last night, I ate a whole jar of pickled onions and had the most horrible gaaaas. Thought I was going to blow up the building."

I am glad the staff took careful precautions to ensure that there are no neighboring diners. I have coffee, toast with marmalade, and make every effort to divert the conversation from gas to Zarr. Being a leaky valve in all ways, B.M. tells me the fifteen people who died did so from paralyzed hearts —as she tries to demonstrate by collapsing on the banquette. Hm. That sounds to me like the effect of Faxidam, meaning the sinister people at Vora-Pharma.

After breakfast, we are to switch hotels, so I help B.M. with her gigantic orange suitcase. It has accidentally opened up like a clamshell in the middle of the lobby and spewing with all sorts of oversized maternity undergarments. The thoughtful concierge has hired a driver to take us to the next hotel, where we will meet up with the hotel-hopping Zarrs. Without waiting for a doorman, the concierge personally walks her orange suitcase out the door, like he's removing a rabid pet. He even helps squeeze B.M. into the getaway car; I'm sure glad to be rid of her.

Chapter 28

Our next destination is the famous Dolder Grand Hotel, which sits atop a mountain overlooking Lake Zurich.

B.M. and I are to have lunch with the father's new wife, aka Number Three, and her daughter, Clover. I spend most of the time during the ride wondering why anyone would name a baby Clover.

Soon we are deposited at the bottom of the mountain cable car—referred to as a funicular—which will take us to the hotel. While awaiting the next ride, B.M. fills me in on Dr. Zarr's third wife. I can tell that B.M. hates her by the way she describes Number Three as "a gold-digging bitch."

B.M. babbles on. "Number Three was Miss Rutabaga or something in her day –like Zsa Zsa Gabor." She studied chemistry somewhere, then married, and had Clover, who became a model and spent much of her life in Paris.

I help B.M. lift her suitcase into the small cable car compartment and soon the contraption takes us up the mountain.

We get a spectacular view of Zurich, but this is not for people—like me—with a fear of heights. One can practically hear the cable of the funicular complaining about the added weight of B.M. and her colossal suitcase. Just one worn gear or snapped cable, and we will slide down the mountain to our deaths. Then I remember that we are in Switzerland, the home of finely-crafted mechanical works, and breathe a sigh of relief.

B.M. says she loves this ride, as well as roller coasters and bungee jumping. Then she tells me that we could have taken a taxi all the way up. After my life passes before my eyes, we reach the top. *'I'm afraid of heights and depths. Maybe that's why I'm afraid of love.'*

The glorious hotel has an old Swiss castle-like section, flanked by glass additions, cantilevered over the mountain. We head to a lounge with 20-foot ceilings, leather sofas, and a terrace —all of which overlook the glistening Lake Zurich. The subdued décor looks like it was done by the twin brother of the Park Hyatt's decorator.

As we check-in, we learn the restaurant has 2 Michelin stars and that their spa was awarded best in Switzerland. *Yay!* It's too early for check-in, *Rats!* So we make our way directly to one of the restaurants.

B.M., with the grace and gait of a Rhino, continues with my briefing on Number Three. "She speaks seven languages, so if she's talking in another language, you know she's saying something baaaad about you." Then B.M. points and announces—for the entire Zurich canton to hear—"There she is."

I follow the end of her finger and see wife Number Three in the distance. She's a thin, attractive mid-50's blonde with big blue eyes. The standard "new wife" profile. This makes me think that they made a whole bunch of them. As I wait to walk with the waddling B.M., I see Number Three moving like a leopard to secure the best seat at the table. We follow her over, and B.M. introduces us.

Number Three takes one look at me, and says to B.M. in German: *"Ich dachte Julian dünne mochte Frauen."*

B.M. laughs nervously and tries to translate. "It was something about Julian liking pretty women."

Judging by B.M.'s nervous giggle, I can tell this was an inaccurate translation. Despite this, I thank Number Three and ask where she is from—Germany or

Switzerland. She tells me that I am wrong. She is from Finland. When I ask why she was speaking in German, she says she doesn't like nosey questions. Okay.

B.M. tucks herself into the middle of the banquette and says she's going to have to learn Swiss if she's going to spend any more time here.

Number Three says, "Stupid! They don't speak Swiss here! They speak Italian, French, German, and Romansh."

As I study Dr. Zarr's new wife, I conclude that men will fall for any woman as long as she has blonde hair, a slim frame —and she's a bitch.

B.M. bounces back from the criticism. "Well, thank God, I learned German from my Grandmother in Pennsylvania." She babbles on about everything, except what Number Three's first name is.

Soon, the giraffe-like Clover ambles in. Whenever I ask Clover or her mother any questions, I'm met with stares. The only thing that I learn from Number Three is that she thinks Maryel is very stupid. And wonders how Julian could ever have been engaged to her.

There is a comment about Mrs. Coquin in some foreign language, probably Finnish. When I ask for details in English, they give each other a look and ask why I need to know.

During lunch, I have to hear all about the baby shower. Now it's to be held at a hotel near Dr. Zarr's holiday home in Lake Lugano. It's in the Italian section of Switzerland, just three hours south of Zurich. The baby shower has been pushed back by two weeks due to poor planning on someone's part in the baby shower committee—meaning B.M.

Number Three looks at her. "I can't believe we have to vait two more months for that baby. You look like you going to explode."

I can see why Julian wanted to avoid this, and now I wish that I had stayed at the Park Hyatt Hotel—or in London for that matter. There is still a debate over the flowers for the tables. I am amazed that Number Three can argue without moving her mouth. She'd be a tricky assignment for a lip reader. I start to wonder if she was a ventriloquist in an earlier life. B.M. tries to pull me onto her side by saying, "What about red carnations?"

The corner of Number Three's mouth suddenly takes a left turn. Then she snarls, "I shall not be seen near a carnation!"

The waiter tries to take our order but is met with dismissive waves from Number Three.

She points to me. "Vat do you tink, Camille — how about Gelsemiums?"

Clover, who seems to have come without any factory-installed personality, finally speaks. "Aren't they poisonous, Mother?"

Number Three waves her hand, "Only if people are stupid enough to eat them. What else are we having? I think we should have Gambas."

B.M. says, "No, we're having a Meringa band."

I say gently, "Gambas are prawns."

Judging by her limited smile, I can see that Number Three has won this round as she announces, "It's all settled then. We will have Gelsemiums and Gambas."

We all sit and drink champagne and glare at each other. I'm so glad B.M. is here, and let her steal sips of my champagne so she can get through the day.

The waiter misunderstands and soon brings flowers and prawns to our table. After a berating by Number

Three, he's now a nervous wreck and spills cocktail sauce on her lap. The manager comes over, and Number Three insists that the waiter be fired. He then becomes emotional and mentions a poor crippled mother he supports. Number Three says she doesn't care —which makes him cry. It occurs to me that if I end up with Julian, this evil bitch will always be in my life.

I am hoping for more Intel on the Zarr company, but know not to bring anything up. Finally, B.M. does. She says, "I'm worried about Julian going to jail."

Number Three seethes. "Serves him right — deleting emails."

B.M. says excitedly, "Well, I'm not supposed to say anything, but I heard Julian tell someone on the phone that he thinks it was an inside job."

I say, trying to open up the topic. "Do tell."

B.M. starts talking like a southern cowboy, "I think he knows who the cul-per-it is."

Looking at Number Three, I ask. "Do you have any idea who could be involved?"

She scowls at me. "Is this any of your business?"

Well, that puts the damper on any newsworthy reports. The topic veers back to the ill-planned baby shower. Pretending to have a headache or scurvy, I excuse myself and make my escape. I high-tail it to the lobby, where the front desk people nicely tell me my room is ready. I practically run to the elevator, hoping I don't have a Rhino, a Giraffe, and a Leopard chasing me.

Chapter 29

Ah, the room is divine, so I close the door and lock the bolt of my new sanctuary. I climb in bed for a nap and think of poor Julian. I hope he's not in danger—or the fall guy for this mess. I can tell that B.M. is on Julian's side, but Number Three is apparently not. I'm not sure about Clover.

I fall asleep until 4:00 p.m. and get a call from Oliver, whose voice makes me melt. He says his wife can't stop crying and won't sign the divorce papers. Oh no. After he hangs up, I replay the base notes of his voice in my head as I run my bathwater. I float in my saltwater bath, thinking of how my life has changed.

Boy, how strange that I'd get so involved with these three very different families: The Zarrs, the Ogilvies, and the Etheringtons.

Julian shows up and pauses in the doorway of the bathroom. He's wearing a suit and loosens his tie as he takes in an eye full of my watery-blur.

He tells me that we are scheduled to meet his father and Number Three for dinner tonight. He must note the worried look on my face, for he kisses my forehead and says, "My poor father. I don't know how he puts up with Number Three."

"What's her first name, by the way?"

Julian answers with a straight face. "Number."

"Does she spell it out or just use a pound sign?"

"Funny. Number Two used to do the hash-tag thing."

"What about Number One?"

Julian gets all quiet and leans against the bathroom counter. "My mother was Number One."

Thinking she probably lives in Monaco or somewhere equally glamorous, I ask about his mother. Julian takes on a robotic tone, "She was killed when I was seven; then my father married Number Two, but then Number Three stole my father from her."

"Gosh, you need to be a mathematician to do your family tree." I get out of the tub to hug him. "I'm sorry, Sweetie."

Julian says his back is sore, and maybe he'll go down and get a massage at the spa. Hmm. He's the sort of man you don't want wandering around the lobby of a hotel looking for a massage, so I offer to give him one.

He seems to like this idea, as he quickly undresses and excitedly asks, "Face up, or face down?" I tell him face down, and then I sit on top of him. I warm up in my hands with almond lotion before deeply massaging his slim shoulders. I slowly work my way down his biceps, then work on kneading the backs of his thighs. He's not very muscular, so it doesn't take long. My mind wanders from Julian's thin ectomorph physic to Oliver's mesomorph physique. *Damn. Why does he pop in my head?*

Julian has fallen asleep, so I climb under the covers with him and stare at his face.

'When I look at his face, I wonder: is it the mystery of him, or the danger that's so appealing?'

Is he the one for me? There is only one way to find out. It's high time to make love to him once and for all. When I turn on the music, composer Erik Satie's "Gymnopédie No.1" is playing. In my mind, it is the most haunting mixture of pale yellow and deep purple notes. If this comes to fruition, I will always remember this as our song and the Dolder Grand Hotel as our first place.

I massage his head and he awakens. When I rub my hand on "him," the corners of his mouth instantly turn up. I lean down and kiss him full on the lips. He's quickly in an upright position. He whispers, "Is it time?"

In a deep voice, I say, "Yes, high time."

He gets up, locks the door, and hangs the 'Do not disturb' sign. He commands, "No matter what, we are not answering the door."

Now, the much slower "Gymnopédie No. 3" is playing, which makes me worry that Julian will fall asleep again. So, I quickly put on "Je te veux," which has a faster tempo. Julian's kisses go from my mouth all the way down my front. Then he stops at the juicy parts and lingers for a while. My sounds correspond nicely with the crescendo of the music. Then he knows it's time. He leans over me. Then slowly works his way inside. *It's finally happening.* God, he's sexy with his lean looks and elegant hands. Now his mouth is hard on mine.

Then Julian's thrusts rock the headboard, making me hope that we do not know the guests on the other side of the wall. He makes light moans. His face contorts in an odd way that makes him look like he's in some sort of horrible agony. This is followed by a long drawn out "ahhh."

And he's done. Poof, it's over. It had all the drama and quick finale of a horse race. He collapses on his back, and in a second, he's snoring—like a cartoon character.

' *Like most things, the best part is the anticipation —the mystery of the unknown.* '

I stare at his serene and chiseled face and think, now everything will be different. Now he's mine.

Chapter 30

I am jarred awake by the landline phone on the nightstand, only inches from my head. Julian pops out of bed and tells me to hurry — it's 8:00 p.m., and we are late for dinner. As I throw a dress over my head, I wonder if Maryel had to dress this quickly.

As I'm applying lipstick in the elevator, Julian whispers, "That was lovely, Miss Carano." He kisses me deeply during our descent until the elevator pings open, and we hear a grandmother clear her throat and cover her grandchild's eyes.

Julian and I dash to the elegant lobby, where I see a dapper gray-haired man in the distance. As we get closer, I see his ice-blue eyes and know it must be Julian's father. He looks like a handsome senator. Actually, he's a dead ringer for that 1970's TV actor, Efrem Zimbalist, Jr.

"Father, I'd like for you to meet Camille Carano. Camille, this is my father."

I am sure after all these years, Dr. Zarr does not put too much stock into any of Julian's relationships. I wonder if he even bothers to learn their names. He probably just keeps track of their country of origin and occupation. I must be 'the American writer.' Hopefully, not, 'the American pet-sitter.'

Julian jokes, "Father, she doesn't believe your wife's name is Number Three."

Dr. Zarr quickly says, "Ah, here she is now."

Err. I still don't know her first name. Number Three makes a grand entrance by standing in the doorway and peering around the room. As we are escorted to our table of Zarrs, and I notice Dr. Zarr looking at me. He finally whispers, "Camille, I don't mean to stare, but you bear a striking resemblance to Julian's mother."

Julian laughs. "God, I hope we're not related."

I don't know what to say, but I come up with, "Thank you, Dr. Zarr. I'll bet you miss her."

He looks down. "She was the love of my life."

When his new wife returns to the table, Dr. Zarr quickly changes the subject. "Camille, I understand you're a writer. What type of books do you write?"

B.M. has a mouthful of food but manages to say, "I'll bet she writes naughty stuff like '*Shades of Grey.*'"

I say, "I'm a food writer, but now I'm working on a novel."

Julian adds. "She's turning it into a funny murder mystery."

With all seriousness, Number Three says, "But how can murder be humorous?"

Julian directs his eyes towards B.M. "I suppose if the person is terribly annoying, it would be funny."

Dr. Zarr laughs out loud and has to hide behind the wine list. Julian grabs it and orders a bottle of Chateau Palmer and says, "You'll like this Camille."

I read aloud, "It says it's a divine blend of 54% Merlot, 40% Cabernet Sauvignon, and 6% Petit Verdot. Who would ever know?"

Julian winks. "I'll bet your tongue can detect percentages."

Number Three clears her throat.

Whenever B.M. says something, Simon shoves a piece of bread in her mouth. He probably does this for legal reasons, as B.M.'s words tend to fly out randomly and unedited.

I sip my wine and conclude that life is one big cauldron of mysteries —with the giant bouillon cube being how Simon will stay married to B.M. I look at Simon and see that he clearly loathes her. The only explanation is that he is just waiting for the perfect moment to enact his nefarious plan. After the baby is safely out of the woods, he'll probably bump off B.M. I ponder the ways: A nice bludgeon to the mouth. Or maybe a small explosion involving liquid rubber that somehow seals her word-oozing hole.

While B.M. babbles on, I study Simon's face. He has a nervous way of looking around — like the mob will sneak up on him at any moment.

Next, I study the father. Maybe I could learn a little bit about Julian from his father. No, better from B.M. I suppose I should take advantage of what could be her remaining time on earth to glean more information.

Whoa. Clover finally makes an appearance in the doorway. She's wearing a peek-a-boo purple gown, and everyone in the dining room turns to look. As she approaches our table, B.M. drags me away to the ladies' room.

In this episode of our secret-ladies-room debriefings, I learn that Julian's mother was crossing the street with him when he was seven. A milk truck suddenly dropped a gigantic fake milk bottle on her head. Of course, Julian was spared, but he witnessed the spectacle and would forever be scarred.

B.M. then tells me that two years after Julian's mother died, Martin Zarr married Number Two, Simon's mother, who is from Prague. Well, Number Two is peeved that she was not invited to the baby shower —especially as it's her biological grandchild, not Number Three's.

I also discover that wife Number Two still loves Dr. Zarr. She lives in Geneva but recently purchased a home in Lugano—right up the street from Dr. Zarr. According to

100

deep throat, "She's got buckets of money, and she practically stalks Dr. Zarr. She's best friends with Polish Paulina, who always knows exactly where he is."

When we finally get back to the table, everyone is quietly enjoying starters of Steak tartare, veal carpaccio, and oysters. While eating continental style, they discuss the potential ramifications of Brexit. Julian thinks it is foolhardy for Britain to leave the EU. Then Number Three manages a laugh and says Maryel thought Brexit was a town in Brittany.

On my next visit to the ladies' room with B.M., she tells me that Number Three wants Clover to go after Julian and wants Maryel out of the way. Hm.

When we return to the table, I notice Clover is seated between Simon and Julian; now, she's leaning close to my man while buttering his bread for him.

After dinner, I survey the Zarr family. I soon find myself wondering: Who are these people? And, how has this family gone so long without killing each other?

Later, when we return to our room, I pity Simon's plight and wonder if Julian does. I find out that, no, he does not pity Simon.

"And if you must know, if anything happens to Simon, all of his stock goes to B.M. He married her without a prenup." Hmm. *Beware of the blonde hillbilly.*

Chapter 31

The next morning, Julian slips out early for another meeting with his father, brother, and their lawyers. They decide to have it at the hotel instead of at the Zarr Pharma offices. It's probably to keep the staff from finding out just how much trouble the company is in. To keep us out of the way, B.M., Number Three, and I are sent to the spa.

It is no surprise that Number Three has monopolized the spa staff by requesting all of her treatments be done simultaneously. B.M. and I are left wrapped in waffle robes and deposited in the Zen room.

While waiting, we hear a horrible siren ring of Number Three's phone. The other inhabitants of the Zen world glare as B.M. answers with her telltale, "Howdy."

She says to me, "It's your Honey Bunny; he needs a phone number for some Kra-kow-ski person."

I grab the phone and ask Julian, "Do you want Paulina or your ex-wife?"

"No, her brother Eddie; Paulina's nephew. He works at our Vienna lab."

I text Julian the info and also put it in my little book. Something tells me this Eddie fellow may be a source of useful information. Right then, B.M. yells, "Oh no!" We can see Number Three approaching in the distance. B.M. gets up and creates a loud distraction—which is not difficult, while I nervously put the phone back in the charger.

Number Three declares, "I just found out they are having a secret meeting on the third floor." She then grabs

102

her phone and says, "Oh, Beth Marie, in light of your condition, I gave all of your treatment appointments to Clover." And off she goes.

Furious, B.M. stomps her wide feet, "I'm gonna kill her."

With a mischievous smile, B.M. says, "Simon hasn't returned my texts, so I think we should go up there to see if he's still alive."

We make our way up to the third floor and spot a room-service man pushing a food cart into a doorway. Soon we hear tense words escaping to the hallway, with Zarr-like tones. Then we hear Simon say, "It's obvious that our competitors got into the Zurich lab."

Number Three is now there and fumes, "Time to fire that Eddie Krakowski dope."

In a determined voice, I hear Julian say, "Not without proof."

Dr. Zarr says, "It's up to the investigators to figure this out. Let's show them we have nothing to hide. Let's give full access to all of the Zarrexifam documents."

Then an unfamiliar voice says, "No documents shall be turned over without first being reviewed."

Simon clears his throat, "Especially none of the lab transfer records."

Very interesting. I'll have to tell Mrs. E. that there is something up in Zurich and it involves this Eddie Krakowski fellow, who is the brother of Julian's ex-wife. I'll bet she has something to do with this. Suddenly the door opens, and Julian helps the room-service man move the cart and catches me listening in. He has a scowl. "Shouldn't you be at the spa?" Then he slams the door without waiting for an explanation.

B.M. and I scamper away as best we can. Now, I worry that Julian is mad at me. B.M. comes back to my room with me to play beauty parlor. She makes a pitiful attempt to reach her toenails for a pedicure, so I volunteer, soon regretting anything to do with her feet. She starts fanning herself like some wilting steel magnolia. "God, I hope we don't lose all our money."

As I dab blue polish on her stubby toes, I say, "I hope no one ends up in jail."

"Or dead!"

She pulls out a mud green facial packet and slathers it on our faces.

B.M. lies on the bed and looks at the night stand. "Oh, look, you have the same Ferra-ga-mo sunglasses as Clover."

"They're not mine."

Her green face says, "Then it looks like Clover paid Julian a visit."

Later, Julian appears in the doorway and cringes at our scary faces. He seems less than delighted to see B.M. under the covers of the bed — the one we recently made love in.

B.M. dangles the sunglasses. "Camille wants to know why Clover's sunglasses are in your room."

Julian's face turns red. Then, in an angry tone, he enunciates, "I have no idea. I told you, I have no interest in Clover!"

But *she* has an interest in him. Competing with her and Maryel is going to be an ongoing problem. I quickly wipe off my mask and start putting on lipstick. Ah, Chanel #102. I wish Mrs. Etherington was here.

Then my phone rings. It's David. "My mother has had a heart attack."

104

Chapter 32

London, England

We are back in London the next morning, thanks Zarr Air. Without any undercover operation, I boldly walk Robert right into the hospital. The nurses don't say a word. Mrs. Etherington is lying there with a tube up her nose, looking so innocent. As I move my chair slightly closer to check her breathing, the monitor starts beeping at a high pitch, and the red blinking line goes flat. *Oh no, is she dead?*

Suddenly, Mrs. Etherington jolts up in her hospital bed. "Oh, Camille, I'm so glad you're here. I'm out of gin."

Then a curtain is abruptly pulled open, and a stern-looking doctor appears. He assesses the patient but seems stumped. Then he points to my metal chair and the bottom rungs that are constricting Mrs. E.'s tubes. *Whoops.*

The doctor's voice bellows, "Ah-hem. Heart attack patients are not permitted to have alcohol. Besides a host of other menaces, it causes dehydration."

Mrs. E. and I hide our faces like naughty school girls. I want to say, *'It's not my fault that the hospital is out of tonic water.'* But I don't. Instead, the doctor adds, "And it may come as a surprise, but pets are not permitted in this hospital."

Mrs. E. pleads, "But he's a trained service dog."

This seems implausible because her dog is now routing through the medical trash. The doctor leaves in a huff.

Mrs. E. says, "I wish David was here. I miss him."

"Yes, me too."

The skinny nurse says to me, "I'll bet you end up with the son."

I say, "No, he's married."

The portly nurse quips, "That doesn't seem to stop her."

I ask them if they might have some bandages that are in need of a roll. Suddenly Mrs. E. has a sparkle in her eyes. "I'm so glad you and David are friends. Maybe you can sort out his marital troubles."

I'll add it to my list of occupations: Dog sitter, writer, gin smuggler, flute player, and now marriage counselor.

Chapter 33

It seems Mrs. E.'s stay at the hospital has been extended, along with my international posting.

As Julian and I head out to dinner, I run up to drop off some supplies for her. When I get to her room, there is a unanimous vote amongst patients and staff to invite Julian up. Mrs. E. says she can't give me any love life advice without meeting him. Soon he is knocking on the frame of the hospital door.

Ratcheting up the charm, he says, "Mrs. Etherington, I'm so sorry to hear about your recent health issue. Are you feeling better?"

She gets a huge smile on her face. "Please call me Elizabeth. Yes, I chose a good place to have a heart attack."

Julian pulls out a bag of items from her Paris wish list. "Sorry you had to wait for this." He produces a small bottle of Guerlain Samsara perfume and asks permission before applying a drop to her wrist. Then, like a magician, he pulls out a pink scarf from Cartier. He gently drapes it around her neck, arranging it just so. Then he pulls out a Chanel lipstick: #102. The nurses are in awe.

Mrs. E. twists the lipstick like she's Audrey Hepburn in Breakfast at Tiffany's ─and applies it to her lips. Cupid bow, just like mine ─no wonder we like the same shade. She looks at Julian and says, "Too bad we didn't meet thirty years ago."

He laughs, and soon a blush appears on his etched cheeks.

Mrs. E. wastes no time in asking, "So Julian, have you ever been married?"

107

He recoils a bit, then scans the audience—which includes the nosey nurses—and says, "Yes, but it didn't count."

Mrs. E. and the nurses lean in with wrinkled question marks on their faces, so Julian fills in the blanks. "She was already married."

Mrs. E. says, "And you didn't think to ask?"

"I do miss things. It seems she thought that her divorce had gone through."

Mrs. Etherington, looking a bit more chipper than before, says. "So you had it annulled?"

Julian smiles. "Like it never happened."

Chapter 34

With the dashing Julian at my side, we head to the Michelin-starred Launceston Place. Word must have spread of our overt displays of affection, as the maî tre d' guides us to a private banquette in the very back. As Julian studies the wine list, I look at his profile. He opts for the 2010 Chevalier–Montrachet —while I opt for the 1969 Mayfair man.

Because I seem to have inherited the meddler gene, I ask more about his ex-wife. It makes sense that a handsome, wealthy man would not remain single for long. Although being married for two weeks is hardly an inclination of commitment. Maybe he's difficult, and I just haven't seen it. He'll probably be a philanderer. Or perhaps he's just too perfect. I ask if his ex-wife is also a supermodel.

"Oh, no. She's a doctor in Krakow."

"How did you meet?"

"Paulina is her aunt."

"You sure are loyal to Paulina."

"I should be. She saved my life."

"How?"

"When I was eight, Simon pushed me onto the rail tracks in Zug. Paulina pulled me up just before the 1:04 train."

The waiter backs away worriedly after he pours the rare wine.

"Didn't *Paulina* know that her niece was already married?"

"Apparently not — she came to the wedding."

Julian and I forgo the multi-course tasting menu for a la carte. Each plate looks like a work of art by Monet with rows of green leaves and purple flowers. He seems a little annoyed with me when I take aerial shots of each dish, but they are just too beautiful to eat. This place is a food writer's dream.

During our meal, I wonder what makes Julian tick. Then I realize that he was not a man who ticked. He was analog in a digital world.

After dinner, we head back to Mrs. E's house to catch up on where we left off.

Julian kisses me fully on the mouth and unzips my dress until it falls to the floor. Soon, we are diving under the covers together naked and his tongue finds my wonder spot. Okay, now I can't remember what exactly is wrong with this handsome man.

He takes me to a higher place; when I'm done, I put my mouth on him to reciprocate. Suddenly, we hear the front door open and a crashing sound. *Of all times to have a burglar!* Julian puts his finger to his lips and hides under the comforter. Meanwhile, the dog snores away. Some guard dog he is.

Then we hear, "Hello, it's me," like it's Todd Rundgren breaking in.

Julian comes up for air. "Were you expecting someone?"

Grabbing a hideous old robe, I head down the stairs. It's David.

I hug him. "You made it back!"

"The only flight I could find was on Aeroflot. I thought they were going to make us parachute out."

He's picking up pieces of a porcelain vase and says, "I hope that wasn't the vase from the Tang Dynasty."

"Um. I think it was."

"Oh well. They don't make them like they used to."

My lover pulls on a pair of jeans and comes down the stairs, warily.

David eyes Julian. "Oh, you must be Oliver."

Julian smiles. "I go by Julian these days."

It's all very awkward as I make introductions. I guess David wasn't expecting to meet 'the dog sitter's lover.'

Julian then turns on the charm. "Oh, I hadn't connected the dots. Are you *the* David Etherington — the famous Dendrologist who is saving the rare Pennatia Baylisiana tree?"

David giggles in delight that anyone has heard of his esoteric livelihood as a tree scientist. "Famous yes, but so far, you are the only one who's ever heard of me."

Sounding sincere, Julian says, "Our pharmaceutical company is always interested in rare plants. Our cancer drug uses Periwinkle flowers and Yew trees."

David is practically dancing. "Perhaps you could help fund our research! There is only one remaining female tree, so all the males have been trying to procreate with each other."

Julian's curiosity mounts. "What are the possible medicinal uses of this rare Baylisiana tree?"

David replies, "Well, we fed some to male goats, and now they seem pretty fond of each other."

"It sounds like a very expensive gay Viagra. I'll have to get back to you on that."

Julian invites us to lunch for tomorrow and slips away.

David says, "My, I see the poet has some competition."

Chapter 35

Julian comes by the next day, but we cannot wake the jet-lagged David, who is comically dead to the world. It's like his body is full of leaden Jell-o, so we leave him on the floor and put a blanket on him.

Julian and I have a long glorious lunch of Devon crab, and avocado with Sancerre pour Deux at, The Royal Automobile Club.

When I return to the house, I soon regret leaving David unattended. I open the kitchen door, and I am greeted by a cloud of smoke and find a smoldering duck. I hear a scream, and suddenly David pops up and pats out the fire with his oven mitts, which are festooned with kittens.

Like nothing happened, he says, "How was lunch?"

"Wonderful, but poor Julian. They are in b--iig trouble." *Oh, no, I'm starting to talk like B.M.*

"What a shame. Julian probably looks bad in stripes."

I think of Julian in his sexy gold and blue striped pajamas and also to his striped boxers.

"He's headed to Paris this week."

David pulls out wine glasses. "Without us?"

"Yes, he's putting his condo on the market. And he wants to meet with that French lady's son — you know the one who died playing Charades."

"The son died too?"

"No. just Mrs. Coquin."

"Mother said she died from Campylobacter poison."

"What's that?"

112

He pats the blackened duck. "From undercooked poultry."

"How did she find out?"

"How else? From that Polish Paulina — when she watched the dog."

"Interesting how now the Zarrs, the Etheringtons, and now the Krakowski's are all intertwining."

"Yes, and mother likes Paulina. Especially since she can get her a discount at Harrods."

"Oh no. I'll probably be out of a dog sitting job soon."

"Not to worry. Paulina is no fan of the dog."

"How is your mother?"

David babbles on. "I stopped to see her, but I can't get Robert past the formidable gauntlet. Especially that large one, who can lift me like a human barbell. Trust me, I know."

I look at David and wonder if he's been over caffeinating.

He continues, "Mother made me sneak her out the side door to pet Robert. I had just put on some lavender hand cream and lost my grip on the handles. Next thing I know, she slid down the hill in the parking lot into an overgrown Ulex europaeus!"

I'm not sure if that is a shrub or a person, but pour David more wine to slow down the dialogue.

We are able to salvage some of the duck —well, just the thin segment in between the blackened outer part and the frozen center. *The dog is not amused.*

After a few more glasses of *Langoa-Barton Claret,* David confesses that he can't bear the thought of going back to Asia and sleeping with his wife. He's wearing a silk smoking jacket but accessorized with fuzzy slippers, making it difficult to imagine him having any kind of sex.

"She expects me to... how do I put it delicately... pull the jib up the mast at a moment's notice." He takes a sip, "I don't know anything about sailing; does that metaphor sound, right?"

"I'll have to ask Oliver."

"The dreamy poet also sails?"

"Yes, he writes, sings, sails, cooks, paints...he's a renaissance man."

"Oh, I'll bet he's a great lover. He'd probably tickle you with flower petals....then he gasps, Oh my God! Here I am going on about Oliver when you must have been intimate with Julian by now."

"Well. Yes, the opportunity did arise finally in Zurich."

"Mother and I were starting to wonder."

After dinner, the hapless David struggles to build a fire in the stone hearth of the library. While sipping brandy and listening to Nat King Cole's amber voice, David regales me with lore-o-the Etherington family. It seems David's father died when he was little, and his mother fell in love with an American diplomat but never married him because he already had a wife. *It's always something.*

Chapter 36

The next day, David and I visit his mother. She says she's bored and needs some pretty things to look at and eat. She hands David a scavenger list of things to get at Harrods.

When David whines about finding such items, his mother says she'll just ask her new friend, Paulina — or Julian. David quickly grabs the list and reads aloud: "Chocolate covered orange peels; Duck liver pate with pistachio nuts; an oyster-colored marabou peignoir and stackable pear-green ashtrays. I'm sure this won't be difficult."

David and I both love Harrods. After a few sniffing and tasting hours, the jet-lagged David realizes that he has left his glasses somewhere. While searching in every department, I catch the near-sighted David chatting someone up in the lingerie department. It's a mannequin. I must have startled him, for he knocks his new girlfriend over, who knocks her bald friend over who comes crashing down. David is now lying on top of three of them. One is now missing her head, an arm, and some fingers. David quips, "Beware of the spontaneous Ménage à trois."

The bald noggin rolls down the escalator one step at a time until it gets caught at the bottom. Horrified shoppers look on and point at the decapitated head. The manager stands akimbo and asks what we think we are doing. Then I see our savior —Paulina.

Julian's favorite personal shopper quickly escorts us to another floor. I want to ask her all sorts of questions, but I know I'll have to wait for another time. Then she says, "I hope Julian finds out more about what happened to Mrs. Coquin when he's in Paris."

David whispers, "I heard it was from Campylobacter."

Just as I'm dying from guilt, I say, "Wait, Mrs. Coquin was the only one who died from eating the duck canapés, but I ate one or two before I dropped them on the ground. And I'm still here."

David says, "Well, you have a heartier system than an old French lady, if that's possible."

I say, "But she said Maryel dropped them off earlier. Maybe Maryel poisoned the early canapés."

Paulina laughs. "But Maryel and Mrs. Coquin were good friends. Why would she do that?"

Hmm?

Safely out of the woods, David and I head back to St. John's Wood. My pheasant with truffle ravioli and green peas works out just fine, although I purposely err on the side of overcooked. We pair it with a few glasses of fine 1990 Pouilly Fuisse. Through his newly loose lips, David tells me his brother recommended this vintage as it's both racy and graceful. When I ask why he never mentioned that he had a brother, David says it's on a need to know basis.

"Why didn't *he* come to help your mother?"

David looks around, "He's in Shanghai. He's in the middle of a secret project and can't leave."

Chapter 37

I wake after a glorious dream of Oliver. Right then, as if our souls are connected, he calls. First, he asks about the dog, and then about Mrs. Etherington. He tells me he has to take his wife to Scotland for evaluation, and asks if I noticed any signs of dementia. She did sing "Late November" three times in a row, but I just thought that late November feels like it goes on forever.

Oh, great, a demented ex-wife. She'll probably kill me — but won't remember doing it.

Oliver says he needs someone to watch the lads; apparently, they've been banned from the local daycare. I guess even the reputations of six-year-olds can catch up with them. I nicely offer to babysit them here, provided it's okay with Mrs. Etherington. Surely she'll veto the idea, which gives me an easy out.

David and I go to the hospital again after lunch. Within minutes, he knocks over his mother's IV stand, and all sorts of noisy alarms go off. He gets a loud reprimand for bringing the liver pate into the cardiac ward and is sent to wait in the car.

Now is the time to ask Mrs. Etherington if Oliver's boys can stay at her house for a week. Not that I want to, but I feel the need to help Oliver out of his latest bind.

Mrs. E.'s non-reply makes me wonder if she heard me, so I continue with details about Enfys' condition, probably called "Enfysema." I tell her that there is simply no one to watch the darling lads.

During the silence, I imagine she's formulating a compound excuse; then she calmly says, "I think it's an excellent idea. It will be a useful experiment."

I hug her. "Oh, thank you. No one else will take them."

"Remind me to increase my homeowner's coverage." She sighs and says it will be good for David to see what it's like to be around children. She says he grew up without any other children around —and "of course, he never had any friends."

I wonder about David growing up alone. Finally, I blurt out, "But doesn't he have a brother?"

Then Mrs. E. gets a faraway look— like her brain took a train ride to the seaside. The room is quiet; finally, one of the machines makes a beep, and she comes back from her trip. She replies, "Oh, didn't I mention my son, James? I must have forgotten."

She takes my hand. "Someday, Camille, I'll tell you all about my life. But not today."

Chapter 38

David wasn't always a nervous wreck. As he downs a glass of Sancerre, he tells me his condition flared five months ago —right when he got married. He secretly eloped! He didn't tell me because he worried it would discourage me from marrying Arthur. I ask for a recap of how he met his wife — having envisioned a tale of them stranded on the high seas, held captive by pirates until he saves her and marries her.

But that is not how it unfolded. Apparently, his wife Fan Yi, is a dermatologist in Shanghai. While visiting his brother there, David needed Mohs surgery on his left nostril. They eloped just before he returned to New Zealand. Her clock is ticking, so he's dispatched to Shanghai each month during her fertile time. His voice arcs with panic when he says the word, "fertile."

When I ask David to describe Fan, he uses words like perfunctory and pernicious, making me think he could be a poet. None of this sounds romantic, so I ask why he married her. He cries, "She had a scalpel in her hand!"

Then he adds, "We'll never be able to have children. And it's all my fault."

I try to comfort him and his presumably low sperm count, "No. I'm sure it's not your fault."

"Yes, it really is." He gulps the last of his wine. "And I'm sure the vasectomy didn't help."

It is impossible to rein it in. "What?!"

He babbles on, "Yes, two months ago, at lunchtime. For some reason, that's when they always do them."

"She doesn't know yet?"

It seems out-of-character for a scientist to do. "You had a secret vasectomy?"

"I don't know what I was thinking. Other than the fact that I am afraid of children!"

Chapter 39

David and I have breakfast like an old married couple – well, more like aging siblings. Still, in his cat pajamas, he reads the newspaper to the dog while eating toast and marmalade. Then we see an old blue Volvo station wagon out front, so David quickly hides in the pantry. Ah, it's Oliver and the boys in the family car–just in time for our domestic experiment. How strange that he'd rely on me to watch his kids. He must really trust me. He comes in, hauling a box of toys and medicines. "Thank you, Camille; you were our last resort."

I look out to see the twins approaching, and ask, "Do they come with any instructions?"

"No, it's just like watching a dog. Feed them three times a day, and hose them down in the driveway once a week. Or is it the other way around?"

As his sons march in carrying little suitcases, he instructs them. "Now lads, no breaking anything. And no jumping out the windows."

I lead Oliver and the boys upstairs, guiding them to the pink room, which has the fewest breakables.

Then, David scampers up the stairs, breathlessly. "Excuse me, but who is that ephemeral beauty in the foyer?"

I look down towards the stairwell. "Is she pasty and thin?"

David gushes. "No, she's luminous and willowy like a Silver Birch."

Oliver looks down. "That's my wife, Enfys."

David beams. "Enfys! As in the Irish word for a rainbow?"

We stand by silently as Enfys comes up the stairs with her old yellow suitcase and starts hanging her clothes in the wardrobe.

Worried, Oliver says, "No, Ennie, this is not where we're staying. We are just dropping off the lads."

As if she's in a trance, she says, "Have they eaten their lunch yet?"

Warily, I lead them all downstairs. David begins to chat up Enfys about Scottish folksongs in the library, while Oliver and I head to the kitchen to set up the boy's lunch. I search for durable plates, as he unwraps the tuna fish sandwiches. Then I hear a gasp. I look to see Oliver's hands shaking. He opens up a sandwich and shows it to me. "It's Fred and Ginger! She made the sandwiches out of the children's goldfish!"

We quickly dispose of the fish, but the dog knocks over the trash, and Fred and Ginger begin the beguine on the dance floor. The dog barks, and then—before we know it, the twins witness the spectacle.

Oddly, Enfys says she has no memory of making the sandwiches. Yet, somehow she can remember their care and feeding instructions in painstaking detail — and repeats them exactly. I'm kind of glad she has this repeating disorder because it gives me a chance to write things down. During all this, Oliver gives me a look that says, 'See what I mean.' When I look at Enfys, I wonder what the attraction is. Perhaps it's that ephemeral quality of hers. Not so much like a Birch tree, but more like butterfly wings.

As the boys run rampant, Oliver guides Enfys out the door and into the car. David and the dog are already hiding in the closet. I think I already know the result of this experiment.

Chapter 40

Poor Oliver. He'll probably be forced to have his wife institutionalized permanently —then we'll have to move to Scotland to be near her. As a fiction writer, my mind leaps to thoughts of Oliver murdering her this weekend— and the various methods. Oh, but then I could get stuck with them when he goes to jail. Even though David is married and lives in New Zealand, I wonder if he could help raise them. Ha! Maybe I'll have to enlist Julian to help with the twins. But Julian seems like he'd be a terrible father. He would become livid if, say, one of the boys got jam on his suit or, say, cut up his shoes with a carving knife.

When I go to see Mrs. E. the next day, she inquires about her crystal and china— and about the Zarrs.

I wonder just how much to tell and think I really should just send B.M. or Paulina over to brief her.

Mrs. E. is nibbling on a shortbread biscuit. "I think we need to have a chat with this Eddie Krakowski fellow."

She is pretty sharp for an old lady. I say, "Yes, he's also the brother of Julian's former wife."

"I see. I wonder if she's involved somehow. Hmm. Now, what did you find out about Simon?"

"He's always nervous about something. And I think he's in love with Clover, but Clover is in love with Julian."

"Oh my; we need to keep this Clover out of the picture."

I then tell her that Julian is in Paris this week to put his condo on the market. The one right next door to Clover and Maryel.

She implores me to keep Julian on a short leash, lest he is stolen by Clover, Maryel, or someone else. She says he's a good catch, and the problems with the family will be resolved someday.

Then Mrs. Etherington hands me a present and a card.

I open the beautifully wrapped gift. "How did you know it was my birthday?"

She makes a flying bird gesture. "I pick up things here and there."

It's a velvet jacket with pearl buttons — in my favorite shade of green. After many attempts with mold green, anti-freeze green, and other green failures with Paulina, I finally figured out my favorite shade: the same as the green cherries in fruitcake. Mrs. E. tells me never to put it in the washer, and if I happen to spill something on it, I'm to send it to her dry-cleaners.

When I get back to the house, I notice the sweet scent of vanilla wafting from the kitchen. Here I find David and the boys covered with flour and pink frosting, admiring a lopsided pancake on a pedestal.

David does a pirouette. "We baked you a birthday cake!"

I find their attempt both adorable and pitiful and thank them. "Is it one of those flourless cakes?"

David says, "Oh, no! I knew I forgot something."

Chapter 41

After a week-o-hell, I tromp back to the messy kitchen in a ratty bathrobe and pour more coffee. I look out the window to see David running down the street like his pants are on fire. In the next comic frame, I see the boys and the dog chasing him. I am interrupted from my moment of glee by the stove timer. *Rats!* Now it's my turn to watch the little buggers. David and I have broken it down to alternating 14-minute shifts. At the end of one challenging shift, I discovered "the caregivers secret" — Irish whiskey. Just as I'm pouring some in my coffee, I notice a face peering in the kitchen door. It's Oliver. *Hallelujah!* He's come to save us!

He picks up the bottle. "A little early, isn't it?" I look at the clock, "Are you kidding? I'm on my third shift."

Oliver says Enfys is staying in Edinburgh for a few weeks, and he has the lads to himself. He looks around and says, "that is— if they're still alive."

It's oddly quiet, so I glance out the kitchen window, and I see David tied to a tree! Even though his shift it not over, we run out to rescue him. He looks humiliated but relieved when Oliver cuts the rope with one of the decorative swords.

David quips, "The irony of a Dendrologist tied to a tree is not lost on the boys."

As Oliver packs up the terrorists, he asks if I want to come up to Felixstowe for the weekend. My brain is desperately trying to conjure a solid excuse while Oliver goes on with the logistics. "So this time it would be at the family house, not the apartment. The lads would be with us full time, but they *do* go to bed at eight."

I'm now drafting a few excuses in my head that involve a sudden goiter operation or a distant relative's funeral.

Oliver goes on enthusiastically, "We could cook, and sing, and cook for the lads."

David, trying to be helpful, says he can take care of the dog and the house, so I'm free to go. Then he finally senses my hesitancy by observing my swiveling jaw. In a high voice, he asks, "Umm, Camille, don't you have to run the blood drive at the hospital this week?"

Like that would ever happen. "Sorry Oliver, as much as I'd like to go, I'll have to see about the blood drive."

David adds, "Yes, let's hope no one needs a transfusion."

Oliver kisses me goodbye and says to let him know. He quietly shuffles the boys out the door. The minute he's out of the car park, David says, "He's a treasure. I like him so much more than Julian."

I say, "But your mother likes Julian, and says to give up on Oliver."

"But how can you not love a man who plays guitar and collects butterflies?"

Now David is lacing his coffee with the whiskey. "Just think Camille, if my mother didn't catch Arthur with his secretary, you be stuck with him. Instead, you've got sweet Oliver and sexy Julian."

126

Chapter 42

The next morning, I find David racing around his room, packing up his clothes. "Oh, Camille, it's so exciting! A rare copses of Wollemi pines have just been discovered. This is even more important than our Agathis australis find. I've got to get back to New Zealand!"

"Will you be stopping to see your wife in Shanghai?"

He comes to a complete halt. "I don't have to. She thinks she's pregnant."

"What!?"

He babbles, "What a nightmare. Last time I was there, she lured me to a fertility clinic, and they said they needed a new sample."

Now he's unpacking his suitcase and hanging up his clothes.

He goes on, "What was I to do? So right then, a delivery chap walked in, and I offered him $400 to give a sample."

Oh my, the things people get themselves into.

He collapses on the chaise like a southern belle. "What if my wife is pregnant with the Fed Ex guy's baby? He's from Delhi, so I think she'll notice when the baby comes out."

The driver is here to take him to the airport. So I quickly repack his suitcase, and guide him downstairs. David says, "Oh, I almost forgot! Oliver came by to get the twins' medicine."

"What? The boys were running around England un-medicated?"

As David says goodbye, he hugs me. "Now listen to me closely. Oliver is like a Monkey Puzzle Tree. And when you discover something rare, you have to hold on tightly."

Chapter 43

Cambridge, England

The voice on the phone is frantic. "My wife has escaped!" *What?* It's Oliver. He goes on using the word "sanitarium" a few times out loud. He asks if I can help him.

"Is she armed?" I ask, straight away. Without waiting for an answer, I say, "Of course I'll help." Thinking I should wash my hair before any type of missing person expedition, I ask how soon. He says it's imperative to find her now. He speaks rapidly, "If you catch the 11:04 train to Cambridge, I can meet you at the station. And bring the dog."

After a bit of preparation and guidance from Mrs. E., I ride the train with my handy search dog. When I arrive at the station, I see Oliver in the parking lot, pacing in front of his green Jeep. We embark on a three-hour journey to Harrogate, a town in North Yorkshire. Along the way, I ask where the twins are, afraid that he's forgotten about them. He tells me he's dropped them off at old Mrs. Rickard's house down the lane. I wonder what he said to get her to take on such a daunting task. Then I realize she probably didn't hear him and just nodded her head as the little devils marched in the door.

If it weren't for the distressing circumstances, I'd say it's fun to be on a road trip with Oliver and the dog. He tells me that Harrogate is considered the happiest town in England. *We'll see about that.* In my entire life, I've never needed to use the word sanitarium. Now, it seems to pop up in every other sentence. That's my new life: Lost dogs, lost wives, lost minds.

We drive around for what seems like hours, with no signs of his wife. I can tell he is exhausted, so I suggest we resume the search after a good night's sleep. Despite not having any reservations, we find a room at a quaint stone and ivy inn. The only room they have has twin beds, so the best we can do is reach across the beds and hold hands. Oliver falls asleep in his clothes, so I take his shoes off and tuck him in. Ah, I love watching him sleep. His dimpled cheeks seem to inflate and deflate with each breath. To me, his breathing is like the sound of the sea. I've made my mind up. Julian is perfect —for someone else. Oliver is the one I want.

In the morning, I wake to the sound of workers outside the window —and Robert barking at them. I look at Oliver and wonder: will we be lovers? Yes, but probably not right now. He must sense that Robert and I are staring at him, for he suddenly awakens and pops out of bed. "What time is it? We've got to hurry before she gets too far!"

Oliver drives methodically up and down the streets, looking both ways, making me think this is a wild goose chase. He tells me he brought along one of Enfys' housecoats for Robert to sniff. I'm not sure if he has those bloodhound skills, but it's worth a try. We stop at a park, and the dog takes in a whiff-o-Enfys and makes a run for it. Yay! Breathlessly, we race across the park, where he makes a dead stop and starts barking. There in the bushes is a couple rolling naked on a blanket; when they come face up, we see that it's not Enfys. The man yells at us, so we make a run for it.

Oliver says it's been over 24 hours, so now we can go to the police station and file a missing person's report. When the police ask Oliver to describe his wife, I am reminded that he is a poet. Instead of descriptive terms like height, age, and hair color, he uses the words: "diffident" and "lugubrious."

No wonder the cops can't find her.

I use the word 'beige' to try to be more descriptive. The officer says he will put out an APB for a woman who is both lugubrious and beige. They ask Oliver if he might just happen to have a photo of his wife. Oliver says, "Right, what was I thinking?" Instead of looking on his phone, he pulls out an old crumpled black and white photo of their wedding. On film, she looks like a negative.

Later, we pause our searching to stop in a little pub for a late Ploughman's lunch. Afterward, we overhear an old man, mutter, "That was the saddest Sandy Denny song I've ever heard." Oliver and I give each other knowing looks. The older man points to a bar across the street.

Here we encounter ole Enfys singing to a crowd of three drunk men in kilts. Six, if one has been drinking themselves. Since Sandy Denny ended up killing herself, I think we should get Enfys to sing something more cheerful, like Bob Marley songs.

As she finishes wafting out about killing someone, Oliver gently tells her she has to go back to the "quiet place."

She clutches her ratty sweater and replies, "I can't go now. I have another set."

"They're waiting for you."

"I'm not crackers! It's those lads who are driving me mad. Where are they anyway?"

"Mrs. Rickard is watching them."

131

Enfys looks out the window and says flatly, "Oh, so it's just a matter of time before she's dead."

Oliver gives me a look.

Enfys perks up. "Oh, where are we staying?"

Oliver doesn't want to tell her about our cozy little room. Thankfully, it is a three-block drive to the sanitarium. Despite this being the happiest of towns, Enfys seems to have dampened the mood.

Oliver tells her that he'll be back to get her. Sounding unhinged, she cries, "When?"

He hugs her goodbye and says, "Soon, Dear. Soon."

As we drive away, Oliver looks in the rearview mirror. She's still waving goodbye. He has tears streaming down his cheeks.

Chapter 44

Chelmsford, England

On the way back, Oliver drives me to our favorite place, The Pig and Whistle. I realize this is the perfect place to propose to someone, as it is so romantic. He orders a bottle of French white wine, so I know something is coming.

Then, instead of seeing dimples on Oliver's face, I see worry lines. Seated together in a corner booth, we both order the Whitstable battered cod again. He sips his wine and says, "Thank you for helping me Camille. I couldn't have done that alone."

He hands me a handwritten poem. I look into his eyes, and my heart starts to pound. I read it twice, but I'm confused. It's lovely and bleak at the same time. He says he's stuck in his marriage for a while. He sighs and says he just can't leave her now with all that's going on. He then takes my hand and says and doesn't want to hold me up. I wonder if he means for the drive home —or the rest of my life.

After the plates are taken away, he clears his throat and looks into my eyes. Then he comes out and says it. He tells me that we shouldn't see each other for a while. "It's just not fair to you." He looks at my fallen face and then says, "I know that someday we will be together. But not right now." He says that is why he didn't try to make love yet.

He says he has spent a lot of time thinking about it, and he wanted to tell me in person. He says when the time is right, we'll meet here again. I ask when. He says, "soon," just like he said to his wife.

During the ride to the train station, we don't say a word. There is so much running through my head, such as how soon is soon? When the train arrives, he kisses me on the forehead. It is a goodbye that might be forever.

I am so preoccupied that I miss one of the connections to get back to St. John's Wood. The dog and I are forced to spend part of our lives waiting on a solitary train station bench like sad hobos. My poor Oliver. I am reminded of all of the letters we wrote to each other. Of all the hope and anticipation. *Damn it! It's raining again, and I'm crying.*

Chapter 45

London, England

The house is empty. No kids; no David; no Julian. Thank goodness, God invented dogs. They always know when you need someone to pet.

I light a fire and sit in the library with Robert, the sofa-hog. We listen to Vivaldi while I have a drop of William Pickering 20-Year-Old Tawny Porto. I feel so relaxed, making me think I want nothing to do with alluring men, pharmaceutical investigations, or pregnant women. Maybe I am happy just being a pet-sitter.

The next day, Julian texts to say he's back from Paris and invites me to dinner at his place. Sure, I say, glad that I won't have to dress up. I'm a little depressed after the Oliver episode.

When I get there, Julian's front door opens, and I see a fat man in a butler suit. It's the penguin waiter!

Penguin says to me, "Ah, the dog-walker."

Julian enters the foyer. "Darling, I would like you to meet my new butler, Penroy. I borrowed him from the Connaught."

Penguin whispers, "Mind you, not a word about this; I'm on probation there."

We sit in the living room, where Penguin serves us tiny glasses of Chablis Les Forets from a silver tray. Julian says, "I don't know how I lived this long without a butler."

No one says anything about Mrs. Coquin. I don't want to bring anything up, what with me being responsible for the undercooked duck canapés. Thank goodness I dropped them on the floor before all the supermodels ate them and died. *Now that I think of it, I'm lamenting my clumsiness.*

Penguin can't help but ask. "So how is the poet?"

Julian answers for me. "She's just come back from a hunting expedition with him."

Penguin sits next to me and inquires, "Did he find his bat-crazy wife?"

I nod my head. Then start to wonder about Julian's staffing abilities; he seems only to hire the bossy, the lazy, and the nosy. Julian quickly changes the subject when he reminds me that we are going to Switzerland this weekend. In my Oliver funk, I had forgotten entirely about B.M.'s upcoming baby shower.

Then I say, "Oh no. Who's going to feed the dog? Paulina refuses."

Julian waves his hand, "Say no more. Perhaps Penroy would like to stay in St. John's Wood, drink wine all day, and leave the dog in the garden."

Penguin holds his hands in prayer. "Would that be the job description?"

Now, I'm a little worried that I could lose my plum assignment, so quickly add, "I'll have to check with Mrs. Etherington."

Julian reports that he's already received an offer on his Neuilly apartment. I am relieved that he will no longer have a pad right next door to Clover and Maryel. I wonder if he saw them while he was in Paris. Experimenting with discretion, I ask Julian about everything, *except* Maryel and Clover. There is no point in being direct with men about other women, as they will just lie.

To open up the dialogue, I ask Julian about his father. At first, Julian is vague, but then he sighs and says they are in deep trouble. "The regulators think we tried to cover up and delete files regarding the bad batches. That and our funds are at risk because the stock is tanking."

Penguin drops a silver tray. He's probably worried about cashing his new paycheck.

Right then, Simon barges in the front door and slams it with great haste. He acts like he's escaped pursuers and found a safe house.

Simon sees Penguin and asks, "New staff? Have you been into the trust accounts again, Julian?"

Julian replies in a curt, "At least I still have access to them."

Simon dismissively requests a drink from Penguin. "Four-fingers of Hendricks, a splash of tonic, four cubes not three."

Penguin pours the gin, his lips pursed, and eyes wild with the look of a man plotting to poison the guest.

I ask Simon where his lovely wife might be. He blots his forehead with a crumpled napkin and pours the cold drink down his throat. "Home with some hideous skin ailment."

Then the doorbell rings, and everyone just looks around. I finally get up to answer it. It's Clover. She's wearing a diaphanous yellow dress — leaving nothing— yet everything to the men's imagination.

Penguin's eyebrows are raised to his receding hairline. "I trust Mrs. Zarr will not be recovering this evening."

Penguin drags me into the kitchen and asks how to turn the oven on. Instead of cooking, he's smuggled in a prepared dinner in from Harrods. He serves Coquilles St. Jacques along with escargot with spinach and Pernod;

Julian complements Penguin on his fine cooking, saying it is nearly as good as Mrs. Coquin's.

Simon says, "How unfortunate that your cook died of food poisoning."

Penguin drops the plate. "I hope it was an accident."

Julian says, "Yes, how odd. We were all here that night. Thank goodness she was the only victim."

As curious as I am, I know not to say a word.

Simon asks Julian if he sold the Paris condo yet.

Penguin, who has perfected the hover, blurts out, "I'll bet Maryel will be sorry to see you leave."

Julian pauses, no doubt trying to recollect the wording of Penguin's termination clause. Penguin's head is reeling as he tries to get the words back in his big mouth. Julian takes a sip of his wine and looks at me without blinking his eyes. "I did not see Maryel."

The typically mute Clover says, "She's in Monaco."

Julian visibly exhales. "Is she? I hadn't known."

Penguin is a joy to have around, making me hope that Julian doesn't sack him today. During one of my many diversions under the table, I catch Simon's hand tucked into the crevice of Clover's lap.

When Penguin clears the plates, he spills the sauce, which lands in her chiffon laced crevice; we soon hear a barrage of foreign swear words come from her mouth. She runs upstairs and stays there for the rest of the evening. I notice that Simon joins her. Hmm.

Later, when Julian and I are alone in his room, I can't help but ask. "Why do you have an £10 million home in Mayfair and a flat in Neuilly, yet Simon appears to live on the edge in Earl's Court?"

Julian spells it out for me. "He has a bit of a gambling problem and had to sell a lot of his shares, back in the day before all of the stock splits." Then he tells me that his father has limited Simon's trust funds because he keeps gambling it away. "Plus, B.M. is addicted to something called QVC."

The next day, I visit Mrs. E., who agrees to have Mr. Penroy watch her dog. She says, "If the Connaught and picky Julian would hire him, then he must be trustworthy. And it sure is better than just leaving the terrace door open." *God, she knows everything!*

As she sips her tea, she asks an awful lot of questions. I tell her all about how Oliver says he shouldn't see me anymore. She pats my hand. "If it's meant to be, he'll come around." She hugs me goodbye and says, "Now, go have a wild time with Julian."

Chapter 46

Lugano, Switzerland

We fly over magnificent green Alps, which look like mossy volcanoes that have erupted through crystal blue lakes. One can practically see the Paleozoic strata a thousand stories high with tiny villages wedged onto sides of the mountains. Our private jet lands at the Lugano airport, which is so small that instead of a concourse area, travelers wait for their flights at a nearby café.

The Zarrs keep a Maybach in the parking lot, and soon Julian is driving me up the spiral mountain.

After driving past both classic and contemporary homes, we pull on a long and winding road and see a huge glass skybox —the home of Dr. Zarr.

We enter red double doors and take a few steps from the foyer to a vast sunken living room with a lake view. Then Julian leads me to the side of the house with color-coded rooms. We are to stay in the yellow room as his old blue room next door is being converted to a dressing room for the father's new wife.

From this blue room, I open a door and see into a red room. Julian says this is his father and Number Three's bedroom. I don't know who thought it was a good idea for all the rooms to have adjoining doors. Maybe that's why they had to color code.

In a flirtatious way, Julian unzips a bag and holds up the pale pink dress inside. "I hope you're wearing this tonight."

I tell him, "I'm sure that it's a bit too tight without some type of steel-belted lingerie."

Julian raises an eyebrow. "Forget lingerie; I can't wait to come back here and have you for dessert."

I'm all about food. "Where are we having dinner?"

"My father loves to dine at the Principe Leopoldo Hotel. It's just down the road."

He kisses me and falls on top of me on the bed. Then we are jolted by a horrible sound. "Yoo Hoo! I'm back!"

Julian puts his finger to my lips. But it's no use, as we see B.M. blockading the doorway with her body.

"Where did you get all those Harrods bags?"

Julian can't help himself, "Ah. Harrods. You should have my brother take you there sometime."

Then Simon appears behind her in the doorway. *So much for privacy.* "Don't give her any ideas. Besides, nothing would fit her now."

Simon and B.M. leave our room and bicker their way down the hall.

Dying of thirst, I wander down the hall in search of the kitchen. I overhear Dr. Zarr, Simon, and Julian talking in a room with a closed-door along the way. Soon their conversation escalates to an argument. It sounds like the father wants Julian to lie about something. No, he wants Julian *not* to lie about something. It switches from German to English just in time. Julian says he won't lie; he'll just omit.

I hear Dr. Zarr say, "You'll have to walk a tightrope between omission and disclosure—without committing perjury."

Then Julian says, "You can forget about Simon walking any tightropes."

Julian flies out the door and catches me, listening at the door. I say I was looking for the kitchen and am grateful when I stumble upon it, proving my theory that women have built-in food-tracking abilities.

Julian sighs, "I'm sure you heard that my brother and I might be facing criminal charges of tampering with evidence."

"What?"

"Not to worry. We didn't — but it appears as though someone has set us up."

Julian is happy to testify, but his father is unwilling to let him go on the stand. He's hoping Simon will do the dirty work. Poor Julian —no one looks more adorable than when they are vulnerable. He's lost the quick arrogance and acquired a slower, softer tempo. His voice has gone from Vivaldi's Storm to Debussy's Clair de Lune.

Right then, a burly Italian contractor barges in the door and says something in Italian, and points to the hallway of bedrooms. B.M. says to him, "Sure, go ahead!" Then she says to me, "Can't understand a word he says. He probably said, 'Okay if I saw your head off later?'"

The contractor's tools start making a loud drilling noise in the blue bedroom. Number Three appears in the doorway dressed in a long metallic gown like they wore in the 1960's movies. Instead of saying "Hello," she says, "Camille, we're dining at 8:00, so I don't want you holding things up again."

Then, Simon bursts in and pours himself a tumbler of gin.

B.M. says, "Now, honey, I want you to behave."

Simon tilts his drink back. "Off my back!"

His wife barks at him. "We don't want a repeat of that night with Maryel when you got stinking drunk."

Simon provides the sidebar. "Maryel drives men to drink."

Number Three moves to the wet bar and pours herself some white wine. "Thank goodness *she's* out of the picture."

B.M. blurts out, "Am I the only one who liked Maryel?"

Number Three says, "Yes." Then she sips her wine. "Probably because you have the same IQ."

When the contractor shuffles back into the living room, Number Three yells at him in Italian. It is not hard to guess what it involves. Something along the lines of, *'When is that god damned room going to be ready?'* Even when she yells Italian, her face and lips barely move.

Simon says to Number Three, "Can you tell him to come back in a few days? I can't stand the racket."

Number Three eyes B.M. "I assume the security system will still be off."

In fluent Italian, Number Three rattles off direct instructions to the man —punctuated with what must be criticisms —judging by his wincing face.

After they both leave, B.M. explains, "They have to leave the alarm off when I'm here. I've accidentally set it off four times, and now the police won't come anymore."

I look around and say, "That's comforting."

Heading to the presumed safety of the kitchen, I pass Dr. Zarr's study and hear him say, "So it didn't turn out as planned. What are you going to do?"

Then I hear Number Three say, "You'll find out soon enough."

Julian comes up behind me in the hallway. "No need to eavesdrop, Camille. If you want to know things about his family, just ask B.M."

"It's fascinating that everyone in your family loves to bicker."

"My dear, if you can't take a little family drama, then I suggest you find a quiet poet."

As if Oliver's family doesn't have its share of drama. At least this is drama in a glamorous setting.

It's not far to the Principe Leopoldo Hotel, so Julian, the father and I decide to walk. Dr. Zarr tells us he bought the property because of its proximity to this hotel. It's a grand 19th Century Spanish-style two-story villa with paprika colored walls, leaf-green shutters, and an orange tile roof. It used to be the summer home of the Belgian Prince Leopoldo. It's on a majestic site that overlooks a split in the mountains as well as the sparkling lake Lugano.

As we enter the bar area, Julian says, "Unfortunately, Simon's mother had the same idea. She bought another house just up the road."

We look to see Number Three tapping her foot with Simon and B.M.

Simon overhears and says, "My mother is the one who told him about the hotel."

Number Three says, "Please tell me she's not coming to the baby shower."

The manager visibly cringes at the thought as he guides us to the dining room.

Soon, a duet begins singing songs by Rodgers and Hammerstein. When "Some Enchanted Evening" plays, Dr. Zarr asks his wife to dance, but she coolly declines. He then asks me, looking to Julian, who nods in permission. Dr. Zarr takes my hand and leads me to the dance floor in such a graceful manner. While dancing, he whispers that I am to follow him. I wonder if he wants to leave here now, or is he talking about the dance. The lyrics are a lovely admonition about knowing when one has fallen in love. They make me realize that I *do* know. I know that Oliver is the one, so why am I here with Julian and this bunch of strangers? As Dr. Zarr holds me, I look to see Number Three's icy glare, so we quickly return to the table. I wonder how much longer Dr. Zarr can remain in this tyrannous marriage.

It is more relaxing to be with the Zarrs when no one is speaking or arguing. I order quail breasts with bacon and chanterelles; Julian has steamed sea bass in lovage stock, and B.M. inadvertently orders a mammoth-sized veal head —which stares at us all evening.

We all head back to the house for after-dinner drinks. After I change out of my tight dress, I see B.M. in the hallway motioning for me to come and eavesdrop with her. She opens a closet in the hallway behind the wet bar and puts her finger to my mouth.

Soon we hear Julian say, "I'll find out who did this if it's the last thing I do."

Simon replies loudly, "No one did anything! For the last time, it's a defect with a few batches."

Julian argues, "So why weren't there any defects for the past three years? The formula suddenly changes, and fifteen people die?"

Then I hear Dr. Zarr say, "Sons, this is neither the time nor the place for this discussion."

When we return to the living room, B.M. fills me in with a sidebar. "Just as we were about to have a stock split, all those people have to go and croak on us. We would have been worth bazillions."

Simon slams his drink down and looks at his wife. "We? Did you invent Zarrexifam?"

Number Three, who has been lounging on the sofa in that feline way of hers, chimes in, "Yes, Beth Marie? You've just become a Zarr. And by force I might add."

What a bitch. And a constant one at that.

Dr. Zarr offers a global apology for his wife and starts playing, "Fly Me to the Moon," on his clarinet.

Chapter 47

With the morning sun peeking in the window, Julian and I find time for a little romp. I don't feel love yet, but I do feel a strong like. At this rate, I'm sure the love will come. This time, there are only two interruptions: one from the glass man and one from B.M., who needs zit cream.

Julian and I are the last ones up as we head to the kitchen for coffee. I am wearing the new long white peignoir that Paulina assigned for the morning. I feel like a princess today.

The glass kitchen door is open, so I can overhear Dr. Zarr and his wife on the terrace. I can only understand snippets of what they're saying, as there is some German sprinkled in. Evidently, something terrible has happened—and they don't know what to do. Unfortunately, I can't hear the 'bad thing' because the glass man keeps making annoying drilling noises.

I spot a breakfast spread on the terrace table and wonder who arranged it, as they don't seem to have any staff. Julian says his father hates having people around. I think it's that people probably dislike working for Number Three. She and Dr. Zarr are dressed in finely tailored clothing and unlike us, are no longer wearing their PJs. Dr. Zarr invites me to help myself to breakfast. I take the top orange off a large pyramid, and it causes the entire pile of fruit to go tumbling off the table—and then off the edge of the balcony and undoubtedly down the mountain and into the lake. Then it occurs me —I've become as clumsy as B.M.

Number Three can't stop laughing so her husband has to guide her inside. I say to Julian. "God, she has sharp teeth. Your poor father."

Right then Simon comes around the corner and laughs. "I think she heard that." Thankfully, B.M. comes out wearing a hideous Chenille bathrobe with a stork fascinator hat on her head. She's doing some sort of comical rap dance. Dr. Zarr comes out and gently asks her to stop. He's no-doubt worried about the structure of the wooden terrace.

Simon, who seems oblivious to his wife's antics, says to his father, "How about if we take the ladies on a boat ride tomorrow?"

"Excellent idea, son." Dr. Zarr, then he tells me that his wife refuses to go because his boat is an antique; he then adds, "I happen to like old things."

Except for wives.

Then Dr. Zarr says, "If the weather is nice, we can go after the party."

While Julian and I remain on the terrace, they all head back into the house.

As I pour more coffee for Julian, I ask if he happens to know what his father and Number Three might have been arguing about. He butters his toast and shakes his head in a way that signals he's not going to tell me. "Oh, typical married people arguments."

The men are having lunch today at the Principe Leopoldo Hotel, so the ladies and I are sent shopping. We take a ten-minute drive down the mountain into town, where we are dropped off at the cobblestoned Via Nassa. It is a chic lane with wonderful upscale shops like Chanel, Gucci, and Hermes. B.M. holds up the price tags and performs a comical charade of fainting. Number Three

148

appears to be mortified by B.M.'s behavior, so she and Clover slink off to shop on their own. I think Number Three hates me now.

B.M. and I head down a twisty lane to a lovely turquoise fountain with a view of Lake Lugano. The lake is lined with Linden and Horse Chestnut trees and festooned with white swans. I love places with swans! In the distance, one can see the snow-capped Alps. I love Lugano. There's magic here.

As we sit, I observe that it is very different from Zurich —much like how the Italian Swiss are different from the German Swiss. It's like Zurich is the mechanical workings of a watch, and Lugano is the soft cordovan leather band that holds it together.

I am starting to enjoy being with this Zarr family. Well, some of them.

Chapter 48

Today is the long-awaited baby shower at The Principe Leopoldo Hotel. I can't decide which of Paulina's many selections to wear, so she sends me a matrix based on the weather and my hourly weight. I try to check the weather, but can't get the wifi to work on my devices, so Julian says to use the computer in the blue room. When I do, I see that someone's got something called SMI—the Swiss Market Index—on the screen. Novartis and Credit Suisse are down a lot, and Zarr Pharma is bright red too. Vora Pharma, however, is very green. That's the suspicious competitor. Hmm.

Julian calls me from the living room to hurry up. I hop in wearing a white body-con dress, hoping someone will zip it for me, so I don't have to use the Venetian blinds. Everyone ignores me as Number Three commands attention. She announces that she cannot fit into her new tangerine Versace dress thanks to B.M. She will have to find something else to wear, and we will all just have to wait. *She needs Paulina.* Dr. Zarr says she looks lovely even though she's wearing B.M.'s ratty Chenille bathrobe. Number Three says, "Well, at least I look better than Camille."

All eyes turn to me in my tight, unzipped dress, so B.M. drags me away. "Come on, I've got pliers."

Once in the yellow room, she waves me over to the blue room door, where the listening is better. We can hear Dr. Zarr and his wife continue to argue. They switch on and off speaking in German, and B.M. whispers the translations.

150

Number Three scolds Martin, "*Ich habe dir gesagt, es war dumm.*"

B.M. whispers the translation. "I told you it was stupid."

Dr. Zarr's muffled voice is very calm. "*Aber Liebling, der dies vorausgesehen haben könnte?*" (But darling, who could have foreseen this?)

"*Tolle Idee was Zarrexifam kostenlos weg!*"

(Great idea, giving Zarrexifam away for free!)

"*Haben Sie nicht wollen, dass jeder Zugang zu dem Medikament zu haben?*"

(Don't you want everyone to have access to the drug?)

Now it's quiet. Then Dr. Zarr says, "I've got to be back here for a video call at three. I'll have to use this."

Number Three scoffs, "Use your own computer! I don't like people using mine."

He says, "Mine's is too slow for a video conference. Come on; we're late."

B.M. pulls me to the far side of the yellow room and says, "Number Three has a lot of shares and doesn't want him to give the drug away."

"How did *she* get so many shares?"

"I think it was in the prenup."

B.M. looks at my dress and tells me to wear something looser. I look at B.M.'s dress, which has gigantic poppies and ruffles at the base. She looks like a cow mother in a *Far Side* cartoon.

Julian appears in the doorway and declares, "I'll be making a run to the hotel; shall I come back and get you in, say, a few days?"

B.M. says, "Camille just needs to find some control top pantyhose or some Spanx."

I can't understand why—after all this food sampling. Julian pivots on his heel and disappears before bursting out, laughing in the hallway.

B.M. looks at my face and says, "I'll be right back." She soon returns and says, "Ta-da!" and holds up a pack of control top pantyhose. "This will do the trick."

After examining the package, I decide that I would rather look flabby than wear these Size AAA long hose, clearly designed for stick figures.

Julian is in the doorway. "Number Three is not ready, and Father is waiting for us in the car."

I grab the pantyhose and head out the door with B.M. and Julian. He says, "You could always walk."

The hotel has two glass wings, which reach out like lion's paws, off the 18th-century main building. We have the best view atop the mountain that overlooks the deep sparkling lake.

We enter the east wing and see elegant tables set with white linen table cloths — and the poisonous yellow Gelsemium centerpieces. I can't help but want to slip some in Number Three's lunch —that is, if she ever shows up.

A jazz band of eight older women dressed in elegant black dresses with pearls are playing instruments in a conga line. We hear clarinets, flutes, and lap-strung keyboards, all playing Dave Brubeck's "Take Five."

One of the musicians wipes off her clarinet with vodka and hands it to Dr. Zarr. He then plays a haunting "Rhapsody in Blue," at the microphone. Then he wipes off a flute and hands it to me. I play, "Summertime," as he looks on smiling.

I look around and see that everyone is here except Number Three. I wonder why it takes so long to find another dress. I mutter, "Where is that evil bitch?" *Forgetting the microphone is on.* Everyone stops talking. Then they all start laughing. Dr. Zarr gets up to make a call outside the dining room, probably so he can swear at her in German.

Grabbing a drink, I slink over to a seat next to Clover. As nicely as I can, I say, "I understand you grew up in Finland." She doesn't strain her swan neck to look up from her phone. Her body language essentially tells me to mind my own business.

I decide to visit Julian and his father who are standing by the piano. They are chatting about the Billie Holiday song, "Don't Explain." Julian's father has a coolness about him—in a saxophone and Drambuie kind of way.

B.M. comes up behind me like a freight train. "Why didn't you put the pantyhose on yet?"

"Thank you for lending them to me, but it's hot, and they're too small."

"Oh, they're not mine. I nabbed them from Number Three's dressing room."

I'm officially mortified. Julian and Dr. Zarr pretend they can't hear, but I can tell that they find this amusing.

I blurt out, "What? She seems like the type who wouldn't want people borrowing her things."

B.M. rests her hands on her ample hips. "That's probably why she's not here. She's probably looking for them."

The staff suggests we wait to eat until the hostess, Mrs. Zarr, arrives. I think this is because they are afraid of her and her sharp teeth. Meanwhile, B.M. starts banging her silverware and demanding food.

Suddenly, Julian's face drops as he looks to the entryway. In walks, the stunning Maryel. B.M. squeals like a pig and runs over to greet her. Dr. Zarr, maintaining a

153

smirk, says from the corner of his mouth, "This should be an interesting day."

As Maryel approaches, Julian says, "I swear I had no idea she was coming."

For just once in my life, I'd like to be as cool as Maryel, who only takes three steps on her long legs to reach our group. "You invited me, Darling."

Julian whispers to me, "I did it just to annoy Number Three —she hates her."

B.M. says, "Maryel is my friend too!"

Maryel says to Julian's father. "Hello Dr. Zarr, I just saw your lovely wife at the residence."

Oh brother, is she staying with us?

Dr. Zarr says, "Ah, what would you guess her ETA to be?"

Maryel reaches for a passing glass of champagne, "Zero hundred hours. Is that a number? She's not coming."

Dr. Zarr looks perturbed. "Not at all?"

Maryel says, "She said she wouldn't be caught dead at Beth Marie's party. She adds, " She's headed to the spa at the Villa Sausage."

I think she means Villa Sassa. Now I wonder if Maryel is always going to pop up at all family events. She then tells us that she's catching a flight to Paris, and won't be staying at the house tonight. *Yay!*

Clover sulks. "I would be in Paris already if not for the stupid fat cow delaying this party for two weeks."

Maryel looks at Clover, "How dare you say that about Beth Marie. She's having a baby."

"*A* baby? It looks like triplets."

Next thing we know Clover and Maryel are having a little slap festival. The men seem to like it as they gather round. Dr. Zarr has to break them up as they are close to falling off the edge of the cliff. *Rats, that would have been handy.*

154

Poor B.M. hears these comments and starts to cry. When I go over to console her, she asks me to get her Kleenexes —a whole box.

The chaotic conversations and jazz music become muted as I head to the sanctuary of the ladies' room off the main lobby. Here I find Maryel putting on lipstick, so to make conversation, I ask if she had a good time in Monaco. She looks at me. "I hate Monaco! I haven't been there in a year." Hmm? Why would Clover say she was there? Maybe she was there in Neuilly and Clover was covering for Julian. Maryel hands me some foundation and says I need some and to also put some on B.M.'s red face. *That was semi-kind of her.*

After she leaves, I hear a voice out side, and look to see Simon pacing out front. He's on his phone. "I am afraid I am going to need a bit more time." Maybe it's the mob calling in a gambling debt. Then he huffs, "I can't drop everything and go to Vienna." Hmm. I wonder what is happening in Vienna. Right then B.M. comes in and starts blowing her nose. I apply some of the make up, and remove the toilet paper trail from her foot as she heads back to her party. *Poor hopeless thing.*

When I head back to the festivities, I find Julian flanked by Maryel and Clover, both vying for his attention. They are so close to him that he looks like a supermodel sandwich. Then I overhear Clover say something to Maryel about me. Julian says I'm just a little *joufflue* today, adding that I have an occupational hazard as a food blogger. I don't have to pull out my French dictionary to know that means chubby.

Finally, the waiters have been given the go-ahead to serve the lunch. Everyone enjoys a lovely lobster salad, Grilled prawns, and a Poire William dessert. But no dessert for me as I'm a little joufflue.

155

Then I notice a text from Mrs. E. asking: *How is it going?*

I text her back: *Maryel here. Number Three AWOL. B.M. crying. Simon needed in Vienna.*

Mrs. Etherington texts back: *Find out why!*

After we finish our late lunch, B.M. starts to open her gifts. She gleefully does a mock demonstration of her new breast pump, the one that Julian and I gave her, along with the five others she received.

Simon beams at Clover in the distance as he chats with his father. "Clover and I arranged for a small fireworks display over the lake, after you finish your conference call."

The father tells him the call is canceled, so Simon then ushers us all outside and makes a toast. Suddenly, a mass of fireworks covers the sky. We hear a loud pounding in the sky —like a bodice ripping; then a booming that acts as a chest defibrillator. We see pink, green, yellow, and blue fireworks spread across the sky, almost as if they had been color-coded by Paulina.

After the grand finale, Julian pulls me aside and whispers, "Let's sneak back to the house."

"Gladly," I say, surprised that he is willing to leave his long-legged beauties. Just as we are tip-toing out of the lobby, B.M. appears and demands that Julian load all of her presents into the car. He hands me the house key and says, "Don't start without me."

I walk up the hill in the dripping heat. When I get inside, I find it's quiet for once, realizing that Number Three must have left for her spa treatments.

To get in the mood for Julian, I play the sexy Robert Palmer song, "Stone Cold." Then I remember something important: chubby or not, there is one Magnum bar left, and I want to eat it before B.M. returns. Ah! It's yummy, and I pause for this bliss moment. I'm so hot, I take off all of my clothes and lick every last bit of the dark chocolate ice cream bar, mentally revisiting one of my chocolate times with Julian.

Then I suddenly remember that I have to return the stupid pantyhose. I have learned one thing in this life: never borrow anything that's hard to put back. I open the door to the blue dressing room and see it: A dead body!

Chapter 49

It's Number Three. She's been crushed by a gigantic window. I try to scream, but nothing comes out, which makes me realize I could never be cast in any of Alfred Hitchcock movies. There she is, squashed—just like a bloody pancake—by a massive pane of glass. She looks frozen in time with her arm up. Her mouth is gaping as if caught by surprise. I try to lift the glass, but my chocolaty fingers are too slippery, and it's way too heavy.

Panicking, I run to the living room but soon realize that I'm stark naked, so I run back and put on Julian's dress shirt — my fingers trembling as I try to button it. Not knowing what to do, I run from the living room to the kitchen and back again.

When I regain some composure, I find my purse and dial 911, but the phone makes a funny sound, and a woman's prerecorded voice says something in Italian.

Then I hear gravel in the driveway and look outside. Ah, thankfully, it's Julian pulling up in the Maybach.

When I open the front door, he sees me. I'm jumping up and down, pointing into the house, but he just looks at me.

With a smile, Julian says, "That's very naughty on you, Camille, but you need cufflinks to pull it off." Then he finally sees the terrified look on my face. "What's wrong, my darling?"

When I try to scream again, it sounds like a chalky yelp. I wave Julian in and drag him by the arm to the blue room.

Shocked, Julian cries a long drawn out, "Fuck!"

He cringes as he looks at his step-mother's body. Then he covers my eyes. This is when I notice the smell of perfume that makes me sneeze.

I observe the tragedy again. "Shouldn't we try to save her?"

"I think it's a bit late for that, but I'll give it a try."

Julian uses a chair to try to wedge it under the glass, causing blood to squirt all over his shirt.

He exhales. "She's already dead, plus there is no possible way I can lift the glass off her. It took a crane to deliver these windows."

I can barely speak, but can't help asking. "How did it fall?"

Julian shrugs his shoulders. "I have no idea."

Right then, we hear the front door open and shut so we head out to the living room. *Oh no. It's Dr. Zarr.*

Julian's voice goes up an octave. "Ah, Father. I am afraid I've got some rather bad news."

Dr. Zarr sees the blood on his son's shirt and turns to his native language. "Was ist das?"

"It's bad, Father. Very bad."

Dr. Zarr and his perplexity follow Julian to the blue room while I hide in the living room. I wait there, expecting to hear a scream, but it never comes.

Then the father appears to sleepwalk across the sunken living room, heads to his study, and quietly closes the sliding door. Julian comes to the living room, slowly walks to the wet bar, and pours two scotches.

Seemingly unruffled, he says, "If Beth Marie comes back, please keep her out of that room."

He takes the drinks and goes to the study to console his father. I sit on the stark white sofa and wonder who will walk in the door next. I also wonder why I ever left Boston.

159

After what seems like a few hours, but has probably only a few minutes, B.M. comes barging in the door. Her face has red blotches so I can't help but ask, "What happened to your face?"

"It burns like crazy! I think it's from your make up."

"Not mine. Maryel gave it to me. " Hmm.

B.M. heads for the bedrooms, so I quickly blurt out, "Don't you want a bite to eat?"

"Yup, I'm starving. There's one Magnum Bar left, and it's got my name on it!"

Now I need to keep her from the kitchen and the blue room, so I put my hands on my hips to create a blockade with my elbows. Then, I try to distract her by asking where Clover and Maryel are. She answers, "Clover went to get her do-dah waxed at the spaaaa. And Mary-el has gone to the air-o-port to go back to Paris."

Well, that's a relief.

I soon realize that it's impossible to keep a pregnant woman away from food, so I follow her to the kitchen. She rummages through the freezer. "Alright, who ate the last ice cream bar?"

I look down. "I think it was Number Three."

B.M.'s face makes a shark-like wince, "I'll kill that bitch."

I grab an opened bottle of Rosé, and pour a glass. Now I feel guilty for blaming the defenseless woman.

B.M. eyes the cognac pate and takes a Tupperware container and starts filling it like she's going on a picnic, "Never mind. Look, there's cheese, liverwurst, and those little Corinthian pickles."

She waddles out to the living room with her stash of food, and I follow her, wondering how I'll corral her. As we walk, I hear the men in the study —too bad they are speaking in German.

In a low voice, Julian says, "*Wir haben dies durchzudenken.*"

It sounds like they will have donuts, which is something I'd do at a time like this. Then B.M. is right beside me, munching on cornichons. She translates. "He said, 'We've got to think this through.'"

Dr. Zarr says, "*Wir sind aus der Zeit.*"

B.M. says, "I left the mustard in the fridge." I think this is an odd translation until she hands me the food and heads back to the kitchen.

The men walk out to the living room with their drinks and silently take seats on the sofa. We sit staring at the jar of Cornichons, trapped forever in the same minute. Suddenly, we hear an ear-piercing scream, and then another. Oh, no! B.M. has taken the back way to the bedrooms.

She comes wobbling—out. "Number Three is dead!"

Julian takes a sip of his drink. "We know."

B.M. looks at me. "Did you see that?"

Trying to mimic Julian's calm composure, I say, "Yes, yes, I did."

She runs in circles like a circus elephant, screaming. "Someone do something."

Dr. Zarr is silent, making me think he's in shock.

Julian takes another sip. "Nothing can be done now."

B.M. throws her fat arms up. "How long till the ambu-lance comes?"

Julian's face turns 90 degrees to his father. Dr. Zarr wrinkles his forehead. "Son, did you call an ambulance?"

Julian's head turns to me. "Camille, did you call one?"

161

"Me? No, I tried but got a funny recording in Italian. I thought you were going to call."

B.M. starts yelling, casting a centrifuge of panicked words fly across the walls, but no one bothers to catch them. Dr. Zarr gives Julian a nod. Julian slowly pulls his cell phone and presses three buttons.

He clears his throat and relays calmly, "Pardon me, but we have an incident we'd like to report."

We can hear the operator respond, but the words sound muffled.

Julian says, "I'm afraid we've had an unfortunate accident." After a muffled reply, Julian speaks like he's identifying his dry-cleaning. "Yes, the Zarrs again. Yes, on Montalban."

B.M. looks at me. "They're just calling them now?"

Julian says to the operator. "Yes, we'll wait for you."

B.M. cries, "Don't tell me you're sitting here drinking whiskey while there's a dead woman in there."

Julian calmly gets up, walks over to the wet bar, and refills the glasses. "No, Beth Marie, we are drinking scotch."

B.M. pulls her phone out and makes a call. She huffs when she gets voice mail. "Simon, get over here right now. Number Three is deee-ead!"

This ability to vent seems to have calmed her down a bit. We all just sit there. No one says a word. That is, until B.M. quips, "Too bad —she just got her boobs done."

Chapter 50

A bit of laughter escapes before Julian can rein it back in. B.M. says, "Boy, do you guys have a lawsuit against that contractor. I tell you it was an accident waiting to happen."

Julian guides me to the wet bar, and whispers in an urgent tone, "This was no accident."

I look up to see if B.M. heard, but she is busy eating ice cream with pickles and pepperoni. Suddenly, we hear sirens approaching. The police arrive in an efficient Swiss pack. I would expect nothing less from them.

Julian greets them with the smile of a host. "Ah, do come in."

Despite the blood on his shirt, Julian appears unfazed. He guides them through the hall entrance to the scene of the crime. I've summoned the courage to take another look, so I follow. I notice that Number Three is wearing her tangerine Versace dress even though she said it didn't fit. Why would she still be wearing this —if she was going to the spa instead of the party? Hmm. Maybe she was looking for her control-top pantyhose. I'll bet if she had found them and could have gone to the party. Then she would be alive today. *It's all my fault!* I decide to keep this to myself.

Next, the police escort Julian's father into the room. He gasps and turns a color that could only be named 'fish underbelly green.'

The police want to know precisely how a large piece of glass could just fall. Dr. Zarr exits the room without answering.

The police tell us not to go back into what becomes officially known as the "blue room." They take a lot of photos, and we are sent to sit together in the living room.

As the police pester Dr. Zarr with a series of nosy questions, the front door opens, and more CSI-type workers enter the home. Dressed in white, they march across the living room and straight to the room. I have no idea what they are saying as they are all speaking in Italian. Oh, if only Number Three was here to translate.

Then someone asks if anyone was eating chocolate in the blue room. Everyone looks at me, and finally I say, "Yes, I had a chocolate ice cream bar." B.M. glares at me and stomps off to the kitchen.

Dr. Zarr continues to answer questions. In a flat voice he tells the police that we were all at the hotel until we came home and found this. No, he doesn't know why his wife didn't go to the party. The now withered-looking man says he'll be in his study.

The police move on to me. I add that Number Three might have been a little peeved that Beth Marie had modified the menu as well as other arrangements, and that's why she didn't show up. Also, her dress didn't fit. The Swiss investigator does not smile once.

Julian comes back into the living room and asks me for help in the kitchen.

I follow him and ask if he wants me to prepare a light snack for the police. He says, "No, I wanted to tell you not to talk." Then he turns to B.M., who is sitting at the kitchen table, "The same goes for you if that's remotely possible." But she doesn't hear him as she's texting Simon.

Julian says to me, "Forget what I said earlier; I think this was simply an accident."

Simon returns to the house and slams the door. He has the crazed look of someone with a ticking bomb strapped to his chest. Julian leads him to the blue room, and we hear a loud, "Yow! That's harsh." When the police shoo them back to the living room, Simon says, "Whoa! Didn't see that coming."

This was no accident. I replay the scene in my head of the baby shower, where family members were coming and going from the glass annex. They were strolling out to the bar, out to make calls, and out to have cigarettes. Dr. Zarr was gone a lot, and so was Simon. Come to think of it, and anyone could have left the party, walked to the house — and killed her. The sweaty Simon looks the most guilty.

Right then, Simon gasps, "Oh no. What if Clover comes back? We can't let her see her mother pressed under the glass like a lab sample!"

Julian looks to see if his father could have heard that.

Simon says, "I know! I'll text Clover and say that B.M. is eating pepperoni and ice cream again. That always keeps her away."

The police take more photos and pieces of evidence, like Number Three's phone and puts things in zip-lock bags.

They ask me why I left the party early and why I went into the blue room — if I was staying in the yellow room. I pause a moment to consider my reply. Julian, his brother, and B.M.—as well as the entire assemblage of the Swiss police, are waiting for my answer. I reply, knowing that my alibi will forever be known as the "pantyhose defense."

Chapter 51

The police escort our party of murder suspects to a village called Norango. This is the designated location for when people get killed on the weekend. Apparently, murder is rare in Switzerland, so there is quite a bit of conversation about what to do.

It takes two cars, as B.M. and her Tupperware container of meats and cheese take up a lot of space.

She says, "You can have some of this if you end up in the pokey, Camille."

I ride with her while the Zarr men ride in the other police car. The police made the seating arrangements without my input. Ah, a lovely ride through the mountains—pity we are in police cars on our way to be arrested.

B.M. is chatty as usual, only in a higher pitch, and fast like a 78 rpm record. "What do you think happened? Do you think someone pushed the glass on her head? That's what she gets for not coming to my party."

Although the police officers speak Italian amongst themselves, I can tell that they understand English.

It feels like we are driving for hours. B.M. asks how much longer. The officer behind the steering-wheel says, "We're still in the driveway." He is young and looks single, so I doubt he knows much about babies or pregnant women.

In a worried voice he says to B.M. "You're not having that baby any time soon, are you?"

As we are near a cliff, I feel the need to reassure him by answering, "She's not due for seven weeks."

B.M. blabbers, "No worries! My mother gave birth to me in a bank lobby. Her water broke all over the marble floor right by the free toasters. Then a man slipped and fell in it, and filed a lawsuit. That stuff is slippery."

B.M. is sweating and decides that her maternity pantyhose must come off right now. So, she reclines into the seat's corner and lifts her legs to the headrest near the other officer's head. Still wearing her big flowered "Far Side" cow dress, she directs me to pull the pantyhose off from the toes. Oddly, there is no glass divider shield in the car to protect them from the perpetrators.

Then it happens: B.M. lets out a fart. No, fart is too short a word to describe what we heard. It was more like the sound of a ship horn on a foggy morning—an extended lingering alert. The police officer who's driving, quickly whips his head around until he realizes the source. I can see in the rearview mirror that the officers are trying very hard not to laugh. One has had to fold his lips into his mouth and I can see the driver's shoulders shaking. Now his eyes are watering, and he is having trouble driving. which is dangerous with these zigzag roads.

B.M. does not think this is funny. "It was my thigh on the vinyl." She pulls her cow dress back down and leaves the pantyhose around her ankles.

Eventually, we make our way to Morengo. I am relieved when they pull up to a kindergarten instead of a police station. Despite bright colored walls and crayon artwork, Julian, Simon, and Dr. Zarr are sitting morosely in the entry. Then, Julian comes over and says they need to see our IDs. Thank goodness I still have my passport in my purse.

One by one, we are escorted to private rooms. I'm guided to a room with pink plastic furniture and a padded floor. An older lady pops in and offers cups of espresso and cookies. After a while, a darkly handsome man of Italian decent comes in and introduces himself. "Detective Roberto Bernardo from the Canton of Ticino."

He has large brown eyes that smolder. My eyes wander up to his dark hair and then down to his square jaw. He has a smile on his face as he looks at my passport. "Tell me how you came to know Julian Zarr?"

The caffeine is kicking in already. "Where do I start?" I try to reconcile the events. "My fiancé cheated on me, so my friend David got me a job cooking for his mother's dog, and she thought I should meet my poet Oliver at Claridge's but somehow her driver took me to the Connaught. And then this supermodel, Maryel—you should pull her in—came and started flinging champagne..."

He makes a cutting motion with his hands like a film producer.

The detective breathes a sigh, "Very well. Ms. Carano, do you have any reason to believe that Penelope Zarr was murdered?"

"Oh my god! That's her first name? Well, you should talk to B.M. about her."

"B.M.? Is that the woman you arrived with?"

"Yes. It stands for Beth Marie, but we think it stands for Blabber Mouth."

"Yes, keep going."

"Well, B.M., BlabberMouth, is also a busybody, which is an unfortunate combination. And I think Penelope—they all call her Number Three. I think Number Three knew too much."

"What do you mean too much?"

"Well, there were some problems at the Zarr Pharmaceutical Company."

The detective leans in like he's got a juicy steak in front of him. "What kind of problems are you referring to?"

I suddenly realize I've said too much, so I wave my hand. "Oh, you know, typical problems like shipping and distribution."

He gets up and brings over a box of Italian chocolates. Then he dangles a pear liqueur one in front of me before offering it.

He says matter-of-factly, "Yes, shipping, distribution, and fifteen deaths. Sometimes we read the papers."

"Well, I'm not sure how much is public knowledge."

His dark eyes bore into me. "Miss Carano, do you happen to have any idea how those deaths could be related to Penelope Zarr getting killed?"

"I have no idea. She seemed a little cranky, and I heard her arguing with her husband through the wall. She was turning a bedroom into a walk-in closet, and the window was being removed so her clothes wouldn't fade. I think the glass just fell by accident."

He gives me another chocolate. "Okay, so now tell me about this argument with Dr. Zarr."

"Oh, I just adore him. He's so sweet and plays the clarinet and the saxophone. I'm sure he had nothing to do with this. They argue, but sometimes it's in German, so I don't know what it's about."

"Now, you were the first to find her. So tell me about that."

"Well, we were drinking champagne all ding dong day at the Principe Leopoldo, waiting for her royal highness to arrive. Have you been there?"

"Yes, it's very nice."

169

I say rapidly, "Eventually, Julian got a little randy, and there's not a lot of privacy—what with walls taken down—not that I'm any sort of screamer. So Julian said to meet him at the house. I was all sweaty, so I took off my clothes to take a quick shower, then I remembered I had to put back the pantyhose."

The dark-eyed Roberto peers into my eyes. "So you were naked, and you found a dead body. Then what did you do?"

I look at him like he's from another planet. "Well, I was worried that there might be a murderer in the house, so tried to put on some panties, but I guess they'd all been flung across the room." I catch him looking at my bare legs, but continue. "I wanted to change, but your officers wouldn't let me."

"We've learned never to wait for a woman to get dressed." He wipes his brow. "So, where were we?"

"I found her smooched body. Boy, that is not a good way to go. Then I tried to call for an ambulance."

"What time was this?" After I shrug my shoulders, he says, "It would be on your phone."

He waits impatiently as I dig through my gigantic purse. After I hand my phone to him, he quickly scrolls through my calls. "I see you made a call at 4:01." He looks at me. "But 911 doesn't work here. You have to call 144 for ambulanza; 117 for police."

"How would I know that? When I dialed, I heard something in Italian, but right then, I could hear Julian in the driveway, so I hung up."

"So then what did everyone do? Did anyone try to hide things or clean up?"

"B.M. had brought out pate, cheese, and pickles. We just sat there in silence. Even B.M., which is rare. She's a chatterbox."

"*She's* a chatterbox?" He hands me a chocolate. "Was it clear that the victim was already dead when you found her?"

"That, or a very good faker."

"So how long until the ambulance arrived?"

"Well, that's the odd thing. No one had called one."

He nearly falls off his chair again. "What?"

"I guess Julian thought I called, and his father assumed Julian had called. And I did, too."

The detective calls out to the hallway: "Tony, what time was the call to 117 on the Zarr incident?"

The Tony guy stands in the doorway, reading off a call registry. "The call came in at 16:48 hours."

"Let see. So no one called for 47 minutes from when you tried to call."

"Was it that long? No wonder I went through two glasses of Rosé."

"So, you all just sat there drinking Rosé and eating pate and cornichons?"

"Well, the luncheon at the hotel started as more of the liquid kind. But we did have a lovely lobster salad..."

"Who was there at the house before the police came?"

"Let's see: Julian, Dr. Zarr, B.M., Simon, and me. So, it was just the five of us. Well, six if you count Number Three. Gosh, that's a lot of numbers."

The detective then gets a call and converses in Italian. He stands up and shakes my hand. "Very helpful, Miss Carano."

'So far, it was the most exciting thing to happen to me. People cared about every word I said. The trouble was, each word added to my prison sentence and sharply dug my grave.'

Chapter 52

When I am released to the hallway, I see Julian pacing the floor. He says we are not permitted to enter the house as it's on lockdown. We are all going to stay at the Principe Leopoldo. *Fine with me.*

I ride back in a police car with Julian, as B.M. and her gas have been detained. He holds my hand, and when I try to speak, he puts his finger over my lips.

As soon as we are deposited at the hotel's entry, I find that everything has been arranged for our stay. Julian silently takes my arm and escorts me across the road to a more modern annex of the hotel. From the windowed corridor, we see a massive emerald-colored pool with orange umbrellas. Glad to know we'll be sequestered in luxury.

When we reach our destination, he opens the door to a large suite. A king-sized bed sits a few stairs above a large sunken living room with a terrace. This would have made a darling apartment for a girl and her pug.

Once Julian closes the door, he says in low tones, "They are calling the incident suspicious. It's too early to arrest anyone, but they have asked us to extend our stay in Lugano."

"How nice of them."

He raises his voice. "It's not to be nice; we are in serious fucking trouble!"

"I thought you said it was an accident?"

"Somehow they thought it odd that no one called an ambulance for 47 minutes. I wonder how they made that calculation."

I avert my eyes. "The Swiss are very precise."

"Also, someone told them that Number Three had argued with my father." He looks at me, "I wonder who told them that?"

I look at the floor. "Probably B.M."

His eyes open wide. "God, save us all if she starts talking."

"If it's just an accident, we'll have nothing to worry about."

Julian continues, "According to my father, the next step is an autopsy. Until then, we are asked not to leave the Canton of Ticino."

Julian opens the terrace door and sits outside, smoking a cigarette. I check my phone, hoping for a text or message from someone normal like Mrs. E. or Oliver. I think of sending them texts, but what do I say? *Nice baby shower. Found dead body afterward.* That will just pose questions, and I'm too tired to deal.

Everything feels a little different now. I had been thinking of turning my novel into a murder mystery, but now it's happening in real life. *Didn't see this coming!* Now, I could see Oliver's wife killing someone or maybe David's wife. But not this.

The only thing to do is climb under the covers for a mini-nap. Julian says his father called to say that Clover had returned to the house, and the police told her what happened. She seems the type to have little if any outward reaction. According to Julian, Clover is staying here in the hotel, and Simon is consoling her. I'll bet!

Julian is going to see his father now, and says if I can manage to be ready, I'm to come down in an hour. Of course, who does he think I am —Clover? He tells me we will not have access to the house for a few days and he's contacted Paulina and the concierge to arrange for clothes. *Who thinks of clothing at a time like this?*

Nothing seems to faze Julian. With no time for a nap, I manage to take my shower. Finding a dead body and being questioned by the police makes one feel less than clean. Just as I'm toweling off afterward, there is a knock on the door. It's a package from the front desk; it is all wrapped up like a present. It's a knit navy dress from Balmain and a pair of sling-back shoes from Chanel. Along with two brassieres, four pairs of panties, and two pairs of pantyhose. Then I remember the pantyhose I had borrowed and suddenly feel a pang of guilt. *Will they find out that I was the one who kept Number Three from the party — that resulted in her death? Oh, no! Will the truth come out that I was responsible for the death of Mrs. Coquin?*

After the guilt pang fades, I manage to get dressed. I walk across the road in the light drizzle and remember how everything was different the last time I came here —even though it was earlier today.

In the quaint lounge, I overhear Julian and his father. Their conversation is not on the topic of being murder suspects, but whether Dave Brubeck was the writer of the song, "Take Five." Dr. Zarr calmly says everyone thinks it was Dave Brubeck, but Paul Desmond actually wrote the song.

"Ah, Camille." Dr. Zarr says kindheartedly, "Come in and sit down." He offers me a soft armchair. "I am so sorry to have you caught up in the middle of this."

Julian says, "Yes, Father, it is a remiss host who lets a guest become a murder suspect."

To the trained eye, it appears that they are more than half-way through drinking a bottle of Krug Grande Cuvee. My face must impart, *'Celebrating?'* so Julian says, "It was compliments of the hotel." Then I think the hotel staff

174

is secretly reveling in the death of the despised Number Three.

Julian bows out to find Simon, who is not answering his texts. I sit with Julian's father in the cozy bar as the waiter opens a bottle of Pouilly Fuisse. They speak in urgent tones in Italian, but I suppose all Italian sounds that way. Julian's father looks ten years older than he did this morning—like his face has melted a little. And somehow, his voice has gone from syrupy to granulated sugar. "I am not sure what Julian has said to you about the situation with the company, but due to our present troubles, this may not have been an accident."

At first, I am surprised and let out an audible gasp. Then I remember that this was Julian's first opinion of the incident.

Dr. Zarr continues. "It is unlikely that the window fell independent of malicious tampering. The contractors are not to blame, as it was well secured."

Trying to be cool, I sip the wine and inquire. "Who do you think, did it?"

Dr. Zarr leans back. "I wouldn't dare to speculate."

"What do the police think?"

"It's difficult to know what they are thinking, and they are certainly not about to tell us."

Despite the recent death, his manner is calm and elegant; I can see where Julian gets his charm and grace. What happened to the brother is another story.

I sip my drink, delighted by its power to transport me from the smell of murder and subterfuge — to the scent of anise and citrus. Finally, I leave the magical aromas and ask, "Are they just going to keep interrogating us?"

Dr. Zarr waves his hand and says, "They are smart and efficient so it won't take long."

Julian comes around the corner right then, looking delighted and asking me to follow him to the lobby.

Here we observe a dozen pint-sized ballerinas, all running down the curved glass staircase. I say, "Look a little flock of swans!"

Julian says, "The correct term is a lamentation of swans."

When David says things like this, I find it interesting; when Julian does, I find it annoying. The four-year-old looking girls are herded by a stern woman who yells at them in Russian, with one or two dancers escaping the "lamentation."

Quickly, I pull out my phone to take a video, prompting Julian to realize he left his phone in the loo; he tells me that he'll be right back.

As I am videotaping, I hear an unmistakable shriek. It is B.M. at the top of the stairs waiting for the adorable pink cluster to move. Then, like it's in slow motion, I see a B.M. tumble forward and fall down the stairs.

There is a louder scream, the kind that curdles bodily fluid. She lands at the bottom, and the little girls run over and circle the fallen woman.

B.M. cries, "Ow! My baby."

The words echo throughout the lobby, so the little ballerinas stay back in a horrified cluster.

There is blood coming from B.M.'s mouth and her face is horribly swollen and red. An efficient waiter runs over with a damp towel and starts to wipe up the unsightly mess from the floor. Dr. Zarr races over and tries to lift her. But then we hear a ripping sound coming from his shoulder and a restrained howl of pain from his mouth. Julian returns, and along with a waiter, helps turn B.M. onto her side. A gush of blood comes out from the bottom of her dress.

With urgency, Dr. Zarr commands: "She's hemorrhaging. Someone call an ambulance!"

I try to remember the Swiss code for emergencies until he huffs, "Not you, Camille."

Julian grabs my phone to make the call. Then, I look up and see Simon casually sauntering from the back of the lobby.

His face makes an exaggerated look of: *'What the fuck?' That's the only way to describe it.*

After a few minutes of suspended animation during our little operatic scene, we hear an ambulance pull up in the hotel's circular driveway. *My, they have outstanding service here in Switzerland!* This is something to keep in mind if one is crushed by a massive pane of glass —or falls down the stairs.

Men dressed in the white race inside and attend to B.M. The top guy looks at us and says, "The Zarr family again."

In no time, B.M. is being loaded on a stretcher and carried out the main door. Under the strain, the gurney breaks, and B.M. falls through. The little Russian girls find this amusing until the stern mistress yells at them.

Dr. Zarr is quietly wincing in pain, so Simon suggests that he go along to the hospital to have his shoulder examined. I think this is Simon's way of getting out of going along. He probably wants to stay with the elusive Clover. He leans against the building and lights up a cigarette as though nothing happened. The emergency workers admonish him in Italian for smoking near oxygen and the little ballerinas.

Dr. Zarr directs Julian and me to stay here at the Hotel. *Fine with me.* I hate hospitals even more than I hate police stations. Both entail bright lights and lots of waiting.

177

Julian and I go back to the bar; he quips, "Nothing like a little drama."

I take a gulp. "My God, I hope she doesn't lose the baby."

"I'm sure the baby will be alright. She looks pretty well insulated."

Later, we enjoy oysters and Beluga caviar with Crystal champagne, like nothing has transpired.

Julian gets a text from his father and reads it aloud. "Baby girl. 8.4 lbs. B.M. fractured jaw. Simon overjoyed."

"I'm glad your brother is overjoyed at being a father."

Julian laughs. "I think it's about the broken jaw." Annoyed with his irreverence, I give him a look.

"My brother was not keen on having a baby with her."

"Oh, don't be so cynical. He'll take one look and instantly fall in love with his daughter."

"Don't be so sure. If Simon hadn't just appeared on the main floor, I'd think he might have pushed her down the stairs."

"Really?"

"Wouldn't put it past him."

"Ah, what a day. A death and a birth."

Julian exhales. "Hopefully, this baby will be just the thing my father needs to help him get over Number Three."

"Do you think you should call her that? Aren't you sad?"

"Of course. After all, she made my father happy for the past few years. And all thanks to Maryel's..."

Then he stops in mid-sentence.

I say, "Isn't it odd that Maryel left so soon after the party?" I sit up in my seat, ready to send her to the dungeons. "Maybe she's the culprit."

Chapter 53

We are rudely awakened the next day by a rapid knock on our hotel room door. Julian opens it to discover it is Clover. She says she wants to see the baby, which I find both odd and suspicious. She has no maternal instincts whatsoever, and it makes me wonder if she intends to bump the baby off.

After a lot of coordination and prompting, Dr. Zarr, Clover, Julian, and I all pile into the Maybach. Dr. Zarr has his shoulder in a sling, so he cannot drive. No one is particularly chatty, and no one even bothers to complain about Clover taking two hours to get ready.

When we arrive, the front desk tells us in Italian that only two visitors are permitted at a time. Dr. Zarr suggests that Clover and Julian go first. I think it's so he can debrief me. He says he's grateful for the baby, and then he admits that this is the only thing holding him together. He rubs his eyes and says, "I can't believe my wife is gone."

I'm thinking of what to say —or instead, what not to say, as he goes on. Julian and Clover finally come out bearing smiles —bordering on smirks. The father holds my hand as we walk to the hospital room and find Simon staring out the window. There is B.M. looking horrible with her face red and swollen — but now with one elbow raised high by a pole, and her jaw wired shut. It's nearly the same pose as Number Three, except for the closed mouth.

I wonder if Simon is secretly thanking his lucky stars that B.M. can't talk. We are guided down the hall to what must be the baby wing. There are a few fat pink babies, and then a nurse shakes her head, and we are led to another section. *Oh, they have a little zoo here in the hospital—what a great way to cheer up sick people.*

I point to one and say, "Look, a tiny monkey."

Dr. Zarr exhales. "That's the baby." He is very matter of fact in his tone. "It is not uncommon for newborns to have hair on their faces. It usually falls off in a few days."

He hopes the baby is alright after the fall and says, "Thank goodness it weighs over eight pounds. It must be a record for a premature baby."

I look at him and realize he is adorably naïve for his age.

Chapter 54

When we all get back to the hotel, we find the police waiting for us. They want to take us to the "station," for more questioning. When Clover complains that there's no champagne there, they acquiesce and interview us in the hotel lounge— probably so we'll blab more.

As the handsome Detective Bernardo stands by, an older police chief grills me. He wants to know why I went back to the house before the others and why my fingerprints were on Number Three's computer. None of this looks good for me. He wisely refrains from asking me what brought me to Switzerland.

Then they ask a lot of nosy questions about the baby shower. Yes, anyone could have walked back to the Zarr house, and no one would have noticed.

They believe the time of the incident—"Incidento" as they call it—was between 13:00 and 15:00 hours.

Oddly, they don't ask anything about B.M. falling down the stairs, so I am careful not to bring it up — especially when I see Julian pacing in the entry of the lounge.

Finally, Julian and I are back in our room together. He looks at me and says, "I'm a little worried. Bad things usually happen in three's."

"A death, a fall—are we calling the birth a bad thing?"

He laughs, but then his voice becomes profound and serious. "It's all very suspicious. I mean, it's not as if B.M. is a likely person to fall what with her low center of gravity."

182

I study his face for clues. "What could possibly happen next?"

We sit on the terrace as he pulls out a Dunhill cigarette. "I've no idea, but we should be on the lookout."

I mutter, "Um. I think I should be heading back to London. I do have to look after the dog, you know."

He tilts his head back and exhales, "I wouldn't count on leaving anytime soon. They found your fingerprints all over the place. Including on her phone and keyboard."

"You told me to check the weather!"

Suddenly, I wonder if my lovely Julian could have possibly set me up. He did suggest that I leave the baby shower early for our tryst. I begin to eye him suspiciously.

Julian tells me he's headed back to the bar to discuss recent events with his father. He fails to invite me, and frankly, I'm grateful for a little time to assess things.

As I run the bath water, I see Simon returning from somewhere. He seems to have all sorts of mysterious activities that take him away from family events. I hope he's not headed here. Then I hear someone knocking on a door in the hallway. It is Simon, calling out to Clover.

Then, I get a call from Mrs. Etherington, so I fill her in on the past 24 hours. She's shocked and says to come home.

Later, as I'm blissfully soaking in the tub while playing Glen Hansard songs, I hear the unmistakable sound of a video call on my laptop. I lean over carefully to press audio-only but see handsome Oliver on the screen.

"Very nice!" he declares, as he catches a glimpse of my naked backside sliding back down in the tub.

He says he's just gotten a call from Mrs. Etherington, and they are both worried about me. I tell him I'm with the Zarr family, so I'm in good hands. Then I say to him that we are staying at the Leopoldo because we can't get back into the house as it's been deemed hazardous due to falling glass; plus, it's a crime scene.

"Doesn't sound very safe to me." Oliver looks even more woeful than he usually does. His dimples do not appear as frequently. He says Enfys is back in the loony bin, actually using those words. He tells me he's been a bit lonely and wishes I hadn't left. Well, he was the one who said to give up on him.

Suddenly, I am startled to hear a tense voice. "Enjoying a little naked Skype with the poet, are we?" I look up to see Julian standing in the doorway.

Oliver thoughtfully signs off, saving me the trouble and keeping me from knocking my laptop in the tub and electrocuting myself.

I try to get Julian off the subject of Oliver, by telling him about hearing Simon at Clover's door.

"Can you blame him? You have to admit that Beth Marie is a bit unfortunate looking."

Later, Dr. Zarr, Clover, Simon, Julian, and I all meet for dinner at the hotel. It's dull without B.M. regaling us with tales of pregnancy and taxidermy. The men formulate the logistics for tomorrow's boat ride.

Everyone pretends all is well, even though we are a collective mess. It is like a family during the holidays, where liquor is poured— and all is ignored. No one dares talk about the incident with Number Three.

Boy, I'm stuck here in a strange country with a dangerous dynasty.

Chapter 55

In the morning, we all meet for breakfast on the terrace of the hotel before our boating trip.

Even in casual clothes, Dr. Zarr manages to look continental with his ascot and leather messenger bag. His shoulder is in a sling, but he says he can steer the boat with one arm —but swimming would be out.

Soon, Clover appears in the lobby looking chic in a large sunhat, a long white skirt, and a halter top, just like Grace Kelly wore in *To Catch a Thief.*

She hands me a bag. "Here, Julian said you needed something to wear.

I open the bag to find a brand new bathing suit still with a tag—a gigantic flowered suit with a ruffled skirt.

"Let me guess. This came from B.M.?"

Dr. Zarr stifles a smirk and asks Clover. "Where is Simon?"

"He's not coming. He's going to visit that baby thing."

Julian looks peeved. "This was his idea."

We all head down to a marina and board the 45 foot mahogany boat. It's from the 1950s, and looks like something from an old movie. I look on the transom and see it's named, "Don't Explain," after the old Billie Holiday song.

Dr. Zarr puts on his captain's hat and begins spouting safety instructions. Everyone but me ignores his plea to put on safety vests. He tells me not to inflate it unless I'm about to drown. I gladly put it on to cover the hideous maternity bathing suit. Clover takes off her ensemble to reveal a tiny purple bikini.

While we are waiting for the dock-hand to untie the lines, I pull out my camera to take photos of the serene lake. Then I notice the video of the little ballerinas comes up, and I replay it. At the top of the frame, I see B.M.'s feet descending the staircase. Then I see a man's foot, hooking her leg and pulling it backward. I knew it!

I wonder if I should show it to anyone. Given that we are in a small boat on a large body of water, I decide now is not the time. I discretely play the video again. It's a man's black European shoe with a brushed-steel side buckle. If Simon hadn't been on the main floor, I'd think it was his. Who else would want to trip B.M.?

It is breezy on the lake, as we are headed to a little sun-kissed village called Morcote. This boat ride is the perfect thing to keep us from talking about the "pressing matter," as Julian likes to call it —Number Three being smooched. My limited German vocabulary now includes the word for smooched: *geknutscht.*

We have a lovely lunch on the shore, where we view old terraced stucco villas and an ancient church. We sit under yellow umbrellas, and the sunlight sparkles on our Rosé wine and grilled Gambas and Branzino. I'm sure this outing will be just the trick to cheer up Dr. Zarr. *Ah, I could get used to his.* As Julian leans over the railing, I study his solemn profile—wondering if he is capable of murder. Then I catch him staring at Clover's tight little bottom. Well, maybe he's not capable of murder, but I am.

Later, Clover taps me on the shoulder and whispers in my ear. She has such an accent that at first, I can't understand her, and she repeats for all in the Canton to hear. She wants to know if I have any tampons. Not

186

wanting to leave her alone with my Julian, I send her down to look in my big purse full of girl supplies and ask her to bring up suntan lotion.

While she's down in the cabins, Dr. Zarr tells Julian they will have to go to Zurich for another meeting with the regulators. Then, he looks around to make sure Clover can't hear and says, "Then, we'll make some funeral arrangements."

Then Julian mutters, "I wonder if they make flat coffins." Dr. Zarr's face crumbles, and Julian's face makes a *yikes* look. That is a comment that B.M. would make, and I'm sure he's bemoaning her influence now.

I look at Dr. Zarr, who is operating the old steering wheel with his right arm. He's very debonair in a Cary Grant kind of way. Too bad he's too old for me. I wonder what he's thinking right now. *Probably: Holy Shit, I'm going to need a 4th wife now, and my grandchild looks like a monkey.*

To change the subject, I tell Dr. Zarr that Lugano is the most beautiful place in the world. Being an analyzer type, he tells me that the Alpine Lake is 63% in Switzerland and 37% in Italy. He is the type to talk in percentages. He has to yell over the boat motor, so he asks Julian why the engine sounds so loud.

Clover comes back up without my purse and I notice her lavender suede sandals are now purple. No, they are wet. When I point this out, she dismisses it. Odd, she seems like the type to complain if her expensive sandals get ruined. Hmm.

Dr. Zarr turns on the radio, which blasts the old Carole King song, "It's Too Late." The lyrics have always depressed me. Yes, time does march on, but there is nothing worse than the feeling of regret. Why did I come on this trip? Why didn't I find out Oliver was still tangled up with his wife before I fell for him? Why did I waste so many years with Arthur? Why have I not finished writing my novel yet? *Ah, thank goodness the song is over.*

Suddenly, Dr. Zarr tells Julian that the engine seems to be overheating. As they discuss this problem, I head down to the galley to get more Rosé from the fridge because I'm now depressed. Then I hear a sloshing sound. As the boat tilts, a slosh of water about four inches high covers my feet. I run half-way up the stairs and sound the alarm: "There's water coming in below!"

Julian looks at his father and then follows me down the stairs below deck. He cries, "Fuck! We've got a leak somewhere."

Dr. Zarr commands. "Camille, come up and man the wheel."

Nervously, I run up the stairs, but my life preserver cord gets caught on the rail. The blasted thing inflates into a blimp-size, causing me to plug the stairway.

Julian tries to push me up the stairs from below. "Get out of the way, Camille!"

Dr. Zarr has to pull from above while Julian pushes from behind. *I indeed have become Beth Marie.* After I make it back to the deck, Dr. Zarr yells to Clover, "Pull out three more life vests from under your seat!"

With her languidness triumphing over the mayhem, Clover leisurely opens the seat cover and pulls out the preservers one by one. She puts hers on first and slowly fiddles with the buckle.

Dr. Zarr stomps to the stern, tripping over her long-legged arrangement. Here, he grabs two preservers and tosses one down to his son. He then puts my hands on the wheel and commands, "Camille, see that Delfino sign on the hill?" Yes, I see it. "Head that way but be mindful of boats on your starboard side." Then, he puts his hand on mine and pushes the lever forward. The bow of the vessel lifts off as we shoot forward.

I hear Julian cry out from below deck, "Fuck! There's a hole!" He pops his head up the stairs, "It looks as though the cooling hose has been cut off the seacock. There's no way I can reconnect it."

God, he's so sexy when he speaks in nautical terms!

"Try to close the valve, Son."

Julian yells, "I can't. It's jammed!"

The father comes back up and tells everyone to stay on the starboard side. Then he looks at Clover. "The side with the wheel." He yells down to Julian, "I've turned on the bilge pump."

I stop to help Dr. Zarr as he struggles to put his preserver on over his bad shoulder. He then grabs the marine radio to call for help. "May Day! May Day!" Then he yells, "Don't Explain!" Then in urgent Italian, *"Quattro passeggeri, near Campione. Fretta!"*

This all sounds like Italian for: "Hurry up!"

Dr. Zarr throws one arm up. "I don't understand it; everything was working fine last week."

Clover just sits on the back deck, admiring her nails.

The father yells down to Julian. "The bilge pump is kaput! Let's see if the engine can be our emergency pump."

Julian comes back up. "It's no use. The pressure has caused another leak. Now we've got an entire section of the hull imploding."

Clover frets. "Don't tell me we are sinking. I can't swim."

"But, I've seen you swimming at the pool," Julian argues.

Clover plays with her hair, "I was just fake swimming; my feet were touching the bottom the whole time."

"Well, you're out of luck here," Dr. Zarr shakes his head. "The lake is 900 feet deep!"

We are sinking faster now. Julian and I waive SOS to a passing tour boat, but the passengers just smile and wave back, not realizing our dire straits. Dr. Zarr calls the tour boat in an urgent May Day call; then, he instructs me to change direction and head towards the tour boat.

The classic wooden tour boat heads towards us, and now the passengers have stopped waving and have a collective look of concern. The ferry captain blasts on the radio in Italian, "Don't Explain. Don't Explain. Pull up to our port side."

When I look down the stairs of our boat, I see the cabin area has nearly three feet of water. The ferry honks its horn at another boat to get out of the way. We are 50 feet from the tourist ferry, but we are no longer moving. Wooden planks are peeling off the sides, and we are sinking rapidly.

The ferry makes it to us, but it's much larger and higher in the water. A crew-member drops a rope ladder to our boat and jumps aboard to help. Dr. Zarr tells Clover to grab our belongings while the crew-member helps her up the ladder. Then he helps me, but due to my suntan lotion, I slip through his hands and into the deep water.

Soon, I'm choking on a mouth full of water — and sinking fast! Finally, I feel of the strong hands of a crew-member holding my waist. I am rescued and pulled up onto the ferry where dry Julian and Clover await. Catching my breath, I see the captain having a conversation with Dr. Zarr in the wheelhouse.

In an intricate process, they try to attach his boat to the back of the ferry. But it becomes submerged and turns into a weighty anchor, so they have to cut it loose. The S.S. "Don't Explain" slowly sinks below the surface. I wonder

190

how long it takes to descend 900 feet. I look at Dr. Zarr's distraught face. How disheartening this must be for him, it was such a lovely boat.

Then, I look and see that Clover has grabbed my sun bag. "Did you grab my purse too?"

She just scoffs at me, which I take as a no.

Julian says, "I hope there wasn't anything important in there."

"Just my driver's license and my credit cards." Now I am glad that the police held my passport. Otherwise, it would have sunk in the boat. At least I have my phone.

The ferry nicely drops us off at the dock in Paradiso. Dr. Zarr remains on site to sort out maritime matters with the Coast Guard while Julian, Clover, and I take a taxi up the mountain to the hotel. Frankly, I'm glad to flee this fresh catastrophe.

In the taxi, Clover does not say a word, making me wonder if she is shy, traumatized, or just plain brainless. One thing is for sure, I'll never go boating with her again.

Chapter 56

While Julian heads to the bar, I trudge to the room to change out of my wet bathing suit. When I get there, I find a delivery from Paulina: a white peignoir and marabou robe —which practically insists I open a bottle of champagne. *Ah, I feel much better.* After downing a glass, I call Mrs. E. to report on recent events. She says she thinks that the boat sinking is suspicious. In her sage tone, she implores me to come back to London. Then she asks where Simon was during this ordeal. I tell her that he was supposed to be at the hospital. She seems to think that he's up to something. I agree and send her the video of B.M. falling and the shoe. After I hang up, I pull out my journal and start writing in swirly cursive about my men.

'Oliver was Lake Lugano. 900 feet of deep calm, but I had an anvil tied to my heart. Julian was Victoria Falls with gallons of sparkling water flying past. I only wanted to watch, not get carried over the edge.'

Right then, Oliver calls on video. "Okay, now both Mrs. Etherington and I are anxious about you. You need to get away from these people!"

I say, "I can't. The police won't let me leave."

The sunset is hitting Oliver's eyes through the laptop screen, and they look very sparkly green. His voice also sounds soothing. I carry my laptop over to the balcony to let him take in the picturesque background. He catches a glimpse and asks, "What are you wearing?" I show him the nightgown under the robe.

Suddenly I hear Julian over my shoulder. "What, no naked Skype this time?"

I quickly hang up and say, "I wanted to tell him what happened."

Julian looks peeved. "Let's keep this to ourselves, shall we?" He lights a cigarette and says, "Thank goodness we sank in the Italian section. We don't want the Swiss police looking into this."

"I'll bet Clover had something to do with this."

"Jealousy doesn't suit you in that peignoir."

"I'm not jealous of her. I've met mannequins with more personality."

He pours himself a glass of bubbly. "I definitely think the boat was compromised."

"This is getting pretty scary."

Julian paces the floor. "Someone is trying to kill one of us —or all of us."

"Well, it must be Clover. She was below deck and oddly failed to mention the water leakage."

"But she wouldn't try to sink a boat if she can't swim."

"It must have been someone who knew Clover couldn't swim or that your father couldn't swim with his bad shoulder."

"If someone is trying to kill Clover or my father, who could it be?"

"Simon seems to be mysteriously absent during all of the mishaps."

"But he fancies Clover and, hopefully, loves our father."

"One thing is for sure: it wasn't B.M.," I say as I pour more champagne. "But what about Maryel?"

"But, she's in Paris."

"She could have paid someone to damage the boat."

Julian looks at me. "Remember, she was invited on the boat ride too? And why would Maryel have an incentive to kill any of us?" Then he smiles and puts his hand on my thigh. "Except for you."

"See! She wants you back."

"Going to all the trouble to remotely sink a boat while putting me—the love of her life—in danger?"

"I suppose you are right. But Maryel could be jealous of Clover, and she would have known that Clover can't swim."

With a long exhale, Julian says, "There's one thing for sure—we do not want the Ticino police looking into this."

"I'll be sure not to mention it."

Julian laughs, "It's probably too late. All is known here."

Chapter 57

I find out that Clover is free to leave Switzerland, but I am not. The police think it's unlikely that she would have killed her own mother — although they don't know her as well as I do. She's leaving tomorrow to join Maryel for a modeling shoot and a party in Paris. Frankly, this is good news. Nobody wants a dangerous supermodel with high cheekbones around.

Clover, and the rest of us murder suspects, head out for dinner at Bottegone del Vino. It is a tiny restaurant in the center of town off the main cobblestone square. The menu is in Italian, so Dr. Zarr orders lots of meats and pasta for all, probably so we don't end up with animal entrails. We have lovely Tignanello wine, described as having an aroma of cherries, smoke, licorice, and rosemary. It is as complex and mysterious. *Thank goodness for mysterious wine at a time like this!*

As I sip the lovely wine, Simon pulls up his chair. This is when I notice he is wearing black Zegna shoes with a polished side buckle. So he's the one who tripped B.M.! He is the most suspicious one regarding the boat sinking too. Maybe he was trying to bump off his brother. Hmm. But why try to kill his brother that way? Then I realize that I'm the only one on the boat he's not related to— or in love with. Maybe Simon is trying to kill me! I slide my chair a little farther away from him.

We have a lovely dinner of succulent veal, lamb, and more Tignanello wine. It calms me to focus on the food and wine at this time. My mind is reeling, trying to figure out this latest incident. Now Simon and Clover's hips seem to be attached, and they're drinking their wine with arms entwined. I'll bet Simon was trying to use the boat ride to bump off his wife, but then she fell down the stairs and couldn't go. Hmm.

After dinner, Dr. Zarr reminds Julian that they are going to Zurich tomorrow. Their jet is undergoing service, so they'll just have to drive. Frankly, I think they just want to get the hell out of town. When Clover hears this, she asks if she can catch a ride so she can get a direct flight to Paris. I think Clover wants to get the hell out of town, too.

Simon invites himself to go with them, but his father says, "No, you should stay here. It will look bad if we all leave town. Besides, you need to be here for Beth Marie."

Dr. Zarr turns to me, "I'm sorry you have to remain in town, Camille. Don't worry; we'll be back in a day or two."

When Julian goes for a cigarette break, Clover follows, prompting Simon to follow her. In a hushed voice, Dr. Zarr says to me, "I know you had nothing to do with it, Camille, but please limit what you say to the police. It would be best if they conclude my wife's death was an accident."

I say, "But what if it wasn't?"

"It would be detrimental to both the firm and the family to be embroiled in a criminal case. They tend to linger for years. It's preferable to solve it quickly and internally."

"But how?"

"Camille, you have a keen eye for details. I would like you to report anything you find directly to me, not Julian, and not his brother. And certainly not to Beth Marie."

"Yes, loose lips sink ships."

When I look out the window, I see Simon pacing. Oh great. I'm trapped here with Simon, the killer.

On the way back to the hotel, I make a point to ride in the car that does not contain Simon — especially along these winding roads.

When we get back to the room, I make efforts to avoid intimacy with Julian. It's not that I'm worried he's a killer anymore—I am starting to think he set me up.

Chapter 58

When I awaken, I find Julian frantically packing his clothes. Apparently, I had called out Oliver's name in my sleep. I guess I'll have to put tape on my mouth before I go to bed.

In an angry tone, he says, "If that's whom you want, don't let me get in the way."

God, he can read my mind too. Instead of his usual methodical packing —he's shoving his shirts into a bag. I hide under the covers, wondering if it's my fault if my subconscious mind works my tongue in the middle of the night.

I ask what I should do—just stay here at the hotel? Without making eye contact, he says, "Do what you like." He tries to slam the door, but his bag gets caught.

Well, I've never been stranded in a foreign country before. The police have my passport —and my driver's license and my best credit cards are at the bottom of the lake. I have one card left and a little cash. I can't go anywhere. I'm trapped.

I drag myself out of bed, and I try to make myself look presentable. Looking good in the morning is tricky. Plus, one has to accomplish this before getting coffee, which is why I usually decline breakfast invitations. Men seem to have a three-pronged strategy for inviting women to breakfast: they can examine you in broad daylight; it costs less than dinner — and the world assumes that they just slept with you.

Once I'm in the charming breakfast room, I sip my coffee and notice how safe I feel in this hotel. It feels like home. Actually, it feels like it was home in a previous life.

As I look out on the foggy lake, I see sailboats listing in the rain. Then, I hear Julian's voice in the lobby. He's on his phone and sounds a bit annoyed. Evidently, Clover is not ready. By now, he should know his father's system of scheduling a two-hour lead time.

I can't believe everyone gets to leave while I'm stuck here. Do I look like a murderer? The waiter seems to think so as he mutters something and refuses to bring me more coffee. It must be in the service provider's handbook never to get murderers jittery. I cannot understand a word he says in his rapid Italian. It is either: "We are out of coffee — or get away from me!" Maybe I should learn a little Italian— so I'd know what they are saying about me. When I act out a charade for getting more cream by indicating a cow being milked, the waiter laughs and brings me ice-cream.

Dr. Zarr finds me at our central meeting place, and the waiter silently brings him coffee and cream. Dr. Zarr says that thanks to Clover's shoe delay, they have now missed one of the regulator meetings, so there is no point in him going. Unfortunately, Julian still has to go.

In his confidential voice, Dr. Zarr tells me that he doesn't want to leave me here alone. There is no need to point out that I'd be stranded here with Simon and Blabber Mouth.

He asks me to meet him in the lobby at 13:00, and we'll have lunch at the Villa Castagnola —but not to tell a soul.

When I go back to the room, Julian is sitting there looking annoyed. He hands me my phone, which I left on the nightstand. "The Poet rang."

I say, "Why haven't you left yet?"

He is tapping his foot and crossing his arms. "I'm forever waiting for Clover."

It is my conclusion that all women need brothers. Why? Because they will train you for a lifetime of having five minutes to get ready—or they will leave without you. Now, it will just be Clover and Julian driving to Zurich, making me wonder if it's a good idea to have my boyfriend spend this much time with a supermodel. Especially, one who seems to have a crush on him. But, what can I do — offer to cut her hair?

There is a fervent knock, and Julian opens the door cautiously. It's Clover. "Hurry, or we'll miss Maryel's party!" Julian looks back at me, indicating he did not want me to hear this. In an overly loud voice, he says, "I have no interest in attending any more of Maryel's parties, or of going to Paris."

I think he's furious because he leaves without kissing me goodbye. After he goes, I play the message from Oliver. His voice is like soft butter when he says he's worried about me. Then I check my emails, I find one from Paulina: '1. Heard about the lockdown. Do you need more dresses and panties? 2. Are you still the same size?' I guess she already heard about the ice-cream for breakfast.

I meet Dr. Zarr in the lobby, and soon we are making our way down the mountain. The incline is so steep that we have to traverse in a "Z" pattern to get anywhere. As we make our way closer to the lake, we pass beautiful old belle époque mansions juxtaposed with contemporary glass buildings. Soon we are at the historic Grand Hotel Villa Castagnola for our clandestine lunch. He tells me it was built in 1880 as a summer home for a wealthy Russian family.

In the distance, we have a lovely view of both the lush gardens and the lake. The grand windows are covered

200

by saffron-and-white striped awnings, making the scene look like an old Monet painting of Trouville.

Dr. Zarr nods to a bottle of Roederer Cristal Rosé Brut. As the waiter pours, I study Dr. Zarr's face and think of how I'd write about it.

'After all the marriages, he has a shiny softness to him, like a silver teapot that's been pummeled and polished.'

He must feel my eyes on him, for he gets a nervous smile. That's when I tell him, "You have the same eyes as Julian."

"Yes, my eyes, but he has his mother's face." Now his eyes are tearing up. "Oh, how I miss my wife."

I say, "I'm sorry, Martin," but I'm not really sure which wife he's talking about.

He must see the look of confusion on my face and says, "I'm talking about Julian's mother, and I suppose Penelope too; but definitely not Number Two."

"Did she have a given name?"

Then he smiles, "Yes, Roslyn. And she was not at all happy when Number Three came around."

"Is Number Two the sort who would want to get revenge?"

He looks down. "Naturally, she held an active dislike of Number Three, but I am not sure about revenge."

I pull out my little notebook. "I'm putting her on the suspect list."

Dr. Zarr asks the waiter for menu recommendations. We decide on the wild gilthead fillet with potato chip trilogy, aubergine confit, and crispy langoustine tail.

I would never have thought of Switzerland as a food writer's destination, but this place is fabulous.

201

Dr. Zarr leans in and whispers—as if the table were bugged— "I sent Julian away so I could meet with you privately."

He continues before I get a chance to ask why.

"Julian won't want you to get involved, but Camille, you are good at finding clues."

"Not always."

"Well, please try. We've got to figure out what happened, and do so without involvement from the police."

"Why? I am sure they can solve it."

"Julian thinks this is connected to the drug sabotage and thinks nothing good will come from a police investigation."

"Oh, I see. That's why he wants it to appear to be an accident."

Dr. Zarr leans back. "Right. Fortunately, the authorities are more focused on preventing terrorism and guarding the borders. They are not too concerned about what the Zarr family is up to, especially if they conclude that my wife's death is accidental."

I say, "So that leaves us to figure it out. Well, let's go through the list. Surely we can eliminate Julian as a suspect."

Dr. Zarr says matter-of-factly, "Yes, he wouldn't have done it that way."

Okay, now I'm a little freaked.

He takes a sip of his champagne. "Besides, I don't think my wife was the intended target."

"What? Then who was?"

"I believe I was."

I look around the room and lean away from him, worried that I might get hit in the cross-fire. "But who would want to kill you?"

"My dear, there would be quite a lengthy list of stockholders. And both Simon and my wife were furious with me."

"Why?"

"I intend to donate the drug patent, but if we sell it, the company stands to make hundreds of millions of francs. I don't need any more money. But, if I'm out of the picture, they'll be rich."

I look out at the rain pelting the striped awning. "But the drug was taken off the market before anyone tried to kill you."

"There is nothing wrong with Zarrexifam. It had to have been sabotage. Most likely a competing drug company."

"Can't someone prove that?"

"Yes, and I am sure it be released again, but by then, I could be gone."

As I look around the room, I note that this would be a lovely place to set an1880's period-piece murder mystery. Dr. Zarr looks at me with pleading eyes. "First, we've got to solve this murder, before anyone else dies."

"Well I'm sure that Julian would never kill anyone." Then somehow, this slips out, "But, I'm not so sure about Simon."

Without missing a beat, Dr. Zarr says, "It is hard to say. Julian once killed a kitten when he was small, and Simon was so distraught that he cried for weeks."

Hmm. I guess I've got it wrong about the brother. I decide that it's time to bring up B.M.'s fall. "When B.M. fell down the stairs, I noticed that someone had tripped her. I have it here on my phone." I pull out my phone to find the video, but it's gone. Now, I get a distinct feeling that someone erased it from my phone.

Our lunches arrive looking like colorful works of Asian art on ceramic canvases.

Dr. Zarr pokes at his lunch. "Even though someone may be trying to kill me, I sincerely hope you do not feel unsafe in my company."

"Um. No, not at all."

"Well, remember that Switzerland is the safest place in the world."

Frankly, I'm starting to wonder.

I sip my champagne while taking in the latest intel. "When do you think we can leave Lugano?"

"My family is free to leave Lugano, but we have to stay in Switzerland. It's odd that they are making you stay here."

I exhale in frustration. "All because of my chocolaty fingerprints."

He laughs. "A true culprit would have used gloves."

"So, my chocolaty fingerprints should be obvious enough to clear me. Plus, it's not like I could lift that heavy window."

Dr. Zarr sips his rose-colored champagne. "While quite substantial, it was held in place inside the house by long pins, and outside the house by wing-nut brackets. If someone removed both, the window would fall. That's why my glass workers put up a warning sign."

"I don't remember seeing a sign. How long do you think it was before someone removed the brackets and pins and when the window actually fell?"

"I'm not a physicist, but it could have been minutes or a few hours. Any strong wind would have caused it to fall if someone had removed both of the reinforcements."

"But wouldn't we have noticed that the glass was just balancing on its edge?"

"My wife and I were in that room before the party, and neither one of us noticed anything."

"Thank goodness *you* weren't in the room when the glass fell."

Dr. Zarr exhales. "That's probably why I'm still alive."

I notice he has barely touched his food. When the waiter takes my plate and hands me a dessert menu, I say to Dr. Zarr, "What a complex way to kill someone. Why not just use poison?"

He pulls himself away from me in a kind of joking way and says, "Because poisoning is unreliable with picky eaters like me."

"But an easy way to kill someone like Mrs. Coquin. Do you think that was intentional?"

"Yes. A French chef gets food poisoning and dies?"

"Who would want her to die? I mean other than everyone who's ever met her."

Dr. Zarr laughs a little. "I think someone else was meant to be poisoned. Someone else at the party."

"Hmm. That's a long list."

Dr. Zarr reads off the desert menu to me. I look worried. "Um. I'll pass. I'm afraid to eat now."

The waiter is standing by, and Dr. Zarr says, "We will split the Cremoso alla fragola con rabarbaro."

When it arrives, I see it's a pile of strawberries, something I'm highly allergic to. "It would be so easy to kill me."

Even though he's a targeted man, I feel so safe with him. Like he's a father to the world.

Chapter 59

After our secret little lunch, Dr. Zarr and I return to the Principe Leopoldo Hotel. When I get to the room, I find Julian still there pacing the floor. Apparently, Clover forgot her favorite shoes in the closet, and they had to come back. He says he missed his meetings and she missed her intended flight from Zurich to Paris, and they are now going to stay here another day. Julian adds that he didn't want to leave me alone here. Then he asks where I was. "Um. At the spa." *Always a plausible alibi with this gang.*

Julian puts his arms around me and asks, "Now, what were we fighting about?"

"You were jealous of my nighttime babbling."

"When in bed, it's best not to mention another man's name."

I take off my damp clothes and say to Julian. "Don't worry. Oliver will be married forever. I've given up on him."

Julian kisses me, so I unleash his belt causing his trousers fall to the ground with a thud of electronics and keys. His shirttail has the telltale lift of lustful thoughts.

There is rain pelting the windows, like hundreds of fingers tapping on the glass. I climb under the covers, and he unbuttons his shirt and is soon naked in bed with me.

He kisses my forehead. "I'm glad I came back."

I whisper in his ear. "The making up is worth the fight."

"Shall I start a war?"

Now he's rubbing himself on me. Then he slides down to the end of the bed—and takes off my panties. Even in the dark, he has no trouble finding my favorite spot to kiss. Oh, life is too short to be mad at anyone with such a dexterous tongue. He reaches up to find my hard nipples between his fingers, and soon he is on top of me under the warm covers. I'm all slippery, and he fits right in. Thoughts run through my head like: *I hope our baby looks like him, and not a monkey.* We fall asleep spooned together on this rainy Friday afternoon.

Chapter 60

We wake around 5:00 p.m. to the sound of pounding on the door. It's Simon. Julian tells him to go away, but Simon says it's urgent. Julian gets up, puts on his striped silk robe, and warily opens the door. I opt to silently hide under the covers.

Simon comes in, opens the mini-bar, and grabs a can of Heineken. He pops it open and chugs half before announcing: "B.M. thinks she was tripped down the stairs."

Julian quips, "I had chalked it up to clumsiness."

Simon invites himself to sit on the bed. "She thinks *I* tripped her." He pulls down the cover by accident and—whoops—finds a naked lady!

Simon says, "Oh sorry, Camille, I didn't know you were in there."

Embarrassed, I yank the covers up over my head. "Just pretend I'm not here."

Simon says, "Camille, don't you remember when B.M. landed? I was on the main floor, so I couldn't have tripped her."

I uncover my face. "But, you could have quickly taken the elevator down." As soon as I say this, I regret it. Simon's face suddenly looks angry.

Julian has a grin that says, '*try taking that back.*'

Covering swiftly, I say, "I honestly can't remember. It was all so fast, and B.M. is so clumsy."

They both nod in agreement. Then Julian asks his brother, "So if you didn't trip her, who did?"

Simon throws his hands up. "I don't know. She thinks there's someone out to get her. She thinks the glass that landed on Number Three was meant for her. And she

208

thinks the poisoned duck canapés were meant for her. She's so paranoid."

Frankly, she's justified.

I peel back the covers and mutter, "Oh brother."

Julian says, "But who would want to kill Beth Marie?" He chuckles at Simon. "I mean, besides you?"

I pull the covers up over my head again to muffle my spontaneous laughter.

Simon does not think this is funny. "I don't want her dead. I just want her to shut the fuck up."

Now I wish I had been able to see Simon as he spoke. It's easy to detect lying if you can see someone's face. I then realize there is just a blanket keeping me from this conversation between two possible killers.

Then I pop up, realizing that this is the perfect opportunity to gather more intelligence. I need to figure out—just like Oliver's twins— which of the brothers is good and which is evil.

This will require a bit of pretense to open up the conversation. I want to hear the full story about Julian supposedly murdering a kitten. I've been told that killers always start with puppies or kittens. I say to Simon, "Your father told me a story about how your kitten died."

"That's right. You killed my kitten, Leslie," Julian recalls sadly.

Simon snaps. "It wasn't my fault. Her head got caught in the refrigerator door."

With genuine emotion, Julian blubbers, "I loved her."

I pop up. "Wait, it was *your* cat, Julian? And *you* cried for weeks?"

"Yes, I'm still not over it. I couldn't even deal with Peteaux's funeral."

209

Hmm. That's strange; the father has mixed up the brothers. *I wonder if he's getting Dementia.*

Julian walks over to the mini-fridge and tosses Simon another beer. "So, when is the thing coming home?"

"Are you referring to my lovely wife?"

Julian laughs. "No, your um, 'baby.'"

Simon huffs, "It's not funny."

That might have been a bit insensitive, for Simon takes his beer and storms out. Then we hear him knock on Clover's door. Julian gives me a look as he brings me chocolates. "Don't you want a glass to put to the wall?"

He is a mind reader.

Julian is now on his computer and gives me updates. "Paulina sends her love. She says she wants to send you a new Valentino dress. She says it stretches a lot and should fit." Julian says we are all going to dinner tonight at a hotel in a village called Agra.

Oh, this will be lovely. As I get ready, I get a call from the police. They are requesting the pleasure of my company on Monday. *Yikes.*

I must look worried, for Julian says, "Not to worry, you are the *last* person who would ever commit murder. I cannot figure out why they would even suspect you."

"That's what I was wondering."

"Maybe it's because you're an American. The Swiss are mad at Americans for ruining our banking system."

"Yes, that must be it."

"Or maybe it's due to your fingerprints. You do get them all over." He points to my chocolate fingerprints all over my teacup.

"If anyone is going to figure this out, they need to find out who was the intended victim. It's hard to determine motive if someone kills the wrong person."

Julian is surprised. "Who else would it have been besides Number Three?"

"It could have been your father, or you, or even me."

He takes my hand, "Now, who would want to kill you? Now, I can see someone wanting to kill my brother— or B.M."

I say, "We need to think of each intended victim — and who had a motive to kill them."

"That makes it complicated."

I say, "Maybe that's what the murderer intended."

"But if they murdered the wrong person, they would have to finish the job."

Yikes.

Chapter 61

After our little love fest and murder-mystery party, Julian and I head down for dinner. We meet Dr. Zarr, Simon, and Clover in the lobby. This is the new nuclear family.

Julian and I are relegated to the Mini Cooper, which frankly is better for threading the narrow winding roads. We pass tiny villages with old pink stucco houses and tall olive and cedar trees. Each little town has a grotto bar and a church, which frankly is all a town really needs. When we reach the top of a mountain lane, we find a fabulous hotel: The Collina D'Oro. Julian tells me that his father would like to buy a hotel, which is understandable, given how much he must spend at them. It's not for sale, but good for doing research.

When Dr. Zarr says the hotel used to be a sanitarium, I think of Oliver's poor wife and how she'd like it here. The lobby is smartly decorated with grays and reds; well, smart for a hotel, but not for crazy people.

We choose one of the lounges overlooking the mountain valley, and I notice that we are the only ones here. I find this a bit odd for such a stellar place, so I can't help but inquire. Apparently, a consortium of left-handed surgical implement manufacturers has had to cancel due to technical difficulties. That's an explanation, which poses more questions than answers. Julian indicates in that way of his that I should leave it at that.

He and his father are in deep conversation about the hotel, so I entertain myself by people watching. Given the dearth of subjects, this leaves me with Simon and his step-sister, Clover. He flirts away, like he forgot he has a wife and new baby. Clover is still hoping to catch a flight to Paris to make Maryel's party. Everyone in the group has been invited to the soiree, but me. Clover say it's because, well, I'm not a Zarr.

As I ponder and plot with a glass of pinot, a major storm is causing the lights to flicker. Lightning bolts that look like spider vein light up the sky. The staff suggests we wait out the storm with coffee and dessert — except everyone orders more drinks instead. *Great, who's going to drive us back?* The father says we should all just spend the night. It must be nice to book hotel rooms all over town. He justifies it as an onsite hotel assessment, but I think it's because he's on the run from a killer.

The manager comes over to announce that the mountain road is closed due to the major torrential rainstorm. We can't leave even if we wanted to. *Okay, so now I'm in a Humphrey Bogart movie.*

Simon gets an impish grin on his face and says, "If there is a room shortage, I can share with Clover."

The manager says because the convention has been postponed, the hotel has plenty of rooms available. Clover looks at the leering Simon and requests her own room.

Dr. Zarr looks at me and winks, "Assuming Camille will share with my son, that will be four rooms, please."

Simon gets a smirk.

The father shakes his head. "I meant Julian."

As we sip snifters of Drambuie and Grand Marnier, the Zarr men argue about the long-ago incident of Leslie, the kitten. I think it is to help avoid the subject of Clover's dearly departed mother.

She has no interest in the cat tale or any other. Simon watches her sinewy frame as she heads up to the desk to get a room key and go to bed.

213

The conversation goes on to Simon's mother. Dr. Zarr says that now she's a neighbor, she comes over all the time to borrow things. "Why did she have to buy a house on my very street?"

Julian quips, "All women are stalkers— it's in their genes."

Simon huffs, "My mother is not a stalker. She's a focused admirer." Then he heads to the terrace for a cigarette, and his father follows.

The minute they are out of earshot, I say, "If Number Two still loves your Dad, she certainly had a motive for Number Three's murder."

"She actively hated her."

I sip my Drambuie ask if Number Two was around *that day.*

"I doubt it." Julian exhales. "She had asked Paulina to watch Esmeralda last week while she was in rehab."

"Who is Esmeralda?"

"Her Chihuahua." Then he says not to mention any of this to the police. I couldn't anyway, as I am not sure who is in rehab: Number Two, Paulina, or the Chihuahua.

I've got to report all of this to Mrs. Etherington before I forget. She enjoys an installment of her latest mystery each night. It could also come in handy in case I end up dead.

Then the lights flicker and go out entirely. Okay, now this is getting spooky. I'm trapped on a mountain with killers and murder target —and it's all Clover's fault! If she had remembered her stupid Christian Louboutin shoes, then she and Julian would be in Zurich. I'd be at the Leopoldo—in Dr. Zarr's safe haven. *Well, kind of safe.*

Another dramatic flash of lightening spreads over the mountains, so I decide this is the perfect time to interrogate the tipsy suspects. Starting with the most suspicious, I ask Simon how he met Clover.

His face lights up instantly. "It was at one of Maryel's parties in Paris. She came in wearing this see-through yellow dress."

Dr. Zarr shakes his head. "No, you met her at the Vienna lab Christmas party. She and her mother were both wearing purple dresses."

It reminds me of the song, "I Remember it Well," from the movie *Gigi*.

Simon, now slurring, says, "No, Father, remember the party at Maryel's flat where we climbed over the balcony from Julian's apartment?"

Dr. Zarr shrugs. "Vaguely."

Simone says, "That's how we met Clover and her mother."

His father says, "But I met her mother at work."

Julian holds his hand up to halt the conversation. "I remember it well. I first met Maryel in April of 2014, when I bought the condo next door in Neuilly. Then, Maryel moved in with me and sublet to Clover. And that is how we met Clover's mother."

Dr. Zarr's eyes are processing the data. "That's interesting; I thought I met her at the lab."

I can't help but ask. "Did Number Three start working at the lab in April of 2014?"

Dr. Zarr thinks for a moment and says, "Yes. I remember because she just earned her five-year stock package. What a coincidence."

I pull out my little journal to make notes. Then I realize I need to make a chart of all the wives.

To complete my chart, I ask Simon, "When did you meet B.M.?"

Julian quips, "Two months ago. In a bar."

His father shakes his head. "Now, Julian, be nice."

Simon answers. "It was in a wedding eight months ago."

Now Simon looks a little sad. As the men continue to loosen up and kid each other, I process the new data.

Maybe Simon is not a killer. It's evident that Simon loves Clover, and I wonder how B.M. can be so blind to this. Maybe Simon poisoned the duck canapés? Maybe he pushed B.M. down the stairs so she would lose the baby. That way, he wouldn't be tethered to her for the rest of his life.

Poor Simon; I can see his predicament. He's caught in a life-long trap with B.M.—keeping him from a field of Clover. The only way out of his hell will be if either B.M. or the baby disappears. Or both.

Now that I think of it, where was Clover when B.M. fell? Where was Clover when her mother died? Who knows, maybe it's like in that old movie, *Mommy Dearest.* Where was Maryel? She may have been the last to see Number Three alive. Wait a minute! I smelled perfume in the blue room, and remember Maryel reeking of "My Sin," at the Connaught. *The perfect perfume for a murderer.* If only I could remember the scent in the blue room, but I was distracted by the dead body. Both Maryel and Clover are after Julian. Sometimes, dating a rich, handsome man is no picnic.

Maybe I was the intended target of the falling glass! Maybe Maryel wanted me out of the way. Maybe she poisoned the duck canapés. She delivered them! Maybe she had Clover damage the boat, so I'd sink to the bottom of the lake due to my occupational-hazard weight-gain. As I look around, I can see that nearly everyone had a motive to get someone out of the picture. What if Simon and Maryel are in cahoots? Maybe Clover is just their unwitting

216

accomplice. Right now, Mrs. Etherington's place in London is looking very appealing to me.

The friendly staff announces that it is time for our little party (of murders suspects) to call it a night. We are led to our rooms with candles. I don't have any of my fancy nighties, so I climb in bed naked. Julian's liquid dinner puts him fast asleep, but I stay up late watching the storm and processing all the new details.

The next morning, I awaken once more to an empty bed. I imagine the Zarr men are in the breakfast room. I dislike seeing other people in the morning—especially the annoyingly cheerful ones.

Thankfully the power is finally back on, but the clock is blinking 12:00, so I have no idea what time it is. I imagine it's the crack of dawn.

Right then, Julian bursts into the room with his brother. *Don't these people ever knock?*

Breathless and agitated, Simon cries, "Clover's missing!"

Chapter 62

Well, this is a surprise— although not altogether tragic news.

Simon asks me desperately, "Have you seen her?"

I look around the room before replying no. Then I say, "Do you think she killed her mother; pushed B.M. down the stairs; sank the boat —and then ran off?"

They both look at me like I'm crazy.

Julian says, "Seriously, no one has seen her since last night, and it's nearly noon."

There is a knock on the door and a thin 30-something waiter wheels in a cart.

Julian says, "That was fast!"

The waiter looks at the order. "Oh, no! This is for another room."

Simon grabs a piece of toast anyway and says to him, "Have you seen the tall blonde woman who was with us last night?"

The waiter tries to pull the cart away, but it's too late. "No."

I say, "She has huge feet."

"Oh, do you mean Clover Fontaine? I haven't seen her since last night."

Julian studies the waiter's broad face. "Eddie? What are you doing here?"

"Um. I got a job here yesterday."

Laying on the sarcasm, Simon says, "That's some promotion; from lab security to waiter."

Eddie's Polish accent comes through as he replies, "For your information, your father directed me to get a job here to protect you."

Simon huffs, "Great job. Only one person missing."

Eddie reports, "The last I saw her was at 11:10 p.m. when she ordered a bottle of 1992 Dom Perignon Oenotheque — with two glasses."

Julian says, "Sounds nice. Say, Eddie, next time you head downstairs, will you please bring us a magnum of Dom and some caviar?"

Simon helps himself to coffee. "Eddie, do you still have access to the Vienna lab?"

"No." He pauses and shakes his head. "Remember Number Three chopped my badge into little pieces? I doubt it will work anymore."

As I study this Eddie character, I slowly connect the dots. Eddie Krakowski is Paulina's nephew —and the brother of Julian's ex-wife. I observe Eddie's features to get some sort of clue as to her look. Eddie has sandy hair and a broad forehead, with a fleshy Slavic nose. While acceptable for a man, but it would not translate well to a woman.

I open one of the tiny sealed jars of marmalade and say, "Maybe Clover took a taxi back to the Leopoldo."

Eddie shakes his head. "No way. The road was washed out during the thunderstorm, so no cars could have come up or down."

After Eddie leaves to get the champagne, I ask, "Has anyone looked over the edge of the cliff?"

Now I've upset Simon with my comment, which is another reason why I should not be allowed near humans first thing in the morning.

Then, there's a knock on the door — it's Dr. Zarr. He hesitates in the doorway until Simon and Julian waive him in. *Oh, great, everyone is in the room, and I'm stuck under the covers stark naked.*

Dr. Zarr says he's called the Principe Leopoldo, but they have not seen her. And, she's not been at the locked-down residence. He seems genuinely concerned; everyone does, except Julian—who seems blasé about everything. He's probably thinking: *'Oh, a missing girl; how is that champagne coming along?'*

Simon plops down at the end of the bed, and I worry he'll pull the covers off. Thankfully, Dr. Zarr guides the brothers over to the separate seating area of the suite.

As I quietly sip my coffee, I wonder—is a missing supermodel the third bad thing, or does the boat sinking count? For many reasons, this is not the time to ask Simon why he didn't make the boat ride.

When I ask Simon how his wife is, he looks startled and confused, making me think I should have used the code initials, B.M. Oddly, he seems to have no interest in his new baby. Well, it does look like it will end up at the zoo, but that's beside the point. Simon lights a cigarette by the window and sets his hefty thigh on the ledge. His forehead has a deep furrow like he's straining to think.

Dr. Zarr asks me, "Camille, did you see Clover at all this morning?"

Not wanting to get into the fact that I slept until noon, I look around and reply no.

Finally, I have to ask: "Um. Simon, what time did you knock on Clover's door?"

They all freeze in silence. The only sound is of me slathering marmalade onto my crunchy toast.

Dr. Zarr says, "What is this? Clover is his stepsister."

Now I've annoyed my only ally on this secluded mountaintop resort. I must look worried because they all start laughing.

Julian finally says, "Hello, Camille, everyone knows my brother fancies Clover. Well, apparently everyone except his wife."

After Simon leaves in a huff, Julian says, "He's been madly in love with Clover from day one."

Curiosity defies discretion, so I ask, "If Simon loved Clover four years ago, why did he end up with B.M.?"

Julian gracefully pours coffee while explaining. "Clover was dating someone else, and wanted nothing to do with him."

The father shakes his head. "It also became awkward when I married her mother, and she became his stepsister."

Julian adds, "You know the rest—B.M. reeled him in with the little sprog."

Suddenly, the door opens. It's Simon, followed by Eddie with the champagne and caviar, smiling as he wheels in the cart with a silver bucket.

Julian says, "That was fast."

"This was for someone else's room."

As Eddie pops the cork, I ask, "Can you let us in Clover's room? Maybe we'll find some clues."

He replies, "I really should call the manager for this, but I do have the key."

When they all disappear next door, I take this chance to get out of the bed. Just as I'm jumping out from under the sheets, Eddie bursts back into the room with the entourage of male Zarrs. "Oh, sorry, left my passkey here."

I grab the sheet and follow them to Clover's room, but find nothing in the room that looks Clover-esque. It's not like we had luggage or anything because we hadn't planned on staying. I go over to the mini-bar. "Look, there are two used champagne glasses —and the empty bottle." On one of the glasses, I see the type of frosted coral lipstick that Clover always wore. In a requisite British spy tone, I say, "I wonder who drank out of the other one?"

We all look at Simon, who says, "It wasn't me."

Eddie says, "We should get out of here before the manager finds us."

I grab the mystery glass as we head back to our suite. Dr. Zarr says, "But how could she have managed to get anyone up to the hotel last night?"

I say, "What if it was someone who was already here."

Eddie says he'll be right back and exits.

Julian takes a bite of caviar and blini and says, "Let's try to keep the police out of it as much as possible."

Then I ask, "But aren't they on the lookout for her? We can't just say 'never mind.'"

Dr. Zarr says quietly, "Julian, call Maryel and see if she knows of Clover's whereabouts. Also, ask if she had a boyfriend who may have come to visit."

We all watch as Julian rings Maryel and reports back while still on the phone. "She's not heard from Clover but was expecting her to attend the party." Julian then asks Maryel if Clover had a boyfriend and we hear him say, "Okay, I don't need all of their names. Thank you, Maryel."

Suddenly there is a crash emanating from Simon's area of the suite. He picks up the caviar lid and says, "Do you think this is funny? I'm in love with Clover, but now I'm stuck with that hillbilly blabbermouth." Eddie pats his head, and Simon stomps out of the room.

Now I think Simon damaged the boat on spec, thinking B.M. would be on board, which she would have if she didn't fall down the stairs. *Poor planning on the tripper's part.*

After due processing, I say to Julian, "It's just like that Theodore Dresher novel, *A Place in the Sun*, where the guy falls for Elizabeth Taylor, but he gets Shelley Winters pregnant..." I start to regret my words.

Julian says excitedly, "And then pushes her in the lake? I read the book too."

Dr. Zarr says, "Now. Now. I don't think Simon would have done anything like that, with us on the boat."

Then, there is a knock on the door. We all become quiet and study each other's features, as the pounding continues. Julian answers the door and sees it's Detective Bernardo. Eddie starts washing the window as if he doesn't know us.

The detective enters. "Ah, the Zarr family."

Chapter 63

So now I'm dressed in a sheet, in the back of a police car. They don't let me change into regular clothes, probably because they know women take forever to get dressed. In a rush, I forget to bring the mystery champagne glass. Once we land at the police station, they take us—Julian, Simon, Dr. Zarr, and me—into separate rooms.

A new officer comes along and asks me what brings me to Switzerland. Detective Bernardo cries, "Oh, Jeez. Not again."

I tell an abbreviated version of my ride to Claridge's and Maryel throwing the Dom Perignon at Julian. Then Detective Bernardo says, "No, it was the Connaught, and it was Cristal Champagne."

Wow, these police in Switzerland are spot on with the details. Oh my god! This mess is just getting worse.

The police release me and say they will drive me back to the D'Oro Hotel to put on clothes.

When I get to the room at the D'Oro, I find Eddie there drunk and crying. He says, "I loved Clover, but now she's probably dead, just like her mother."

It doesn't take much to divert Eddie's attention so that I can uproot the obscure glass from under the bed. I follow Julian to the lobby, where he announces the latest plan. "Let's check out of this hotel and head back to the Leopoldo. Tomorrow, we'll drive to Zurich."

I say, "But they told me that I had to stay in Lugano."

"No worries. We'll leave the tab open for you."

Chapter 64

The police are looking for Clover in Paris, Zurich, London, and Lugano. If I'm ever missing, I hope my cardboard milk carton mentions such glamorous ports.

We head back to our forgotten rooms at the Principe Leopoldo Hotel. How do these people keep track of where they are? They are still probably paying for rooms at the Dolder. No wonder Dr. Zarr wants to buy hotels.

When I ask who would want to kill Clover, Julian says, "Who says she's dead? Let's just wait and see if she turns up." While he looks like he could play a detective on T.V., his deplorable lack of curiosity would hurt the ratings.

Once back in our room, I soldier on with my own in-house investigation. Julian is not in the same mode as I am. He says, "If B.M. were smart, she'd find a way to get Clover out of the picture. But then again, she's not that smart."

I say, "I think she's done pretty well for herself." Julian puts his finger to his lips to indicate I should lower my voice. Then we hear yelling in corridor. It is not difficult to tell who has the room next door. Despite thick walls, we hear a cacophony of sounds from Simon, B.M., and the "baby." A water glass to the wall helps clarify the topic. Simon and B.M. are arguing as much as she can with her jaw wired shut. She accuses him of abandoning her and the baby in her time of need, which is true.

What's to become of B.M.? I tell Julian I'm going to see if she's alright. I throw a dress over my head, and go and invite her for afternoon tea. She agrees but, unfortunately, brings the squealing creature.

As we wait for tea in the dining room, I gently bring up the subject of her fall. She says she only remembers a light tumble, like it's a dryer cycle, and then waking up in the hospital. I decide not to mention the black buckled shoe.

Then I ask her theory on Clover's whereabouts, I'm hoping she says she knows all about Simon and Clover. Instead she thinks it has something to do with Maryel. "I think Maryel wants my Simon. That's why she put Poison Ivy, or whatever in that makeup. So she'd be prettier than me."

It's hard not to laugh, but I manage with lip biting.

B.M. puts a half stick of butter on her scone, "Sometimes I think Maryel is only friends with Clover so she can come to family events again."

"But Maryel is *Julian's* old fiancé. I think she wants *him* back."

"He's with you now. That is unless you dump him and go with the married poet. Then he'll go back to Maryel."

I pour my tea. "What about Clover? Aren't you jealous of her?"

She got the whole scone assemblage in her mouth and mutters, "What? Well, not if she's dead."

"We're not sure. Clover could just be missing."

Now I wish I had time to call Mrs. E. to run all this past her. As we wait for more scones and jam, I try to determine precisely what is wrong with this baby. Ah, the mouth is gigantic, and she has ginger hair, the color of an Orangutan. B.M. starts to breastfeed the infant right in front of me, and her entire breast seems to go directly into the baby's mouth. *Yikes.* Dr. Zarr approaches from behind and appears embarrassed to catch her in mid-feed. He picks up the baby and engages in all sorts of cute Suisse-

Deutsch baby talk with his new grandchild. He takes the baby's long arm, gestures for the waiter, and in a mock baby voice, says, "Cup of tea, please."

When I get back to the room, I send emails to Mrs. Etherington, David, and Oliver. I see that there is an email from Paulina. She wants to know that I'm stuck in Lugano with the baby, if I need any more clothes that are drool-proof. Evidently, news travels quickly.

Ah, finally, time for my bath. As the water is running, I pull out the glass with Clover's kidnapper's fingerprints. Since this could solve all the crimes, I just might have to give this to the police. But what if it ends up pointing the finger at Julian or Dr. Zarr?

Julian returns from breakfast to pack. And when I look over at him, I notice that he is wearing black shoes— with a side buckle! Yikes. Maybe he's the tripper!

But why would Julian want to trip B.M.? Could it be that she knows too much? No, perhaps because she's annoying. No matter what, I've got to get away from this family.

They can all go to Zurich for all I care. Now I'm grateful that I have to stay in Lugano. As he packs, I see Julian's worried-looking face in the closet mirror. He pats me on my head, "Now, try to say very little to the police, or—for that matter—anyone."

As Julian walks away, he says, "I'll be back in a few days." He leans to kiss me goodbye.

After he leaves, I soak in the tub for a long time. How *did* I end up here? Well, it all started when Mrs. E. and David were busybodies at the Dorchester. What if they hadn't seen or "heard" my fiancé Arthur? I would now be a married woman instead of a murder suspect.

Oh, how I wish Oliver would write me back. I haven't heard back from him in days. Now I wonder if he's run off and killed his wife.

There is a friendly knock on the door; Julian must have forgotten something.

I grab a towel and open the door. It's Oliver.

Chapter 65

What? Oliver hugs me, and I catch the welcome scent of nutmeg and butter. Then I smell a wet dog. Oliver says, "I couldn't very well have you stranded here all alone."

He kisses me while the dog hugs my leg. I look down. "They let him on the plane?"

"No. We drove. Well, I did most of the driving."

"You drove from England to Switzerland?"

"We took the ferry from Dover to Calais, and then drove all day yesterday through France. It took twelve hours with a dog, and those damned Alps in the way."

I can barely hear what he says as I'm watching his sensuous lips craft words like 'Calais' and 'damned.'

"Why didn't you fly?"

"Mrs. Etherington suggested I take the dog to help find you. And I think she is also worried about that Penroy character getting too comfortable in her house."

I look at Oliver. "So how are the twins?

"Not biting people and dogs as much. It helps when the one stays on his meds."

God! Oliver never looked so gorgeous. His hair is tousled and messy. What was I thinking, signing up with Julian? Look at this mess I've gotten myself into. Oliver pulls me in for a kiss, and my arms come up around his neck. Ah, I'd forgotten about his sweet pudding kisses. The jealous dog pulls at the corner of my towel, causing it to fall off. Right then, the door opens. It's Julian and his father. They just stand there until Julian regains his composure and says, "I left my phone." Julian's face is red with fury as he grabs his father and leaves.

Oliver apologizes. "Sorry, should have called first."

I quickly grab the towel and run barefoot down the hall, chasing Julian and his father. They are trapped, waiting for the elevator.

Julian finally blurts, "I can't take this anymore, Camille."

His father remains silent, with his eyes focused on the elevator lights. Older men like him have probably seen it all, and have learned not to interfere. Then I hear the cacophony that is B.M., coming towards us, yelling, "Hold the elevator!" She and Simon and their assortment of suitcases and baby paraphernalia load into the elevator with a silent Dr. Zarr. Julian and I remain behind.

Julian, his tempo decreasing from Presto to Largo, says, "I was really falling for you, Camille."

His eyebrows are turned down in the corners with a look of sorrow. This is a big surprise because I didn't think he let go enough to fall. Now, I feel terrible.

"I'm sorry, I had no idea that Oliver would show up."

The elevator door pings open. Julian steps in without looking at me and presses the buttons several times to get the door to close —clearly anxious to end this right now.

He exhales. "I think Oliver loves you—and you love him."

Chapter 66

I slowly walk back down the hallway, realizing that I've messed up. Now, I've ruined any possibility of a relationship with Julian. I hear the elevator ping again and hear the doors open. *Ah, maybe he's come back for me — like in one of those British rom-coms—he'll run down the hall, and we'll embrace.* Instead, I hear what sounds like an approaching circus and see B.M. "The idiot forgot the baby."

Without getting involved in that drama, I slip back into my hotel suite door and find Oliver nodding off on the sofa. The dog is asleep in my clam-shelled suitcase on the floor.

Oliver rolls his head up. "What was all that?"

"Just the Zarrs."

"When are you going to realize the Zarr's are dangerous?"

"Not all of them. Not the father and not Julian. I do, however, think Simon is a bit of trouble."

He looks at his watch. "If we leave right now, we can catch the last ferry from *Calais.*"

"But I can't leave Switzerland."

"I think you're in danger." He rubs my feet. "I wouldn't have driven for hours with this dog if I weren't worried about you."

"It was sweet of you. But I can't leave before Monday."

He's kissing my toes and looking at the door. "Let's get out of here. I doubt that your man would like me staying here."

"I don't think he's my man anymore."

231

Now, I'm worried that Julian will walk in the door again. "Um. There's a nice hotel down the hill, The Delfino. Let's go there." I say as I grab a few things. It feels like I'm running to a safe house with my protector.

Oliver drives down the steep incline and spots the Hotel Delfino. He runs in to check it out and gives me a thumbs-up. Soon we are headed up the staircase of the modern hotel bedecked in wood and glass. We are given the keys to a large room with a lake view and twin beds. Oliver says it was the last room. He opens his suitcase and hands me my green velvet jacket and my flute. "I thought you might have missed these. With the drapes blowing in the breeze, I play a Debussy song for him, but then Robert starts to howl, so I have to stop.

Oliver strips down to his boxer briefs, and I can make out the shape of things to come. There is a little moonlight coming in the window and I catch a glimpse of his muscular chest. Oliver tells me that he thought of me the whole time he was driving. Ah.

After a delightful dinner in the hotel, we come back to the room. He sleeps in the bed with me—and so does the dog. The whole time my heart is pounding, and I know he's the one I love. Oliver, that is. As much as I want to be lovers with him, I don't want to fall into his ocean. He doesn't try anything romantic, making me wonder what's going on in his head. Then I hear snoring. It's emanating from both man and dog. The poor things must be exhausted.

Chapter 67

In the morning, I find a note from Oliver; the penmanship is so beautiful that I want to frame it.

'Downstairs for breakfast. Didn't want to wake you.'

When I head down with the dog, I am greeted by an elegant man who appears to be the proprietor of the Delfino. He asks what brings me to Switzerland. I ask if he wants the long or the short version. He smiles and smartly says, "short."

He gets the two-word explanation. "A man."

His eyebrows rise. "A man?" Now I think he wishes for the medium version, so I say, "Suppose I'm writing a murder mystery set here, and someone is a witness or maybe a murder suspect; can they just leave the country if they want?"

He shakes his head. "I'm afraid not. Just stay until after your meeting tomorrow with Detective Bernardo, and perhaps he'll let you go."

God! Everyone knows everything here!

I find Oliver seated at a charming table on the terrace, reading the local paper. He looks up. "Good Morning." He pours me some coffee. "It seems your Clover is quite a colorful character."

I don't have my glasses, so he reads to me.

"Super-model missing after dining with Zarr Pharma Scions. Clover Blinova, had been well known in the European jet set for dating royalty and tech billionaires."

I interrupt, "Clover Blinova? It sounds like an ointment."

He now pretends he's reading to the dog. "She was despondent about the death of her mother, Penelope Venalailen Blinova Zarr, also known as Number Three."

I pull the paper from him. "It doesn't say that."

Oliver offers me toast and marmalade. Then I ask about his wife.

"She's better, but I don't know what's going to happen with my marriage. Right now, I feel stuck."

He must see the look on my face. "I think of you every day, Camille. You've even inspired me to write a book of poems."

"Oh, sweet. Can I see them?"

"Yes. Someday."

He's Mr. Someday.

Later in the day, we walk down the mountain to the marina, and Oliver suggests a ride. After the last boat ride, I am not too keen. Oliver says it will be fun and signs up for a boat rental. Well, okay, hoping maybe my purse will resurface.

Oliver's face is so serious that it makes me wonder what he is thinking about—so I ask him. He laughs, "Sailing the bloody boat, and keeping the dog from falling in."

After our ride, we drive up the mountain, past the Zarr residence. I point it out to Oliver and wonder out loud if I can sneak in and retrieve my suitcase. He says I'd probably better not.

We head back to the Delfino for a steak dinner and a bottle of the local *Ticino Merlot*. I decide I love this town. It's like going back in time.

When we get back to the room, Oliver pulls out his guitar, and I think of a line for my book.

'When he played the guitar and sang, it was like he hit my notes and strummed my soul.'

We have another night of innocent slumber. Maybe he doesn't want to be lovers because I was just with Julian.

Chapter 68

It's Monday morning, so Oliver takes me to the kindergarten posing as the police station. He asks me if I'm worried.

"What are they going to do – put me in a playpen?"

I march in, well aware that they could lock me up forever. Wearing the innocent-looking navy dress, I carry the bag containing the champagne glass, which will set me free.

'I vaguely remember the old days, when I was a dog sitter wearing Gap. Now I'm a murder suspect in Balmain.'

Detective Bernardo greets me in the interrogation room, which looks like a "time out" room for kindergarteners. The older gray-haired police chief is there too.

Excitedly, I pull out the evidence, which I have carefully wrapped in underpants to protect from breakage. I tell them that I believe that the fingerprints will be an exact match with those of the killer. They give each other a silent look.

I continue. "Clover was probably kidnapped by the same person who killed her mother. All you have to do is send this to the fingerprint lab and see if you have a match with your database of killers."

The older one says, "Very interesting. Julian Zarr says the glass window falling was just an accident. But, you seem to think we have a kidnapping and a murder."

Why do I speak? I should just get some duct tape and seal my mouth.

"Oh well, that is just one theory. Maybe it was made to look like kidnapping and murder, to make us look bad. Then I hand them the suspicious bottle of make up.

"I think Maryel is the murderer. She put something in this."

Bernardo reads the label. "Ivory foundation is hardly a murder weapon."

The chief says, "Do you mean Maryel Bouvier, who was sitting on the runway at Lugano airport at 2:14 p.m., well before the death of Mrs. Zarr. That Maryel Bouvier?"

"Well, yes, that one."

Detective Bernardo shakes his head. "Try to think who else would have wanted Mrs. Zarr to die?"

"Well, certainly not Julian or his Dad, and probably not B.M. or Clover."

The chief says, "Ah, Clover Blinokov." He then uses his hands to make a smooching sound. "That's Russian for a pancake!"

"I thought Clover's last name was Fontaine."

Detective Bernardo answers. "She must have changed her name to Fontaine. And what makes you think she's been kidnapped?"

I look around. "Well, we can't find her."

The chief says, "Ah, you are an imaginative writer, Ms. Carano."

"You can't make this stuff up! Especially the boat sinking. I wonder who was supposed to die on that trip."

Bernardo slaps the desk. "I forgot about the boating accident. The damned Italians were supposed to investigate that one."

Somehow, I answer all of the questions without trying to frame anyone, well except for Maryel. When I get back to the car, there is my adorable Oliver, all blurry behind the windshield in the rain. He runs out with an umbrella to help me.

It reminds me of that first day — when I was to meet him but met Julian instead. If only the stupid taxi driver had taken me to Claridge's — then I never would have met Julian and been involved in this murder. My whole life would have been different.

When I say this to Oliver, he says, "What I'm wondering is: who is this Polish Paulina woman who is always sending you clothes? She seems suspicious."

"Paulina Krakowski. Hm. Maybe you're on to something. She's a friend of the family and aunt of this Eddie guy who worked in the Vienna lab."

"Maybe *she* killed Penelope Zarr."

"But why? She'd lose so much Zarr business."

"I have no idea. It's just a thought."

Later that day, the rain lets up, and we sit by the lake to watch the elegant swans. Then Oliver holds my hand. "It was difficult to sleep in the same bed and not make love."

"I was wondering about that."

"Camille, I don't want to be unfair to you. I don't think I can afford to get divorced —ever."

Suddenly, the swans do not look so elegant. The once-beautiful scenery becomes a grey blur.

He tells me he'll have to pay for part of his wife's private treatment — and he's not getting his tenure at the University. It might be because he wrote a controversial piece about how studying Ancient History will only get someone a job as a waiter.

I think of my life. I'm now a foreign murder suspect riding in an old station wagon with a married man, while clutching a bag of underpants.

Chapter 69

The next morning, I am awakened by a French kiss — more fervent than ever. *Oh, Oliver has come to his senses and will get divorced after all. We'll finally be lovers once and for all.* Then I open my eyes. It's not Oliver — it's the dog.

Oliver is sitting in a chair, wearing his adorable glasses, and looking at his laptop. "Do you two want to get a room?"

"I thought it was you."

"I'm afraid I can't compete with that tongue."

He pours me a coffee and says, "If we leave now, we can make it to *Calais* by nightfall."

I smile and start packing. *Yay! Free at last.* Then the phone rings; it's the front desk. They say the police want me back for another little chat. *Hmm. I'd better wear my lucky jacket.*

When I get to the station, I find Detective Bernardo and the old police chief in the interrogation room. They want to know how B.M. was injured and more about the boat sinking. They say they had considered them accidents until I blabbed. I ask if they found out anything about the make up or the fingerprints on the glass.

Bernardo says, "That make up had hydrochloric acid in it."

"There's a reason to arrest Maryel."

"From the sounds of it, anyone could have tampered with her makeup."

The old one says, "Like Clover, whom she had a fight with."

"Well, then what about the fingerprints —did you trace them?"

Bernardo says, "Yes, but we are not at liberty to say."

"I'll bet Clover has a secret lover!"

They look at each other and laugh. Finally, Bernardo says, "No, it was her father."

"What? Where did he come from?"

"Apparently, he wanted to get her away from the Zarrs, so he came and got her."

Detective Bernardo gets up and says, "Thank you, Miss Carano. We can no longer suggest you remain in Switzerland."

"That was just a suggestion?"

"Yes, but you are so full of information that we hated to have you leave."

The older one slaps down the file. "You are free to go back to London with the poet."

How did they know all this?

When I ask for my passport, Detective Bernardo says, "We don't have it. We don't usually keep passports."

They call in the lady who brought me the espresso that day, who is also the passport copier. She says she handed it back to — "The sexy man with the black hair and blue eyes."

Julian has my passport!

"We know you recently had words with Julian Zarr at the hotel when the poet arrived."

When I walk to the car, I see my sweet Oliver doing tricks with the dog. When I tell him my passport is now in Zurich, he doesn't say a word and starts the car.

I decide not to tell Julian that we are on our way. Stealth moves are the best.

Chapter 70

Zurich, Switzerland

It's an enchanting four-hour drive through the Alps with the dog. Without a dog, it would be an enchanting three-hour drive. We stop in the lakeside village of Brunner for a late lunch of cheese sandwiches. We should make Zurich by 5:00 p.m. now, which means we'll have to sleep over and drive to Calais tomorrow.

It's not hard to guess where the Zarrs are staying—either the Dolder or the Park Hyatt Hotel.

Oliver sees the prices of $700 per night as he researches on his phone. "Ahem. That might be a little out of the budget for me."

We stop at the Park Hyatt first and scan the common areas for Julian. I ask the polished concierge to call me immediately if they see any of the Zarrs. Most politely, he tells me that he is not at liberty to divulge such information. When I ask him if he remembers B.M., he laughs and says, "If I see or hear her, I'll have her call you."

Now, we've got to find the Zarrs and a place to stay before nightfall. Oliver pulls out his phone to sign up for an Airbnb. We see a nice one with a man named Edwin for $75 per night. They have a system where one has to be approved, so we have to wait. We decide we might as well check out another Zarr hangout—The Dolder Grand Hotel.

We are given directions to the bottom of the *Dolder Bahn*. We leave the Volvo at the bottom and consider leaving Robert there, but his incessant barking implores us to bring him. As we are riding up the funicular, I could swear that I see someone who looks exactly like the missing Clover Fontaine passing by in a descending car. She is so tall that her head is practically hitting the top of the cab.

When we get to the top, we head to the bar. Knowing Julian Zarr, it's likely he'll be there. The staff welcomes our dog and us. Frankly, I'm a little displeased with the pet policies of European hotels. They will let anything in, putting my cunning dog smuggling skills to waste.

We head to the expansive lounge overlooking the lake. But no Zarr sightings. I hesitate to text my prime source, B.M., because she is a two-way street when it comes to information. If all else fails, I'll text Paulina. She's got Zarr-dar.

Ah, my stressful day is winding down as Oliver, and I settle in one of the comfy butter-colored sofas. A lady is playing the harp in the distance, like an angel in heaven. Today is turning around.

Oliver orders two white wines as we wait to spot Julian. We wait so long that we have to dip into the budget for another round. While we're waiting, Oliver checks to see if we've been approved by Airbnb yet. "Bloody hell!" He moans, "My card has been declined." He cleans off his glasses. "That's odd. There should be £3,000 in available credit."

He tries another card. "Fuck! This is also declined."

I say, "Maybe it's because you're traveling internationally."

As I sip my wine, I discreetly check the balance on my one remaining credit card—the one that is not at the bottom of a lake. The robotic voice says, " Available credit $5.43." *Really! Do they have to say it so loudly?* I fish through what's left of my possessions and find 43 Swiss francs.

This is a predicament that requires venting. "I have no wallet, no passport, and less than $50 to my name."

"Doesn't Mrs. Etherington pay you?"

"Um. Yes, but I subtract all my time off, and deduct for all the gourmet food and aged port I consume."

Oliver laughs. "Oh, so you owe her money."

We toast each other with what will have to be the last of the wine — unless we feel like washing dishes. Oliver checks another credit card online. "It's not blocked, but it just has £58 in available credit. We'll need more than that for petrol and the ferry."

"What are we doing to do?"

Oliver pets the dog. "Have you ever slept in an estate wagon? It's not too different from camping. We can find a nice spot with a view."

I look around the luxurious hotel and say, "Let's pray, it doesn't come to that."

Oliver looks a little peeved. "Perhaps you should have stayed with your rich boyfriend."

Right then, Simon walks into the lounge. *Bingo!* He doesn't see me as he snaps his fingers at a passing waiter and orders a gin and tonic. Now he's on the phone on the other side of a wide column. He's pleading with someone to give him some more time. As he paces, I see he's wearing black Zegna buckle shoes. He's the tripper, not my Julian!

Right then, Julian saunters in and settles on a sofa near the window. He looks quite content with the world, so I walk over to him and stare.

He looks up. "What are you doing here, Camille?"

With my hands on my hip, I say, "You're in big trouble, Mister!"

He seems startled by my sudden authority. "Why is that?"

243

"You've had my passport all this time! The police lady says she's handed them all back to you."

"Err. Um. I was doing you a favor. I thought if you had your passport, you'd leave Switzerland at your own peril."

I huff, "I'd like my passport back if you don't mind."

Julian hems. "I couldn't very well hide it in my suitcase, so I put it in my father's bag."

Right then, Simon runs over to make an announcement. "Camille, have you heard? We think we've found Clover!"

Julian says, "She thought someone was trying to kill her. So she's been on the run."

I reveal my latest intelligence. "Did you know that was her father who came and got her from the D'Oro?"

Simon looks shocked. "What? She told me he was dead."

I say, "Well, where is the lying bitch?"

Julian flings his hand. "Our father flew to Geneva to look for her."

"What? Your father is in Geneva now?"

Oliver is waiting off in the distance, so I amble over to give him the news. "My passport is now in Geneva with Dr. Zarr."

Oliver exhales. "Then we are both in a bit of a pickle. It seems my wife bought £4000 worth of farm animals. She's maxed out all the cards and left £34 in the checking account. I honestly don't know what we are going to do."

"I guess we'll be sleeping in the car with the dog."

Julian is hovering nearby and can undoubtedly hear us, judging from his smirk. He clears his throat as he approaches and kindly invites us to his sofa area with Simon. Here we find the sommelier opening an expensive

244

bottle while describing it like poetry. "The *Domaine de La Romanee St.-Vivant* charts its own mysterious path..."

Simon quips, "Just pour it!"

Julian toasts. "Cheers."

Oliver says, "I'm not feeling very cheery. My wife just spent all my money."

The waiter suddenly halts pouring for Oliver, who gets up to make a call.

Julian says, "That's terrible. Can wives do that?"

Simon says sarcastically, "Hello!"

Julian clinks my glass, "Now, I've heard about your predicament. Not to worry, I'll get two rooms for you and Oliver here tonight."

Julian asks the waiter to make reservations for a couple of rooms.

The waiter says, "I'll check, but I think we're nearly booked."

Right then, B.M. comes down and plops herself on the sofa. With her mouth wired shut, she can still talk, but she sounds like Long Island Lockjaw. Frankly, it's a vast improvement.

Julian looks around. "Dare I ask where the baby is?"

B.M. replies, "Oh, I left it in the room."

I say, "Is that legal?"

B.M. replies, "You have to! That thing makes so much noise, you can't think."

Oliver returns, and B.M. fixes her gaze on him. "You're even better looking than Camille said. Is your wife still in the loony bin?"

Oliver replies, "No, unfortunately, she escaped again."

B.M. enters unchartered territory by asking him how long until he gets divorced.

Without missing a beat, Oliver says, "I just called her shrink. He thinks my wife is only pretending to be crazy. This farm animal bit proves it."

B.M. says, "So now you can get divorced!"

Simon quips, "Divorces are expensive. Maybe you should just bump her off."

B.M. hits Simon on the shoulder. "That's not funny!"

Simon gulps his wine. "I'm sure he's already thought of that and is just wondering how."

Julian quips, "He could always use Zarrexifam."

Chapter 71

We all sit in the lounge drinking the fine wine with a spirited debate on whether Oliver should divorce — or murder his wife.

Then we see Clover saunter by!

Simon runs over to her; then returns with a news flash. "She took the train from Geneva yesterday. She's staying upstairs!"

My phone beeps with a timely text from Mrs. Etherington, so I excuse myself to visit the safety of the ladies' room. She wants to know what's happening. I text back: '*In Zurich. Oliver's wife faking it. Clover found.*' She types back, '*Any more accidents?*'

I text back. '*Not yet.*'

I guess we'll have to take up Julian's offer to get us rooms. It is nearly 7:00 p.m., and this sure beats sleeping in the car. There aren't a lot of rooms left, so someone will have to share.

While I have a moment to contemplate my future, I realize that if I stay in the hotel room with poor married Oliver, I'll really kill any potential second chance with Julian. This is tricky. There are moments in one's life when one makes a seemingly simple choice, but that choice had profound consequences when looking back.

Simon leaves to make a call. I hope he's not dialing a hit-man to bump off Oliver's wife — but that could simplify things.

As we sit, Julian orders everything on the tasting menu, which includes lobster, crab, and caviar. *Yay!*

Oliver looks at the food warily, probably worried about getting stuck with the tab. Even though I know he must be starving, he will not eat anything.

Clover slinks over. She has an innate insouciance about her, but maybe that's from being a super-model. The entire country of Switzerland has been on the lookout for her, and she acts like she was just getting her hair done.

Simon shoves B.M. off the slippery leather sofa and offers Clover a seat.

Clover says, "No, I'm off on a date at the Bar Au Lac Hotel."

Simon looks Crestfallen. "A date? Is that a good idea?"

"Yes. And do not send a search party."

Then we hear a horrible approaching noise. It's the waiter pushing the crying baby in a rusty old pram. "Does this belong to someone here?"

B.M. slaps her forehead. "Now, I remember why I came down here! I'm out of diapers, and that thing needs changing."

Clover holds her nose. "Oh, really?"

B.M. says, "Clover, if you're headed down the funicular, can you can you bring back some diapers?"

Clover gets up to leave. "Yeah, right. Like I'd be caught dead with them."

Sweetly, Oliver says, "I have to get our things from the car at the bottom of the mountain. I'll get you some nappies in town."

B.M. gets a big smile and says she'll go along to help him pick them out, because even though it's a preemie, the baby is huge. I also think this is so she can continue to ask Oliver probing questions.

The hotel staff suggests that they take the baby, the noisy pram, and the dog with them. B.M., with a gigantic bagel in her mouth, creates a noisy scene as they exit the lobby.

After the carnival leaves town, I'm left alone with Julian. He pours me more of the fine French wine and says, "So, you're driving back to England with Oliver?"

"That's the plan. The Swiss police finally let me go."

He puts his hand on my knee. "Don't go."

I sit silently, somehow feeling that my entire future may be decided during this one evening. Do I continue on to London with Oliver with his crazy ex-wife and evil twins? Or do I just throw my hands up and embrace Julian?

"It pains me to think of you sleeping with the poet."

I look at Julian. "I never have."

He crosses his arms. "I find that hard to believe."

"We had twin beds at the hotel, plus, who knows if he'll ever get divorced."

He takes the tiny mother-of-pearl spoon and puts some Russian caviar in my mouth. "And he's broke to boot."

Then I think of my past week. "But what a mess you've gotten me into. I've been stuck here in Switzerland as a murder suspect with no passport and no money."

"Why didn't you say something?"

He pulls out a roll of Swiss francs. "What do you think? Will four thousand will get you through the week?"

"I just need enough to get back to London. I'll borrow two hundred if that's alright."

He puts the whole roll of money in my purse. "I wish you would stay to help us figure this out."

"That's funny. That's what the police said."

"If they ever suspected you, they must have thought you were being set up."

Now I realize that I was wrong to accuse Julian.

"Who would set me up?"

Then he leans back on the sofa. "Well, who would like to see you out of the picture?"

Without thinking, I say, "Oliver's wife for one."

Julian toasts, "Yes, I think you had better stay in my room tonight."

Now I really have a big dilemma.

Chapter 72

Suddenly, the waiter runs in. "Come quickly! There's been an accident."

We follow him down the elevator to a ramp that leads to the funicular stop.

There is B.M. She's screaming as much as one can with one's jaws wired shut. Her hair is caught in the door hinge of the cable car. An observant lady bystander gives us a rapid-fire report: "Her bagel rolled onto the tracks, and the dog tried to get it but was tied to the baby carriage, and the baby went rolling down the hill, but the leash got caught in the funicular gears."

The funicular driver is waving his arms. "Someone cut the brakes! If it hadn't been for the dog, people would have been killed."

Julian quips, "I can see the headlines: 'Dog saves lives.'"

Oliver pulls me aside and whispers, "Camille, let's get away from these people."

Poor Robert. His stumpy tail is on the track of the train. He's whimpering and bleeding. I start to cry. *I love this dog.*

In a few minutes, the Swiss police and an ambulance arrive in an efficient pack. They look at me and say, "Camille Carano, we presume."

After a bit of negotiation, Oliver volunteers to ride in the ambulance with B.M. and her hair. Julian accompanies me to the local vet with the baby and the remains of Robert's tail. It's in a plastic ziplock bag given to him by the innocent bystander lady.

In less than a minute, I get a call from Mrs. E. "What has happened to my baby?"

"Nothing major. We're taking him to the vet because they don't have ambulances for dogs. I'll have to call you back."

While the friendly hotel staff drives us to the vet, Julian says, "How the hell did Mrs. Etherington know something happened to her dog — did you text her?"

I shake my head, no.

Julian jokes, "Maybe she's the one killing people so she'll get her dog-walker back."

Julian, the baby, the dog, and I are at another vet office, just like that first night when Robert ate all the buttons.

The vet office nurse gasps when she sees the baby and says, "Sorry, we don't accept monkeys." Then she realizes her mistake and hides behind the counter.

The dog and his tail are escorted to the inner sanctum by the nurse.

Julian sighs, "What next?"

After a while, the vet comes out to the waiting room with a solemn look on his face. Then he holds up an x-ray of the dog's tail. It looks like a tumor.

He says, "It's some sort of GPS tracking and listening device. It's quite sophisticated. See, if you bend his tail, there's a toggle on/off switch."

Julian shakes his head. "It all makes sense. Mrs. E. seems to know way too much."

Suddenly, I start to replay the tape of Mrs. Etherington. She always seems way too curious about my whereabouts.

The doctor says, "One question. Before we sew it back on, do you want us to take that out?"

I say, "It's not our dog. I'd better call Mrs. E."

Julian jokes. "No need to call and ask; she can hear us."

The vet doesn't find any of this funny and says he doesn't have all day. Mrs. E. doesn't answer her phone, so we elect to have the original tail sewn back on if there is data in the device that could be useful.

Robert is invited to be an overnight guest at the vet's, so Julian and I head back to the Dolder with the baby. Then it occurs to me that all of my possessions are still in Oliver's station wagon. When I send Oliver a text, I get no reply.

We go to Simon's room next. Julian deposits the baby in Simon's arms and says, "I believe this belongs to you."

Simon barely touches the infant and puts her on the floor. "Did you hear? Oliver is in jail. They found a wrench and chain cutters in his car."

"Oh, no! We'd better go and see him."

Simon tosses a pretzel, like a dog treat for the baby. "He's in for the night. He hands me the baby. "Mind watching her for a bit Camille?"

"Sure. Where's B.M.?"

"She's still in the hospital, getting her scalp sewn back to her head."

Julian asks me to come back to his room, thinking this solves my dilemma of who to share a room with. I call the police station to ask about Oliver, but they cannot release any information. Julian says that Oliver must have been set up and adds, "But who would want Oliver out of the picture?"

I say, "You."

"Hey, I found a room for you two. It wasn't I."

"Well, your brother seems to be mysteriously absent during all the mishaps."

253

"Yes, but he's just so obvious. It's not Simon. The question is, who are they really trying to target?"

"I think Clover. She was planning on riding the funicular to her date, and she was an obvious target on the boat sinking."

The room service people bring us a trolley of warm milk options for the baby. Julian winces at the sight, reminding me that he's got milk-o-phobia and making me wonder how he'll ever be a father. We make a little bed for the baby using towels and a dresser drawer, just like in the *Thin Man* movies. Julian tries to burp her, but it comes out all ends—with the sound effects of a frat boy.

Finally, Julian kisses me good night. I enjoy his nice long French kiss. H*mm, almost as good as the dog.*

Chapter 73

At 9:00 a.m., there is a knock on the door. I throw on one of Julian's shirts and open the door. It's Oliver. He comes and collapses on a chair. "What a nightmare! The next time anyone needs nappies, they can get them themselves."

Julian gets up and puts on a robe, "That must have been awful. I heard the food's not very good."

Oliver says the police let him go, as it was too evident he had been framed. The chain cutters were in the front seat of the car, but my suitcase is missing.

Julian says, "The authorities should be on the lookout for someone wearing pink La Perla lingerie."

Oliver hands me my flute. "It was sitting out in plain sight, but no one pinched it." Then he asks about Robert. I can tell that Julian is about to mention the device in Robert's tail, so I shut him up quickly.

Oliver holds up the baby and says, "Who put on this nappy? It's backward."

I say, "It's for a cat."

Then Oliver stands up and says, "Well, time to go. I've got to get back to Felixstowe to sort out my wife and my bank accounts."

Julian gets up to shake his hand. "I assume you'll be taking the dog."

Oliver looks at me. "Are you ready, Camille? We can pick up Robert on the way."

Oh no. I'm not sure whether to leave with Oliver or stay here with Julian. Once again, Oliver or Julian? The baby cries, and I try to fix the diaper while searching for the answer.

Oliver waves his hand over my face. "Are you coming?"

Finally, Julian says, "Actually, Camille, even if you take the ferry over the channel, you'll still need a passport."

"I don't even have a driver's license. It's at the bottom of the lake."

Oliver sits back down. "Hadn't thought of that."

Julian rubs his chin. "I suppose you could hide in the boot and go through the Chunnel."

Oliver tells him. "It's an estate wagon, and I'm not in the mood for any human trafficking. I'm afraid I'll have to go alone."

Julian looks at me. "Not to worry. I'll get your passport and fly you and the dog back."

Well, sometimes, the universe makes the decisions for you.

I follow Oliver to the hallway to say goodbye.

"Camille, I didn't think I'd go back alone." He looks so sad. Like an orphan stranded by the railroad tracks, I watch his tight butt walk away down the hallway as he gets smaller and smaller. My heart wants me to run after him, but my brain says to stay with Julian.

When I come back to the door, Julian is getting dressed. He says, "I've had it with the screaming baby. I'm taking her, the drawer, and all to my brother's room!"

Julian comes back after a few minutes and says, "He's in there with Clover!"

"Where's the baby?"

"I left it with the waiter."

He tugs on my shirt and says he needs it back.

"Right now?"

He runs his fingers up the buttons. "Yes, I think I have a job interview."

I smile. "You've never had a job interview in your life."

He begins unbuttoning my shirt with his mouth. He kisses me softly, and pulls me to the bed. He dives under the sheets and sends my panties flying across the room. Julian is in me again, but slower this time. It's dark in the place, and there was really no time to think. Julian rolls on his back and says, "I missed you, Miss Carano."

Now, what have I done? We lie under the covers in the afterglow. Then there is a knock on the door. It's Oliver.

Chapter 74

I hurry to put my clothes on, but Oliver is already in the room. He takes one look at me, and I know he can smell the sex. People always know. He marches in with his head down. "I haven't got enough quid to get home."

Julian silently hands him a stack of £100 bills. Oliver takes two and says he'll pay it all back. He looks so sad and embarrassed. Now I feel guilty for having sex with Julian. Poor Oliver, I'll bet he's sorry he drove all that way to fetch me and now has to leave me with the other man.

He thanks Julian and walks out the door. Woosh! He's gone. Perhaps gone forever.

Julian and I get up and make our rounds, which we have to do with the baby in tow. First, we stop to visit B.M. at the hospital. She looks even more unfortunate. She doesn't even seem to want to hold her own baby, who screams at the sight of her.

I ask her who could have tampered with the funicular brakes. She quivers as if she's being electrocuted and tells me she can't remember. I decide that it's not the right time to mention that her husband was in bed with Clover. B.M. will be staying at the hospital for a few more days. She probably likes it here because it's so quiet, and no one is trying to kill her.

Next, we head to the vet to get the dog. Okay, now I'm a murder suspect with a dog and a baby, but no clothes and no passport. At least I have Julian with me and 4000 Swiss francs. We stop to do a little shopping, but it's not easy with the animal entourage.

While I shop, Julian gets a call from his father. No one bothered to tell him that we found Clover. He says he's relieved, but he's shocked when we tell him about B.M.'s funicular accident and Oliver's arrest. Someone is apparently trying to get B.M., Clover, or Oliver, so it's best to getaway. Dr. Zarr feels bad about Oliver getting implicated in all this, and he wonders what sort of gangsters B.M. and Clover are running with.

Dr. Zarr says to come to Geneva. He's staying at the Four Seasons Hotel, and he will get us a suite here and send the jet to retrieve us. Ah, things are looking up in Camille world. That is until he says to bring the baby and the dog. Julian gets on the phone to call Paulina and sends some dresses and lingerie to Geneva. *Hallelujah!* I'll have fresh underpants after having to go without for days.

While I wait for Julian to pack up, I call Mrs. E. but get no reply, so I call David.

I fill him in on all things dog, men, and murder.

David says, "Let me see if I have this straight: The dog saved everyone from dying in a runaway cable car, Oliver ended up in jail, and the brother ended up in bed with the kidnapped super-model."

"Yes, that's pretty much it."

"But wait, who are you, um you know, with? Oliver or Julian?"

I bashfully indicate Julian, who is dawdling nearby.

David says, "Poor Oliver."

"It will be a while before he gets divorced. His wife just bought two cows and spent all his money."

"That's madness!"

Then I remember my reason for calling him. "Um. Why does your mother's dog have an electronic device in his tail?"

259

There is no sound. Then he says, "Does mother know you know?"

"I don't know."

He hesitates, then finally says, "Robert used to belong to my brother." His voice accelerates once he gets to the thread of the tale. "Yes, he was kind of a special work dog, and they might have put the device in at his brother's place of work." Now, when I hear the words "special" and "might," I know he is hiding something.

When I hang up, Julian says, "I think there's something up with David. I mean, who has ever heard of a Dendrologist? Frankly, it sounds like a cover."

I finally hear from Mrs. E. She says she can explain the dog tail, but not to breathe another word about this device.

Mrs. E. says she's been looking into things for me. She says she looked at the little Russian ballerina's video, and the person who tripped B.M. has a woman's ankle and large feet. Maybe it was Clover wearing Simon's shoes! But why would Clover try to trip B.M.? Perhaps she wants Simon to herself. Or maybe it's because B.M. is a woman who knows too much and blabs too much.

Mrs. E. says it's too bad about Oliver. She thinks his wife is using faux-dementia to get him to come back.

Chapter 75

Geneva, Switzerland

With the dog and baby in tow, we arrive at the sumptuous Four Seasons Hotel in Geneva. Dr. Zarr takes the baby from us for the afternoon, so Julian and I head to the room for a little "nap." I can hear early warning moans indicating that Julian is just about to reach his long-awaited goal. Then, sure enough, there is a knock on the door. Julian loses the moment and sighs in frustration. I find a robe and peel the door open an inch. I see lovely olive-green dress bags from Harrods. Yay! My shipment has come in. I love this!

Afterward, we head downstairs for a late lunch in *Le Bar des Bergues*. The Swiss are so resourceful that they're probably inventing of "cone of silence" to put over the wailing baby.

Dr. Zarr tells of all of the adventures he had with his new little parcel today. Dr. Zarr has no trouble mixing formula, changing a nappy, or handling any other gross procedures. Julian looks on with disgust.

We are one happy subset of the Zarr family: Julian, his father, the baby, the dog, and me.

Then I hear the words, "Oh, no!" come in synchrony from the Zarr men. I look and see Simon sitting in the distance—in drag. No. Fooled again! It's Simon's mother in a signature green outfit.

Now I see why Dr. Zarr had upgraded to the dearly departed Number Three. Right then, Polish Paulina shows up. She greets Number Two and starts pulling out a series of Chanel purses. I think, "What a coincidence," but then Dr. Zarr tells me that Number Two and Paulina are best friends, which is how the family knows her. God, with all this gossip, it is like Dr. Zarr has become B.M.

Paulina must be raking in the dough on Number Two, who has all of the markings of a compulsive shopper. Then there are the rest of the Zarrs. Paulina could probably pay her mortgage just on them. She comes over to our table to compliment me on my pink dress. She says she hopes I like everything in my latest delivery. Then she adds loudly, "I hope you don't mind thong underpants. That's what all the other ones liked."

Paulina fluffs her hair and looks at Dr. Zarr. "How convenient that you're all in Geneva." Then I realize that Paulina is the tracking device for the entire family.

Dr. Zarr and Julian both seem a little annoyed with her, so Paulina quickly says, "Don't look at me. I didn't tell her you were here."

Julian says, "I doubt it was a coincidence."

Paulina avoids eye contact. "She's Simon's mother. Maybe he told her."

Julian answers, "Oh, I suppose you are right."

Dr. Zarr adds, "He must have told her that the baby would be here."

Off the hook, Paulina toddles away in her high heels back to Number Two.

Dr. Zarr quietly proposes an escape plan and heads into the hotel to make a private phone call. I decide to powder my nose. Once inside, I hear Dr. Zarr talking behind a column. I listen in a bit, mostly because I want to know about our next not-so-secret location.

I hear he's trying to buy back more shares of Zarr Pharma stock. I guess with the recent setbacks, the stock price must have tumbled. Then I hear him ask, "Who else is buying up shares?"

Maybe he's better off without blonde Number Three. Not so sure about brunette Number Two, who looks a bit controlling. With Number One dead, I guess he might have to go for a Number Four. I'll bet this time he goes for a redhead. I wish I knew someone. Hey, wait a minute. What about Paulina with the magenta hair? Hmm. Now I wonder if Oliver could be right. She seems suspicious, and she seems to like Dr. Zarr. Meaning, she would have needed Number Three out of the way.

Chapter 76

The next morning, we find Dr. Zarr sitting alone at the outdoor restaurant having coffee. When we ask where the baby is, he says it's up in the suite with Paulina. He chuckles, "Simon's mother said it must take after Beth Marie's side of the family."

Julian asks his father, "Is she still mad that she didn't get invited to the baby shower?"

"She should be glad. If she'd been in Lugano, she would have been a suspect."

I decide I'd better check on the dog. We all go up to the suite but can't find him. Dr. Zarr opens the door to the adjoining suite, and we catch Paulina feeding the baby. When we ask where the dog is, she tells us that Number Two took him a while ago.

With her Polish accent, she says, "Oh, Martin, she put something in your suitcase."

Dr. Zarr looks through his suitcase and finds a tiny box with a silver baby bracelet monogrammed with "Little Monkey." He continues to rummage through the suitcase. "Wait a minute. I had a small leather case in here. Now it's gone."

Julian looks at Paulina, who is hiding behind a Vogue magazine. "Don't look at me."

Dr. Zarr searches through his suitcase again. He says his thumb drive is missing as well as his security card to the lab in Zurich. He tells me that my passport is also missing from his suitcase. *Oh, brother! The universe will not let me leave Switzerland.*

Julian shrugs his shoulders at me.

I say, "Should we call the police and alert them to a theft and a dognapping?"

Dr. Zarr calms down. "Ah, not yet. Don't worry, we'll get them back for you, Camille."

Julian paces around. "Father, do you think Number Two could have also been responsible for the drug sabotage?"

Dr. Zarr closes his suitcase. "No. She's not that clever."

Paulina says in broken English. "The big mystery is, why steal the stupid dog?"

Dr. Zarr says, "I'll bet she's on her way to Zurich now."

Right then, I remember the handy dog-tracking device. I call Mrs. E., who always knows everything, including the whereabouts of her pet. When I ask her about the tracking device, she says it's been a bit spotty ever since the funicular incident. Frankly, after all of the dog incidents, I'm surprised she hasn't fired me. As a baseline test, she asks if the dog was in the lounge at the Four Seasons Café in Geneva last night. Dr. Zarr says, yes.

Mrs. Etherington reports back, excitedly: "Okay, I'm getting a reading. Robert is still in Switzerland! He's in the village called Solothurn, in a church." This is very precise, but I think this is an odd locale for a compulsive shopper and a dog. I can just picture Mrs. E. in her hospital bed, with all the nurses around watching a little red dot on a map of Switzerland that shows the GPS whereabouts of her dog's tail.

Boy, did wife Number Two choose the wrong dog to nab! Dr. Zarr is impressed that we can track his ex-wife through a dog's tail, but says there are 11 churches in Solothurn. Then Mrs. E. says, "Never mind; now they're on the highway headed to Zurich."

Finally, Mrs. E. mummers over the speakerphone, "Can someone retrieve my darling, Robert? Oh, I should have left him with Penguin."

Julian replies, "Of course, Mrs. Etherington."

Dr. Zarr chimes in. "Yes, we're on our way."

Paulina smartly declines to go to go with us, saying she has to get back to London. I think she sees nothing but chaos —and lost revenue in this adventure. Frankly, I'm a little irked that she let poor Robert get dognapped on her watch.

Dr. Zarr directs, "It will take longer to get a flight plan, so we'll just drive."

Julian, his father, the baby, and I hit the road. I am wearing my green velvet jacket and am deputized to feed the baby. It latches on to my breast. After prying the powerful jaws open, I strike what I think is an alluring Madonna pose, praying the baby doesn't spit up all over my jacket. Ah, what is to happen? Will I settle down with Julian in an old house with a child of our own? Or will we be one of those jet-setting childless couples?

Chapter 77

Zurich, Switzerland

With Julian at the wheel, we make a mad dash to Zurich. We decide that we've got to get rid of this pesky baby. There is no way to sneak up on a dognapping killer with a shrieking baby in tow. Then it occurs to me that we might benefit by keeping it as a hostage swap.

Julian calls Simon, but there's no answer. Then he calls B.M. and gets a twang-spiked earful. She's out of the hospital and back at the Dolder Hotel.

Mrs. E. is not answering her phone, so we've lost the critical contact with the dog tail and the dog-napper.

Not knowing where to go next, we drive to the faithful Dolder Hotel.

It is not difficult to find B.M. echoing in the cavernous lobby. Julian asks again if there have been any signs of Simon. This seems to be a running theme: Where is Simon? As usual, B.M. has no idea. If half of all marriages fail, this strikes me as one that falls into that half of the bell-curve. She tells us that she overheard him booking a trip on the Orient Express to Vienna. This time she's full of useful information; most other times its snippets of misinformation. She's convinced that Simon is going to surprise her with a romantic train ride. With her superior eavesdropping abilities, B.M. would have made a great spy but would have failed in the entrance exam's clandestine portion. If I had to guess, I'd bet Simon is taking Clover— and not his beloved wife on the Orient Express.

Julian, Dr. Zarr, and I take seats in the lobby as we wait for the keys to our latest hotel rooms. They call Paulina for tracking help. She thinks Number Two is headed to Vienna tomorrow too, saying she asked for warmer clothes. This means we'll have to catch her tonight. Dr. Zarr says his missing pass key also works for the Vienna lab.

I hesitate to ask Dr. Zarr, but I don't seem to have any self-control. "Do you think Simon is in cahoots with Number Two?"

He sighs in a matter-of-fact tone. "She *is* his mother."

I wait for him to go back to the concierge before asking Julian, "Do you think Number Two killed Number Three?"

Without hesitating, he says, "Now *that* I can see."

As much as I want to get the dog back, I feel a little uneasy about confronting Number Two, the dognapping killer.

Chapter 78

After being radio silent for the past two hours, Mrs. E. finally reconnects. She sends a text to say her dog has excellent taste. Robert is now sitting in the Zurich Park Hyatt Hotel.

Dr. Zarr, Julian, Simon, and I head down the mountain to find our culprit. Boy, this tracking system is handy! *I should have put one on my passport.* When we reach the hotel, we see Number Two sitting in the lounge drinking a bright-green Absinthe with her Chihuahua.

I ask abruptly, "Alright. Where is he?"

Number Two seems startled. "Who, my dear?"

"Robert. You dog-napper!"

"He's out there tied to a tree." She waves her hand dismissively. "I didn't take him. He was a stowaway in the trunk of my car."

Julian scoffs. "And hand over Camille's passport, if you please."

She pets her Chihuahua. "Really, must you all be so hostile?"

Dr. Zarr is more composed. "Do you care to explain why you stole my lab key?"

Number Two looks down. "Not really." She takes another sip. "Martin, you know I would do anything for Simon. And this was to help you, too."

Simon lopes over to explain. "I told my mother to get the pass-key. I think I can prove that Number Three tampered with Zarrexifam and tried to frame us."

Julian interrupts. "How?"

269

Simon is breathless. "I think I figured out how she did the tampering. Zurich was out of Periwinkle, so there was a transfer from Vienna."

His mother says, "Out of Periwinkle? How tragic. That's a color that flatters every skin tone."

Dr. Zarr says, "No, the plant, Catharanthus roseus." He shakes his head. "But there are protocols for these transfers."

Julian huffs, "We've talked about these component transfers. They *are* a weak link in the system."

Simon says, "I think Number Three used me as the cover for *her* sabotage. If I don't get there, the regulators will think *I* masterminded the cover-up of the transfers."

Dr. Zarr is baffled. "But why would she do that?"

Number Two looks pleased. "Simon and I knew she was trouble from day one."

Dr. Zarr says, "So how did you find all this out?"

Simon says, "Eddie in security. He caught her in the Vienna lab one weekend night."

His father asks, "Why didn't he tell me?"

"Eddie was suspicious when he found her there alone, but she said she had forgotten her phone."

Simon says hurriedly, "I just need to get into the Vienna lab before the regulators do!"

Dr. Zarr puts his hand on his son's shoulder. "But why didn't you tell us what you were up to? We would have helped you, son."

Simon looks at his watch. "Because I didn't want to implicate you. I have to talk fast before Clover comes down. She's headed to Vienna with me."

I feel the need to interject. "But, why are you bringing Clover if you are trying to blame it all on her mother?"

Simon wipes the beads of sweat from his brow and gulps his drink. "Clover doesn't know this. She thinks we are going there to undo the cover-up and pin it on Eddie."

Julian scoffs. "Are you nuts? You'll just get yourself in more trouble. You'll put us all in jail!"

Number Two touches her son. "Simon, Dear, how can you trust Clover? I think it's some sort of trap."

"Your mother could be right." Dr. Zarr sighs.

Simon stands up and announces, "I love Clover, and she loves me."

"Ah, I hate to mention it," Julian says casually, "but has it slipped your mind that you have a wife and baby?"

Simon tips his drink and says, "It's not my baby."

We are all stunned. *What?*

Number Two's face springs in relief. "I knew it! That baby is too hideous to be any grandchild of mine." She hands the baby off to a passing waiter.

Julian speaks for us all. "And when did you discover this ?"

"I just got the DNA results."

Julian frowns. "Ah, so you didn't need to trip her on the stairs or push her in front of the cable car."

Simon scoffs, "I had nothing to do with either incident."

I realize that we have got to stop Simon from going to Vienna with Clover. The only way to do this is to prove to him that she's trouble. *But how?*

I then remember the video. Thank goodness I sent a copy to Mrs. E. "Wait a minute," I say as I play the video of the ballerinas, revealing the Zegna shoe buckle.

Everyone looks down at Julian's shoes. Julian says, "Well, I certainly didn't trip her."

Dr. Zarr points to the video. "It's Clover. I'd know that bigfoot anywhere!"

271

Simon says, "But my sweet Clover would never do such a thing."

I feel the need to interject: "I think she tripped B.M., sunk the boat, and caused the funicular accident."

Dr. Zarr shakes his head. "What a mess. No, Simon, you are not going to Vienna. We will tell the regulators everything. It is the right thing to do."

Oh my, I completely forgot about the dog tied to the tree.

Simon looks to all of us. "If you think Clover is to blame for everything, then who killed her mother?"

I notice that Number Two is sneaking out of her chair to leave.

Dr. Zarr points to his ex-wife and says, "Don't tell me you had anything to do with this!"

I decide the dog can wait.

Suddenly, we look up and see Clover standing there, holding a suitcase. She glares at Number Two. "I'll bet you killed my mother! You did this just so you could have Martin Zarr back!"

Simon shakes his head. "But my mother was in Geneva at the time. Weren't you, Mother?"

Number Two's eyes try to find the nearest escape route. "Well. Um. Yes, I was in the morning."

Dr. Zarr looks at his second wife. "Were you in Lugano that day?"

Number Two looks down, "Perhaps. I was hoping I'd get a last-minute invitation to the baby shower. It was my grandbaby, not hers."

Clover hisses. "So, you killed her!" She leaps over and wrings her hands around Number Two's thick neck. Simon has to pull her off his mother.

Number Two says, "I removed a couple of wing nuts. I thought maybe she'd just lose an arm or something."

Simon scoffs and shakes his head. "Mother, really?!"

Number Two pleads her case. "I had to do it. First, she steals my husband, and then doesn't invite me to the baby shower."

Julian says, "Is that any reason to try to hurt someone?"

She looks around. "Yes." Then she continues, "She tampered with the drug, and ruined Martin's lifelong dream. That woman had it coming."

Clover suddenly starts swearing in Russian. Then, thankfully, she reverts to English. "I'll kill you, bitch!"

The waiter comes over to ask if everything is alright.

"Yes. Yes. We're fine." Julian holds up his empty glass. "Does anyone else fancy a drink?"

Number Two sits back down. "Jeeze. I just loosened a couple of little wing -nut thing a-ma-jigs. Is that a crime?"

Julian says matter-of-factly, "Wait a minute! That was on the outside. There was a long metal pin on the inside. Both needed to be removed for the window to fall."

Curious, I ask, "So who pulled the final pin?"

Number Two points to Clover. "You! I think you wanted Martin to die, but your timing was off."

In a thick Russian accent, Clover spews, "I was at the salon when the window fell." She picks up her suitcase and starts to make a break.

Right then, Robert comes around the corner— followed by —Mrs. Etherington!

In an imperious tone, she commands, "Not so fast, Miss Blinova."

Chapter 79

Shocked, I say, "Mrs. Etherington, what are you doing here?"

We spot Clover making a beeline for the door, but the security men grab her in time. Number Two also starts to make a run for it, but it doesn't get far due to her chunky legs.

Mrs. E. says to Clover, "You pulled the pin that made the glass fall, didn't you?"

Simon is not sold. "But why would she try to kill her own mother?"

Mrs. Etherington points to Clover, "You were trying to kill Martin Zarr!"

Simon is shocked. "What? But she was at the salon at the time."

Sticking my nose in it, I say, "Maybe she pulled the pin earlier, and the window fell later."

Simon looks at Clover in a new harsh light. "Wait a minute — it was your idea to have the fireworks! Maybe the vibration of the fireworks made the window finally fall. You thought my father would be back at the house at 3:00. And your mother was supposed to be at the salon then."

Clover just looks down.

In the background, Number Two is trying to peel the guards' arms off her chunky arms. "See, it wasn't my fault."

I point to Clover. "You wrecked the boat, didn't you."

Clover shakes her head. "No. Why would I do that if I was on it?"

Dr. Zarr shakes his head. "Yes, that was risky for a non-swimmer."

Mrs. E. looks at us. "Clover was a competitive swimmer in Russia."

Clover shakes her head. "It wasn't me."

Julian says, "So who was the boat saboteur?"

I jump up. "I think Number Three did it in advance. Maryel was supposed to be on the boat and Number Three wanted her out of the way"

While we're still absorbing this news flash, Julian says, "But what about the tripping incident and the funicular accident?"

Mrs. E. points both hands at Clover, like a flight attendant point out the exits. "Clover was trying to get rid of Camille and B.M. They were starting to become busybodies."

Julian mutters, "Starting to?"

Mrs. Etherington goes on. "And Clover is the one who poisoned Mrs. Coquin."

Julian collapses. "Oh, no. Why?"

Mrs. E. says, "She knew too much."

Clover now lets her Russian accent come through as she cries, "My father had a brain tumor, so we needed to get him the drug!"

Dr. Zarr says, "You only had to ask, my Dear."

Julian stammers, "Yes, why try to kill *my* father?"

Mrs. Etherington sits down to explain to us. "Clover, her mother, and her father—Vladimir Blinova—are part of a Russian spy ring."

We all sit in stunned silence.

Mrs. E. continues. "They were using Swiss pharmaceuticals to fund their operations."

Simon says, "I knew something was up with Number Three!"

Mrs. E. continues. "Zarrexifam stock would have made a fortune, but when Dr. Zarr wanted to offer the drug for free, the value of the shares would have collapsed. So Clover's mother —Number Three as you call her — decided to short the stock."

She grabs a drink from a passing waiter and takes a sip. "But then Martin Zarr changed his mind, and it went back up."

Julian exhales. "So, that's why Number Three had to sabotage the drug! When the stock dropped after the deaths, she probably made a fortune by shorting the stock and buying up Vora-Pharma shares."

Mrs. Etherington says, "Yes. By manipulating Swiss drugs and stocks, the Russian mob made millions."

Julian's forehead wrinkles. "But why try to kill my father after they made all the money?"

Mrs. E. explains, "It was only a matter of time before he and Eddie Krakowski figured out that she did the tampering."

Clover turns to Dr. Zarr and says, "Mother was not supposed to fall in love with you."

Dr. Zarr quips, "That was love?"

Simon looks at Clover. "Does that mean you don't really love me?"

Clover practically spits on him. "Are you kidding me?"

With firm authority, Mrs. Etherington says, "Take them away, boys." The plain-clothed security men march off with Number Two and Clover.

Simon points to Mrs. E., "Now who exactly are you?"

Chapter 80

We all sit in silence. In awe of her, I say, "Wow, Mrs. Etherington, how did you figure all that out?"

She says modestly, "I had a little help from Mi6. They let me come out retirement to help crack this."

Julian says, "What?! You were with Mi6?"

She walks over to touch my green velvet jacket and opens the lining. "Thanks to the wires in your jacket, we have everything recorded."

Julian's face drops. "Oh, and to think of all the naughty things, I said to that jacket."

I look at her and say, "Do the doctors know you're here?"

"Oh, I never actually had a heart attack. It was simulated to keep you here. And to get David to visit."

Simon looks at Mrs. E., and asks, "You're not going to put my mother in jail, are you? After all, she helped you catch a Russian spy."

Mrs. E. says, "No need to worry, dear. After a little debriefing, we'll have her out in no time."

Dr. Zarr jokes, "No, hurry."

Chapter 81

After the dust settles, I fly on the Zarr's private jet back to London with Mrs. E., Julian, and the dog.

Mrs. E. pets her dog. "You were more than just my dog walker Camille. You were my spy."

Julian says, "Just think. If I hadn't met Camille by accident, none of this would have worked out."

Mrs. E. mumbles, "Err. That wasn't really a coincidence. I had my driver take Camille there because I knew you frequented the Connaught."

I am surprised. "It was my first night. And you were recruiting me as a spy?"

Mrs. E. starts rifling through her purse, probably wishing she could hide in it. "I hadn't planned it that way. You had flown all this way to meet some poor married poet. And here I knew this rich single Pharmaceutical heir."

I ask. "But you were already investigating the Russians and Zarr Pharma. Didn't you know there would be the trouble?"

"Well, I have to admit, it was handy to have you date Julian, but I honestly had no idea it would go so far."

Julian says, "I can't believe Mi6 brought you back from retirement to investigate our company."

Mrs. E. leans back and sips her martini. "Well, technically, they didn't ask me back."

I look at Julian, who is also confused.

Mrs. Etherington looks out the jet's window. "I had to take matters into my own hands. My son is being detained by the Russians."

Shocked, I gasp, "What? They have David?"

She laughs. "God help us, if he was ever captured. No, my other son, James."

Julian says, "So is Mi6 getting him back?"

Mrs. Etherington gets a sly look. "Camille, with your help and the lucky jacket, we're going to do a spy swap for Clover."

Julian puts his arms around me, protectively. "I love Camille, and I don't want her in danger."

I look at him. "You love me?"

"Yes, Darling, ever since I saw you crying in the vet's office."

"Really, the day the dog's tail was cut off?"

"No. That first night when he was choking on the buttons."

Mrs. Etherington shakes her head. "I'm glad you're not watching my dog anymore."

I look around. "I'm fired as your pet sitter?"

"No. You're getting promoted. You're going to be my little spy."

Julian exhales. "A spy! But I want you to be my wife."

I look at Julian. "Really?"

Mrs. Etherington says, "Well, my dear you have a big choice to make now."

Julian says, "Whether she's my wife or not, I will not let you put her in that kind of danger."

"I've never put her in danger. Frankly, she's safer as my spy than your wife."

Julian says, "But you don't love her —not like I do."

Mrs. Etherington kisses my forehead. "I love her too."

I say, "You do?"

She says thoughtfully, "Of course. Every mother loves their child."

Julian and I look at each other. Julian says, "Wait? You're her mother?"

Mrs. Etherington starts to cry and hugs me. "Yes, Camille is my baby girl."

The End.

<u>Dramatis Personae: Cast of Characters</u>

B.M. or Beth Marie, 37, American, obese, pregnant, "blonde" wife of Simon Zarr.

Camille Carano, 41, American writer, pretty, turquoise eyes and reddish hair.

Clover, 28, Russian and Finnish, tall thin beautiful blonde; daughter of Number Three. Step sister of Simon and Julian Zarr. Friend of Maryel.

Mrs. Coquin, 74, French, mean. Friend of Maryel. Julian's cook.

Detective Roberto Bernardo, 48, Swiss Italian, handsome with dark features.

David Etherington, 48, British, reddish hair, pear shaped. Dendrologist, Son of Mrs. Etherington. Friend of Camille Carano.

Mrs. Etherington, British, 74, grey hair, green eyes. Wealthy old Grand Dame. Mother of David and James Etherington.

James Etherington, 44, mentioned character, son of Mrs. Etherington and brother of David.

Maryel, 30, French; tall thin beautiful brunette model who live in Paris; former fiancée of Julian Zarr. Friend of B.M.

Number Two, 68, Czech and English, chubby, auburn haired, mother of Simon Zarr, and second wife of Dr. Martin Zarr.

Number Three, or Penelope Zarr, 55, Russian and Finnish, tall, thin blonde; Mother of Clover Fontaine, and Third wife of Dr. Martin Zarr.

Oliver Ogilvie, 44, British, handsome poet and professor. Green eyes, light hair; Married to Enfys Ogilvie; father of twins.

Trevor and Tristian Ogilvie, 6 year-old twins. British, sons of Oliver and Enfys.

Enfys Ogilvie, 44, Scottish, Thin pale wife of Oliver and mother of twins.

Penroy or Penguin, 51, British, fat pasty busybody waiter at Connaught.

Stella, Camille's Pug 16, Big eyes. Eats wedding cake.

Julian Zarr, 48, Swiss and British CEO of Zarr Pharmaceuticals; Elegant with black hair and pale blue eyes, tall and thin. Son of Dr. Martin Zarr, half brother of Simon Zarr.

Dr. Martin Zarr, 74, Swiss, Elegant physician with silver hair and pale blue eyes; father of Julian and Simon Zarr. Ex husband of Number Two and Number Three.

Simon Zarr, 46, Swiss and Czech; Hefty, light-haired, brown eyed brother of Julian Zarr, son of wife Number Two and Dr. Martin Zarr. Married to B.M.